Media Acclaim for *Rescued*
by John Bevere & Mark Andrew Olsen

. . . a gripping thriller that goes beyond a rescue from certain death to deliverance from a fate far worse. . . . Through his suspenseful tale, Bevere addresses Christian hypocrisy and challenges easy grace theology.

—**Lynne Thompson**, Christian Retailing, Altamonte Springs, FL

" "

. . . the message catches you off guard, sucks the breath from your lungs and makes you rethink everything you've ever believed about God, eternity, and what it means to serve such a Holy Being. I challenge you to get *Rescued*. It will be the most important thing you do in this new year.

—**Deena Peterson**, wholly-devoted.blogspot.com

" "

Bevere and Olsen set up the opening collision sequence in a Tom Clancy-esque string of random events (that really aren't so random). . . . But even so, it's when the connection to eternity becomes clear that the true meaning of the story is finally revealed. . . . Highly Recommended.

—**christianfictionreview.com**

" "

While *Rescued* is plotted and shaped as a suspense thriller, the message is strong with spiritual depth about the ramifications of life choices. . . . a page turner that I strongly recommend.

—**W. Terry Whalin**, FaithfulReader.com

" "

. . . the perfect blend of truth and grace. . . . *Rescued* isn't just a hold-your-breath thriller, it's also the story of redemption. . . .

—**Jackie Baumgarten**, armchairinterviews.com

Experience the Full Effect With Audio Theater!

More Than Just Life-Altering Choices Await Them...

Reminiscent of the timeless classic *Pilgrim's Progress, Affabel* follows the powerful otherworld story of King Jalyn and his kingdom of Affabel.

Follow six of King Jalyn's subjects as they journey through a world very similar to our own to meet their lord. Yet things aren't always as they seem in Affabel, and each sojourner meets joy, sorrow, astonishment, and powerful revelation along the way.

Recorded by a Hollywood cast, this riveting drama features the voice of John Rhys-Davies (*Lord of the Rings* and *One Night With the King*) and brings to life the powerful story woven into John Bevere's bestselling nonfiction book, *Driven by Eternity*.

***Affabel*, Dramatized Audio**
4 CDs/2:30 hours

Edge-of-Your-Seat Suspense...and Something More!

As a dramatized audio experience from John Bevere's novel *Rescued*, Audio Theater portrays the consequences of sin, the power of redemption, and the certainties of the afterlife—for everyone.

A father trapped in a terrible underwater accident. A son desperate to do something—anything—to save him. A digital readout ticking down toward certain death—and a fate more horrible still...

For Alan Rockaway, his teenage son Jeff, and Alan's new bride, Jenny, it's been little more than a leisurely end to a weeklong cruise... then the horrifying crash and the plunge toward the unknown...

Everything Alan has assumed about himself is flipped upside down. In the ultimate rescue operation, life or death is just the beginning!

Featuring a cast of professional actors, including John Rhys-Davies, this amazing listening experience will leave you on the edge of your seat, contemplating everything you thought you knew about eternity.

***Rescued*, Dramatized Audio**
4 CDs/2:00 hours

RESCUED

a Novel

JOHN BEVERE
& MARK ANDREW OLSEN

BETHANY HOUSE PUBLISHERS
Minneapolis, Minnesota

Published by Bethany House Publishers
11400 Hampshire Avenue South
Bloomington, Minnesota 55438

Bethany House Publishers is a division of
Baker Publishing Group, Grand Rapids, Michigan.

Printed in the United States of America

ISBN-13: 978-0-7642-0447-0
ISBN-10: 0-7642-0447-5

The Library of Congress has cataloged the hardcover edition as follows:

Bevere, John.
    Rescued / John Bevere & Mark Andrew Olsen.
        p. cm.
    ISBN-13: 978-0-7642-0200-1 (alk. paper)
    ISBN-10: 0-7642-0200-6 (alk. paper)
    I. Olsen, Mark Andrew. II. Title.

PS3602.E8436R47   2006
813'.54—dc22   2006018024

I wish to dedicate this book to five very special men:

First, my father,
John P. Bevere Sr.

Thank you for being a faithful husband
of nearly sixty years of marriage,
and a dedicated father who always provided for his family.

Second, to my four sons,
Addison David Bevere
Austin Michael Bevere
Joshua Alexander Bevere
Arden Christopher Bevere

I love and am so proud of each of you.
Live in truth, love deeply, and glorify God in all you do.

—JOHN BEVERE

———————————

I wish to dedicate my work on this story of father and son

To my father, Walther Olsen:

I have been so blessed to have a father
whose unfailing love and faithfulness
to his family is matched only by his dedication to Him.

And to my son, Benjamin Olsen:

God has blessed me with a wonderful son whose loving heart
teaches me more about Him than a hundred sermons,
and with whom I will always love to share "boy-time."

—MARK ANDREW OLSEN

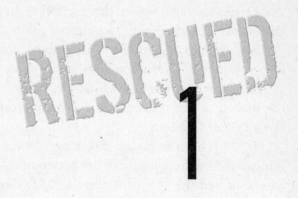

New Jerusalem

The young woman glanced at the smoke but thought nothing of it—except as a sight vaguely, unsettlingly, out of place.

She was too far away to identify the acrid smell.

Or hear the screaming.

The bliss of her pilgrimage glowed brightly upon her face. Like hundreds around her, she was merely basking in the glory of the previous few hours, wandering about the vastness of the Eternal City, gazing at the beauty on every side, raising a hand into the golden light, and humming praises under her voice.

Then she strolled across the terrace of the Temple Mount and glanced over. For the first time since her arrival, her smile fled her countenance.

The smoke's appearance seemed dramatically, even violently out of place. The thick column etched a darkly knotted cord against the cobalt blue sky, the streaks of crimson and ochre vividly contrasting with the city's warm, welcoming palette.

Finally the odor reached her. In an instant she felt herself transported back to a far earlier time, that childhood summer at the Orphans Farm when the caretaker had slaughtered a deformed calf and burned it whole, out against the far tree line.

The sweetish, slightly nauseating fumes finally registered in her memory. She frowned and walked over for a closer look.

The other pilgrims around her glanced solemnly her way as she moved toward the edge of the railing, the overlook above the Valley of Gehenna.

Had she been more careful, more observant, perhaps less transported by the splendor of her previous few hours, she might have followed the flow of walkers, quickly crossed to the other side, and averted her face like everyone else. Had she remembered her Israelite history a bit more thoroughly, she might have recalled the ancient lore of the chasm approaching her— *Gehenna*, a cursed pit, a valley of hideous child sacrifices, of burning corpses, of hellish rumors and terrifying legends.

Instead, she made her way to the edge, consumed with curiosity.

She peered over.

And then she heard the wail of torment, as dreadful and bloodcurdling as any sound ever created.

For a few seconds, she did not move a muscle. Then, after a moment, her left hand flew to her mouth. Her knees gave way, legs nearly betraying her. She stumbled away, her face turned white, her eyelids quivering with horror. The stream of worshipers paused, one older female pilgrim close to her wincing in sympathy.

The young woman stared at the sympathetic faces, silently begging them to explain how they could walk calmly around what she had just witnessed. Feeling driven to verify what she had seen, she moved forward again and looked more closely.

"O Lord," she whispered, still staring down. "This can't be . . . Don't let this be . . ."

Now her knees failed her completely, and she grasped the stone railing for support. She was utterly torn between, on one hand, a desperate wish to retreat as far away from the horror as she could and, on the other, a compulsion urging her to return and look down yet again, as if one last glimpse would somehow prove it was only an illusion.

She did not wish to attract attention, and she was dismayed at the thought of somehow diminishing someone else's joy. Yet she could not help herself.

She grasped at the wall, panting heavily, and sagged down against it.

Why this? Why here, and now. . . ?

She could not understand. Her bliss had billowed away alongside the smoke. Her cause for joy, the entire ecstasy of her pilgrimage, was now tarnished in light of the images still swimming before her eyes.

A strong hand touched her arm and gently pulled her upward. She lurched to her feet, stood, and swayed until she could look into what proved to be the warm gaze of a young man.

"May I be of some help to you?" he asked in a comforting tone.

"I just—did you see that, down there? Do you know how horrible. . . ?"

"The sight is always terrifying for those who glance down," the man explained. "Particularly for the pilgrims who come here and see it for the first time. But I assure you that what you have just seen is not intended to undermine all that you've experienced here. In fact, it's meant to reinforce it. I've been sent here to find you and to help you comprehend it. Perhaps, if you could walk with me awhile, I will tell you a story, a rather long one. The hearing will help you to understand what you have seen."

S.S. *Aqua Libre*—105 *miles east of St. Lucia, Windward Islands, Lesser Antilles*—years earlier

For most of his last hours on earth, Marshall Rhodes just knew he was already in heaven.

After all, the bare-chested thirty-year-old had tropical sunshine lighting up his face, sea breeze ruffling his hair, a brand-new, luxurious sixty-five-foot motor yacht purring beneath his feet, a hundred miles of achingly blue Caribbean waters before him, and the warmth of three—no, four, maybe five—tumblers of Mount Gay Rum pickling his frontal lobes.

Oh man . . . He chuckled to himself, shaking his head with a grin. *Doesn't get any better than this!*

He laughed as he held up the rum bottle and shook out the last drop. To think he was getting paid for this. And good money, too.

He set the boat on autopilot and turned for a fresh bottle in the galley. He reviewed his good fortune. After all, he *was* solely responsible for the safe delivery of a twelve-million-dollar vessel from the Newport, Rhode Island, docks to the Port of Spain pier in Trinidad. The yacht was now owned by one of the world's wealthiest sportsmen, an impatient man who had waited on this marvel of marine technology for two years now and who would brook no delay. A man who would make Marshall's life a living nightmare if he failed in his appointed mission.

Still, Rhodes reminded himself, uncorking the next bottle and swallowing a gulp straight from its mouth, *some men don coat and tie and stew in hours of traffic just to fawn before their bosses all day long. How lucky can a dude be?*

The one thing more he could have asked for was a girl. The teak deck below him cried out for a companion in a bikini. Rhodes was no Adonis, yet he knew that with this kind of cruiser at his disposal, he could have surely snagged one, if only he'd had the time. But no ports of call were in the offing, not on this trip. The world's loveliest seashores had glided past him during the last three days, often out of sight, sometimes beckoning their distant palm fronds and white surf ribbons from just beyond his horizon.

Oh well. Can't have it all . . . He let out a long sigh and reminded himself that the end of his journey lay just hours ahead. The bittersweet realization enticed him into throwing his last ounce of caution to the wind. *Go for it.*

The ship's innovative autopilot had proven rock solid since leaving Newport. Almost too perfect. Marshall knew its half a terabyte of onboard memory would compensate seamlessly for a few more hours of alcohol-induced haze. He had run all the necessary tests, finished the dozen or so pages of notes his employer expected of him. Everything checked out. He had only one broad turn to make on the open sea, a single adjustment which would change his course from one flanking the bow-shaped layout of the Windwards to another, sharply angled toward the southwest and Trinidad. But that correction wouldn't be needed for an hour or two.

He took his longest gulp yet of Mount Gay and creased a heavy-lidded smile. The rum hadn't taken long.

His eyes flew open. An icy hand seized the center of his chest. A viselike grip clamped down on his heart like it was no more solid than a damp washcloth.

Marshall let out a strangled gasp, but there was no one to hear it.

He clutched at his thorax and stumbled. He opened his mouth to scream, but it remained buried inside him. Grimacing tightly against a red-hot agony that pierced his torso, he felt his balance shear away from him and collapsed.

He hardly felt his fall, at least until the hard deck slammed against the back of his head.

Silence.

An incredible stillness enveloped him, a peace far greater than silence or darkness or even sleep. It was a calm that immediately, overpoweringly, signaled *this existence just ended.*

Then he was looking down at a bare-chested man, lying on the deck of a yacht. From far above, the image was growing smaller, as was the *Aqua Libre*—swallowed up in an eternity of ocean blue.

He felt no fear or regret. Only a vague, almost mischievous curiosity about what was happening. He was flying.

Cool. He'd always wanted to fly.

And then he wasn't. Suddenly he felt himself falling. Only, he wasn't above his world anymore. He was over . . . nothing.

A void. Nothingness. Blackness.

A crushing sense of malice, of evil, filled every inch of him. His self, his being—whatever this was now—was being jerked downward by a merciless, proprietary tug.

For the first time *ever*, Marshall Rhodes learned the meaning, the devastation, of absolute fear.

The *S.S. Aqua Libre* now sailed unguided, a fifty-seven-thousand-pound, sixty-five-foot long torpedo with a trajectory relentlessly maintained by the world's most advanced autopilot system. Without Marshall Rhodes there to correct its course, however, the sleek new yacht now plowed unswervingly toward the easternmost of all the West Indies, the lush island from which his rum had originated—the former British protectorate of Barbados.

COAST OF BARBADOS—2 HOURS LATER

Just four hundred yards from the Barbados coastline, and only thirty-eight nautical miles ahead of the *Aqua Libre*'s errant trajectory, floated the towering hundred thousand-ton *S.S. Pearl of the Seas*.

At anchor in Barbados's Deep Water Harbour, just outside its capital city of Bridgetown, the floating resort was in the process of disgorging groups of its 1,400 passengers onto the dock. Some were merely out for a day's port of call, while others had been transferred to smaller tender boats which would speed them to a variety of pleasurable activities at sea.

The last small-craft captain's voice rang out against the vast, imposing hull.

"Final call!"

Standing on the boat's deck, Pastor Alan Rockaway looked anxiously over the waves slapping the *Pearl*'s black waterline. Forty-seven years old, handsome and lean, with light brown hair riffling in the breeze and a winsome gleam shining in his clear blue eyes, Alan lacked only one aspect of his usual demeanor: a calm state of mind.

"Please, sir," he called, leaning over the railing toward the captain, "my son is on his way down and it's very important he make the launch. *Very* important."

The man glanced at his watch. "He's got about fourteen seconds. That's all I can manage. The sub schedule is tight. The boarding pier is two miles out, and we have only a three-minute window to make our rendezvous."

Rockaway turned to his wife, Jenny, and sighed heavily. In years past, he would have indulged his frustration and yelled up to the perpetually late boy. But this trip was special, and for many reasons. He would not embarrass his eldest son like that. He would hold his tongue and send up a frantic prayer instead.

A high-pitched shout echoed from the deck above. "Coming! Hold on—I'm coming!"

Jeff Rockaway, a lanky, good-looking seventeen-year-old, scrambled down the stairway and onto the ramp leading down to the dock. In one fist he gripped a black briefcase, in the other a video camera which bounced against his knees from the flimsiest of leather straps.

"Come on, guys! The boat's waiting!"

The elder Rockaway turned to the group of thirty adults clustered around him and smiled wryly.

Chuckling, the group followed the boy down the gangplank. After they had all arrived and begun climbing into the boat, the youth loped across the dock to his father's side, ending his run with an abrupt stomp and a contented exhale of breath.

"Is everything okay, son?" Alan asked in a voice somewhere between exasperation and admiration.

"It wasn't my fault, Dad. I'm coordinating with the ship's bridge to tap their satellite portal, and they had some kind of crisis. Trouble with their docking. Something with the current."

Jenny Rockaway locked eyes with her husband. "They did seem to struggle with their positioning this morning," she said.

Laying his hand gently upon the young man's shoulder, Alan smiled. "I believe you, son. It's just a little nerve-racking, that's all. Not only do we have to meet the sub on time, but we've got about fifteen hundred folks back home waiting for this whole link to come off smoothly."

"They won't be disappointed," Jeff replied. "I've got it all worked out."

"With *that*?" Alan shot back, pointing down at the single case with mock amazement. "Is that all the equipment it takes?"

"What do you mean *all*?" the young man huffed. "There's a laptop in here, plus all the accessories. Try and lift this thing. It must weigh ten pounds."

Alan turned to Hal Newman, his closest confidant and anchor of Denver's six-thousand-member Summit Chapel, where Alan was pastor. He raised his eyebrows and gave a good-natured shrug. "Wow. Ten pounds. All for a mere transcontinental live video satellite relay hookup. Something that five years ago would have required a truck weighing three tons and costing three million dollars."

"Five years is an eternity in techno-time, Dad."

"So I've heard, Jeff. I told you I'd trust you to pull this thing off, and I do. So I'm not going to question you anymore. I'll just give you one last opportunity to reassure me. What you're holding is so . . . compact, it doesn't seem enough to link us live with no hassles all the way back to the sanctuary in Denver."

Jeff broke into laughter, an unforced guffaw that creased his tanned face. "Trust me, Dad. Things have advanced. This is the latest ultra-compact, Internet-linked array."

"All right, then." Alan gave the bemused shrug and rueful grin of the technologically outmatched. "At least we can agree on that, Jeff."

They sat down onto benches as the launch's outboard roared to life and surged away from the mother ship. Alan looked about him, exhilarated to be out on open water, a sailing wind gusting in his face.

"Things *have* advanced," Alan said as he nodded to Hal and

Jeff sitting to one side of him. "Remember when you were a little boy and I'd just started my first church?"

"Barely."

"I do," interjected Newman with a smile.

"Of course you would!" Alan exclaimed. "Our first retreat we drove up to your weekend house out near Buena Vista. Rafting and fajitas."

"That's right. One near-drowning and charred skirt steak, if I remember right."

"I haven't forgotten," Alan laughed. "And how about when I wanted to call back to the rest of the congregation during Sunday worship back home? Help them feel not so forgotten and left behind? Of course, there were only about fifteen people left, but I was so insecure, I just *had* to touch base. So I drove down to the little country store, dropped twelve quarters into their pay phone, and old Mike Barfield managed to feed my phone call through his stereo speakers. Not a church P.A. system, mind you, but his own living room Radio Shack specials. And yet I felt like Alexander Graham Bell, phoning that assistant for the first time."

"Boy, do I feel old just remembering that," Newman said with a chuckle.

"And boy, does it make *me* feel young," Jeff quipped. They all laughed.

"Know what's strange?" Alan said. "I haven't felt that kind of thrill in a long time." He stared out over the swiftly passing waters. "Everything. The faith. The church. The pastorate. Seems like just last week I was baptized in good old-fashioned ocean surf, Seal Beach at sunset, high tide—by a hippie pastor who still thought Woodstock was the greatest church service ever held."

"Really. I'm sure Jeff never heard that story before, Alan," Jenny interjected with a smile and touch of irony in her voice.

"I know. I've told it a thousand times. It's just that we didn't have all these—all these bells and whistles back then. Things seemed more real, more passionate. If the guitar didn't resonate enough, and the song leader's voice wasn't strong enough, then whatever—people didn't notice. Perfect sound wasn't the point. We were there to worship with all the breath in our lungs. We were lucky to have microphones, let alone live, global hookups. And if we wanted to have a couples' retreat, we'd borrow somebody's cabin, not fly a thousand miles to board a Caribbean cruise ship." Alan's voice had dropped low enough that his companions almost didn't hear his last statement.

"I'd say things have improved," Jeff said with youthful vigor.

"I'm not complaining. I'm just saying that I remember being more in awe, more in touch with a sense of wonder, with fifty people in my church than today with six thousand. Things seemed more authentic. Even dangerous, in a way. We were driven to find God—even if it killed us."

"Well, I'm sure there's still plenty of ways for this hookup to fail, Dad," Jeff said. "We're out in the open, on the water, with a real-life submarine picking us up. I'm sure we'll run into a little excitement before it's all over."

2

On the open seas, miles away from the tourist submarine's launch site—an anchored boarding pier sitting in calm waters a mile and a half off the Barbados coastline—the final piece of a disaster was falling into place, within the microscopic registrations of an oceangoing onboard computer.

The *Aqua Libre* sported the most advanced navigation system available, featuring the utmost in precision settings, including one that Marshall Rhodes had neglected to address. Its radar-linked collision-avoidance system, designed to navigate around obstacles while on autopilot, in fact depended upon a myriad of user-defined preferences.

One of these was a refined speed sensitivity. The avoidance system could be told not to activate at or above speeds of the captain's choosing. The logic dictated that on open seas, when a craft would reach its highest speed, some might consider it less safe to have the controls abruptly taken over by a machine. Most captains would be satisfied with a set of warnings such as a Klaxon or siren, as well as prompts to the captain's beeper, private quarters, and cell phone. So the system compensated for the higher speeds by alerting the captain of any obstacle ahead, granting the necessary time to react.

The default factory setting, which Rhodes had never thought to change, told the *Aqua Libre* to avoid collision below ten knots, when most boats might be maneuvering through crowded harbors or shipping channels. The *Aqua Libre* was now hurtling at its top speed of thirty-five knots, which had already earned it the anxious scrutiny of the Barbados coastal patrol's radar system.

By now, each ship's successive warning was fully activated, but true to its programming, the collision-avoidance faithfully declined to engage.

As for the man charged with managing this system, he still had the warm Caribbean sun shining on his face. The wind still ruffled his hair, and the pure blue ocean still lay wide before him.

But Marshall Rhodes was definitely no longer in heaven.

BARBADOS—UNDERWATER EXCURSIONS BOARDING PIER

The moment his feet touched the sun-bleached planks of the pier, Jeff flew into action. He abruptly knelt, swung the case with a careful flourish to rest on the pier, and opened its contents to the sky. Four swift hand motions later, a thick telescoping antenna reached three feet into the air, and the laptop was whirring to life.

Despite an earlier vow to focus on his fellow travelers and not on the mechanics of the broadcast, Alan stood over his son, mesmerized.

"You figured all this out by yourself?" he asked.

"Pretty much," Jeff said without looking up. "I called the cruise company and confirmed that their bridge had a satellite uplink. So I started making friends with the captain's crew as soon as I got aboard. The rest was easy. I'd already rented this briefcase transmitter from my buddies over at Channel 10, and a camera. I had to make sure this pier was within line of sight of the ship, which checked out. All that was left was renting the satellite time. I Googled for that, sealed the deal on-line with the church credit card. No sweat!"

Alan was shaking his head in amazement when suddenly something blinked red on the laptop's screen, followed by several loud beeps.

"We have our link!" Jeff shouted.

"You mean it's all set?" Alan asked, incredulous.

"Yep. Not only are we linked straight into the church control board, but high-definition to boot!"

Alan leaned down and grasped his son by the shoulder. "I'm sorry, Jeff, for ever doubting you," he said. "But you said you could do it, and you did it in spades. I'm so proud of you."

Jeff looked up, clearly embarrassed by his father's display of affection. "Thanks, Dad."

A split second later, with his attention back on the video project, Jeff was all business again. He snatched up the video camera, plugged it into the computer's FireWire port, and raised it to his shoulder.

"Camera's ready! Action, everybody!"

DENVER, COLORADO—SUMMIT CHAPEL

Click! Click!

The upheld drumsticks struck together twice in the golden half-light, alerting 1,500 worshipers that their packed auditorium was about to be flooded by a melodic tidal wave. The tsunami began with a minor chord, strummed once on an exquisitely distorted Les Paul guitar. Hard on its heels came the distinctive tremolo of the Hammond B-3 organ, star of the classic-rock era. No synthesized imitation here at Summit Chapel, not when it came to the music.

A Steinway grand joined in, pounding out the same chord,

accompanied by a deafening cymbal crash, three sharp snare beats, the thumps of not one but two bass guitars, and the soaring *aaaahhhs* of half a dozen smartly dressed worship singers of both genders and three races, who smiled and clutched their microphone stands as though their lives depended on it.

The resulting sound was a veritable blast of auditory delight.

"Let's worship Christ!" boomed the voice of worship leader Michael East, boyishly handsome with dark curly hair, neatly trimmed goatee, wearing an untucked button-down shirt and faded jeans—the look of a guy winning his war against middle age.

The congregation leaped to its feet like thirty-somethings at a U2 concert.

Executive Pastor Larry Collins looked out over the crowd from his last-row perch, clapped loudly, and smiled. He loved the way Summit's crowds seemed to convey every possible demographic. African-Americans stood beside Anglos and Hispanics of every age, not to mention skateboarders, college students, older folks, the suits and the casually dressed, business and community leaders alongside the jobless and down-and-outers and the recently paroled. And all of them unselfconsciously swaying side to side, most with hands held high, basking in the emotion invoked by eighty-five decibels of intricately produced, FM-radio-worthy worship rock.

Sometimes Larry closed his eyes, let the music roll over him, and tried to picture Jesus at one of their services. Would He have enjoyed this kind of music?

Sure. Why not? thought Larry. *Jesus is cool . . .*

Occasionally during the worship times, like when the key change in "I Could Sing of Your Love Forever" kicked into high gear, or when that single drumbeat detonated "Agnus Dei's" slow *alleluia*s into a soaring bridge, Larry could sense God's Spirit so powerfully that he would find himself overwhelmed, weeping and fighting the urge to bolt from the sanctuary. For he was certain that God had created resolving harmony, electronic distortion, and reverb as surely as He'd made trees and sunsets.

He'd crafted it all to make human beings' hearts throb to the heartstrings of His beauty.

The third verse ended with a sustained chord from the Les Paul and a scattering of ecstatic applause. Larry always felt a palpable sense of disappointment at the end of worship time.

Now, from a hidden slot high in the ceiling, a thirty-foot-wide projection screen came humming downward. The screen was halfway down before most of the worshipers, still caught up in the last song's afterglow, even noticed it had cleared the proscenium arch and its amber-lit suspensions of denim and crepe-paper decor.

Come on, already . . . Larry Collins urged the screen under his breath. The silent pause for it to finish lowering had dragged on way too long. He never forgot that today's congregations, weaned on television and averse to dead air, did not tolerate long hesitations.

Finally the screen was down, and immediately a huge, vibrant image filled its every inch. "Hello, everyone! Good mornin' from Barbados!" a familiar voice greeted through the speakers. The man's tanned face loomed bigger than a movie star's, and as expressive as always.

"Morning!" the watching crowd replied in perfect unison.

"I'm sorry, but I didn't hear you from all the way over here! You must have run out of coffee or be running a little slow. I said *mornin'*!"

"Mornin'!" the crowd chanted, louder this time.

"Much better," said the man on-screen. "For those of you who are new among us, I'm Alan Rockaway, senior pastor at Summit Chapel. I'm speaking to you all live from the first annual Summit Chapel Couples' Cruise, and man, has it been a blessing so far. And I'm not just talking about the wonderful cruise ship or the beautiful Caribbean surroundings; I'm talking about the incredible lessons we've been unpacking together, about how to strengthen and deepen our marriages and return to the priorities our busy lives often strip from us."

Now it was Larry's turn in the spotlight. He flipped on his

portable microphone and began to stroll down the center aisle as casually as possible. *Keep it casual. Never forget the low-key approach* . . .

"So, Alan," he spoke into the mic, launching into his prepared script. "Come on. You're telling us you're on a cruise ship in the Caribbean and spending your time in some room listening to someone teach?"

On-screen, Alan pressed on a small earphone and laughed on cue. "I hear you, Larry! Doesn't sound likely. But if you heard the wisdom and life-changing counsel we're digging out of God's Word, you'd understand. Dr. Meltz from North Central Seminary is one of our country's finest experts on how to recharge a marriage. His *Stoke the Fire* seminar has so far refueled a quarter-million marriages around the world, and I can tell you, he's about to add seventy-five more to his list!"

"And afterward, you better be enjoying all the cruise ship has to offer."

"You bet! Except for one couple I won't mention, who got so . . . stoked up, they raced straight back to their cabin and haven't been seen since."

Laughter swept through the audience.

"Well, Alan," Larry continued, shaking his head, "maybe we'll leave that for another service."

"Right!" Alan said. "I can see it now—the world's first church service just for grown-ups!"

"Moving right along," Larry said while glancing at the faces around him and wondering if the routine had gone too far. "What are you guys up to now? You don't look like you're onboard the ship."

"I'm glad you asked, Larry. We're about to take one of the cruise's most interesting side trips. We're about to climb into a submarine, specially built for tourists, and take a ninety-minute dive to sample the best of Barbados's underwater sights. As a matter of fact, here's our ride now. Jeff, would you pan over a second?"

The view on-screen tilted away from Alan's oversized face to the greenish-blue tropical waters. There, churning the turquoise surface into a pale froth, emerged the unmistakable profile of an upthrust conning tower.

Beneath it swam the shiny spine of a forty-foot submersible.

3

DENVER—SUMMIT CHAPEL

"So here we are, about to go under the waters and back again!"

Alan Rockaway's voice reverberated from the church speakers with the image of the now-docked submarine filling the screen. Behind him, passengers departing the previous dive filed cautiously across the pier and climbed into a waiting tender boat.

"Although it's not really a baptism; we just thought you'd enjoy the symbolism. And if we resurface in time, we may just come back on and give you a full report! Have a great service, everyone—I love you and miss you all!"

BARBADOS—UNDERWATER EXCURSIONS BOARDING PIER

As the camera panned to him, Alan waved and turned around to give Jeff another *way to go* gesture before leaving him on the pier. His eyes sought out his son and winced in disappointment when they found him, of course, behind the camera. Jeff would think his father was merely signaling to the crowd.

Oh well . . . Alan decided to do it anyway. He raised his right thumb and brandished it high, pumping it forward twice for emphasis. Even making the gesture now felt alien to Alan, the flexing of a long-forgotten muscle.

Good job, son.

It was the gesture he'd always flashed Jeff during those adorable toddler years, whenever the towhead had achieved a boyhood triumph like catching a fly ball or snagging their Nerf football by his fingertips during their backyard playtimes. Jeff had become so thirsty for his father's thumbs-up of approval that he would literally stop in the middle of his soccer match after every single encounter with the ball, eagerly scanning the sidelines for his father's gesture. Once locked on to his father's grin and upheld thumb, the boy would beam like a world champion, his countenance alight with joy.

Alan bit his lip against the sudden pang of regret. It had been almost a decade since he'd given his son that sign of approval. And half that long since he'd seen the old grin transform Jeff's handsome face.

Sign of the times, he told himself. *I'm making it again, but he can't tell it's meant for him. Because now he's the one holding the video camera, where I once used to* . . .

He abandoned the thought and focused on negotiating his entry into the conning tower. But just as his head lowered out of sight, Alan saw his son's free hand extend high into the air, turning into a thumbs-up sign.

"Later, Dad. See you soon."

Alan wished he had a free hand of his own to wipe away the mist in his eyes, but his fingers now gripped the submarine's entry ladder, and he wasn't going to let go for pride or money.

Behind his son, the tender boat turned away, its engines churning up the waters as it headed back to the *Pearl of the Seas.* Again Alan fought a pang of guilt over leaving his son alone on the pier with only its operator for company, baking in the sun.

Oh well, he reassured himself. *It's what he wanted.*

SUMMIT CHAPEL

Jeff's camera now framed Alan's wife, Jenny, and also an older couple who waved enthusiastically at the camera.

"Sounds good, Alan," Larry Collins said into the microphone. "Have a great dive! Oh, and hi, Hal and Audrey!"

The camera lingered on the subjects of Larry's last greeting, the older couple struggling to climb down into the tower. Their excitement over the excursion seemed mixed with self-conscious smiles at making such an awkward entrance under the gaze of the large remote audience.

They disappeared inside. A long moment later the submarine pulled away and began to sink slowly beneath the surface.

"I'm sure most of you regular members recognize Hal and Audrey Newman, probably our oldest and most faithful members," Larry said, trying to fill the void. A whole new set of titters broke out, and he realized his mistake. "I didn't mean *oldest* as in physical age; I meant that they've been with our fellowship since its very beginning. In fact, I'm not sure there would be a Summit Chapel without Hal and his wonderful bride. Of course, for the new folks in our midst, you probably know Hal from those Hal Newman Homes and Hal Newman Mortgage ads . . . And there they go under—"

A high-pitched shout rang out across the sanctuary.

Rumbling sounds, deep and mechanical, vibrated out from the speakers. The camera swirled back around—jerking past obscure flashes of water, blue sky, the distant prow of the receding tender boat, and then a strange white object which suddenly hurtled into view, racing fast toward the lens.

The last image was that of black stenciled words floating upon the large white intrusion.

S.S. Aqua Libre

A deafening CRUNCH shattered the sanctuary's shocked silence. Instantly the on-screen image went black.

Then it seemed as if each of the church's nearly 1,500 voices had blended into a single ear-splitting scream. The anguish of their cries rose to engulf every inch of the place, finally trailing off into sobs and sporadic shouts.

Next, an awful silence fell upon them all. There was nothing to watch, nothing to listen to. No commentator to guide the experience. Many of the women sat with hands pressed over mouths, rocking back and forth in their seats as though trying not to vomit, while the men sat with their hands gripping the seats' arms, biceps flexed, ready to rise and do something. *Save someone. Take action. Anything!*

What now? Larry thought as he struggled in vain to regain his composure, but all he could do was stare openmouthed at the blank screen.

You! a stern voice warned him. *It's up to you now. Step up and take control . . .*

He raised his microphone and began to speak. *Casual* was forgotten. He was lucky to form words at all.

"Folks . . ." Larry said in his most solemn voice, then paused. "Let's, uh, stay calm and . . . say a prayer. Yeah . . . let's all bow our heads and say a prayer for our brothers and sisters and whatever it is they're going through right now."

Pastor Larry Collins bowed his head for thirty of the longest seconds of his life.

After inwardly pleading with God for a happy explanation for what they'd just seen, he raised the mic to his mouth and said, "Friends, at the moment I have no more answers than anyone else. We've witnessed something we don't really understand. Because this was a live broadcast transmission, it's unclear whether what we saw was a serious accident, or some prank, or a fluke—like maybe Jeff Rockaway, Alan's son, who accompanied his dad to film the cruise, slipped and fell or something. We just don't know. All we can do is keep praying. Elders? Could we have all the elders who are present come up to the front to assist?"

Larry noticed someone at the control booth waving wildly.

He squinted and shielded his eyes from the overhead lights, then shrugged, for he could not hear what the individual was saying. Finally he spoke through the microphone. "I'm sorry, control booth—do you have something for us?"

A loud crackle erupted over the speaker system. Then a voice—young, masculine, out of breath, very frightened. "Oh no! Oh no!" Jeff's voice repeated. "Some boat came out of nowhere and smashed into them! It hit the submarine! I've lost sight of them!"

New Jerusalem—Many Years in the Future

The distraught young pilgrim and her mysterious new friend had now walked a good distance from the pit of horrors. They blended into the huge crowd of smiling, singing pilgrims who continued to mill about the farthest edges outside the Temple Mount. The dark smoke continued to rise, but the pair now stood with their backs to the sight.

"But I don't understand," she said through her tears. "Something huge and awful just happened, there at the end. What kind of story is this? One of those old fictions?"

"Fictions?" he said, smiling.

"Yes. Back in . . . those former days, I remember how people used to distract themselves by reading these long and involved stories."

"You are very perceptive, Lydia."

"Who told you my name?"

He glanced over at her sharply.

She was unusually beautiful. In these times, such perfection was commonplace. Yet he noted a special luminous quality in her eyes, her hands, her pale skin, and hair so fine and blond it appeared almost white around features as petite and delicate as her frame. Her air of vulnerability only magnified the impact of the horrible sight the young woman had just witnessed.

He nodded as though considering a reply to her question,

then thought the better of it. Instead, he took a deep breath and decided to change the subject.

She beat him to it with another question.

"I'm just wondering," said Lydia, "how such an unreal story is going to help me deal with what I saw down there?"

"You're going to have to trust me. First of all, let me assure you this story is not fiction; it really happened. And please do not form any judgments about what part of the story is most important, because you'll be surprised. Very surprised. Just bear with me and listen. All right?"

She let out a sigh. "All right. I trust you."

"Now, I'm going to back up a bit and give you more background. We'll start at the beginning of the cruise, then catch up to the catastrophe."

4

For Jeff Rockaway, the first leg of the trip had begun with a too-early departure time and drop-off by his mother at Denver International Airport. Running late as usual, with a razor-thin margin in which to clear security and reach his party at the gate, the teenager leaned over to give his mother a good-bye kiss.

"What's the matter, Mom?" he asked as he pulled back and noticed a tear on her cheek. "Don't worry about me. I'm gonna have a great time."

"Oh, it's not that, honey," she said with a brave smile. "It's just—seeing all this. Knowing that I'm kind of avoiding the crowd, not wanting to see people who used to be my best friends. Knowing how uncomfortable they'd be to see me, too." She stared out through the windshield and sighed wistfully.

"They'd love to see you, Mom," Jeff insisted.

"No, they wouldn't. That's just the way it is." She grew pensive, then abruptly came back to the present. "Look, don't worry about me, either. I'll be fine. I've moved on—you know that.

Really. So go have a blast. I love you."

"Love you, too," Jeff said, reaching for the door handle. "I'll call you later, let you know how it's going."

He leaped from the car without remembering to close the door behind him. With a weary, bemused look on her face, Terri Rockaway pushed the gearshift into park, opened the door, and walked around her car to close the passenger door as her son disappeared into the airport terminal for the flight to Galveston, where the church group would embark.

She waved to him but did not glance at the terminal, then hurried back into the anonymity of her car.

GALVESTON, TEXAS

For the first time in his life, Hal Newman, one of Denver's leading businessmen and founding member of Summit Chapel, was wearing a flowered-print Hawaiian shirt, along with other adventurous attire, all of it mismatched.

In fact, Alan Rockaway had taken great pleasure, while walking across the gangway, in pointing out Hal's black socks—comically inappropriate in combination with his tan leather walking shoes and ill-fitting khaki shorts. Even Hal's wife, Audrey, couldn't keep herself from laughing, reminding Hal, after he'd turned on her in irritation, that for once she had not chosen his clothes. *"You're on your own, honey,"* she'd told him as she watched him pack those black socks.

Before long, a buildup of laughter like that of a grand party echoed out from the pier, the bridge behind them, and even the ship's nearby decks. For a throng of Summit Chapel couples were now gathered in the vicinity, watching and enjoying themselves as the rest of the group arrived.

"Feels like a family reunion," Alan said to Jenny as they stepped aboard. And then he leaned over and kissed his wife on the lips.

One of those following the Rockaways, who overheard the pastor teasing Hal and awarded it a careworn smile, was Carrie

Knowles, forty-five, a mother and church icon. Norm, her accountant husband, had dared to reach over as they stepped onto the gangway and pull out Carrie's hair clip, releasing a cascade of blond-gray hair which no one at Summit Chapel had ever seen unbound before.

"Norm!" she shrieked, turning around, yet unable to stifle a playful grin.

"I told you we were gonna let our hair down," he joked. "And I was serious."

"I should have known what you meant," she replied with a teasing smile, "since I'm the only one of the two of us who *has* any hair."

"Oooohhh," he mock groaned and stepped onto the welcome deck. Norm turned to the church member beside him and grinned. "Took me three months of constant badgering to get her here," Norm said out of the side of his mouth.

"How will the church nursery or children's program manage?" the man asked.

"I don't know," Norm laughed. "I hear they're canceling all activities while she's away." Even though Norm didn't know the man very well, the stranger smiled and nodded. Carrie's commitment to the church was so legendary, even new members were aware of her diligence.

"So far away from all those obligations," he noted, "what on earth will she do with herself?"

Norm turned to him, raised an eyebrow, and whispered, "That's for *me* to find out."

The gigantic ship edged effortlessly away from the pier, the power of its engines surging to a low hum, and soon the mainland gave way to a sea glittering under beams of late-afternoon sunlight. Onlookers cheered as reggae music played over the decks' speakers, with confetti flying across the railings in an offshore breeze. The whole scene proved so enchanting that the Rockaways and many other church couples found it difficult to tear themselves away to find their way to the cabins.

Probably the only attendee not smiling and cheering was Jeff, who stood to one side and watched with an expression of wariness mixed with deep reserve.

Jeff did not live with his father, and normally he would have considered the prospect of spending a week in a romantic setting with his dad and stepmother, Jenny, an ordeal to be endured. But a month earlier, his father had met him at a local Starbucks and made him an offer he could hardly refuse.

"Come with me on a free Caribbean cruise. You'll have tons of free time. Some of it, when I can get away, you and I will spend together. Just boy-time—you and me catching up on a lot of hanging out we've missed. And here's the kicker. You can bring your video equipment and shoot a documentary of the event for the church. A real commercial product the attendees will want to buy when it's over. Plus you'll have a great piece for your showcase reel."

Jeff desperately wanted to enter the field of video production, so the offer to tape the trip was indeed tempting. Besides, it wasn't the worst working environment in the world. The only part Jeff truly dreaded was the indoor sessions, and, as it turned out, for good reason.

The Summit Chapel couples contingent met that first night in one of the ship's meeting rooms to great fanfare and carefully staged enthusiasm. An actual trumpet blast blared from a speaker as Dr. Meltz, of *Stoke the Fire* fame, bounded forth in a getup of flowered lei, Hawaiian shirt, Bermuda shorts, and Birkenstock sandals.

Filming the display, Jeff had cringed at the sight, grateful that his reaction was hidden behind the camera.

"Welcome, Stokers!" the speaker called out in a clear and eager voice.

"Welcome!" they echoed loudly, for these diehard Summit Chapel folks had been conditioned to amplify the energetic salutations from the platform.

Now with microphone in hand, the speaker asked, "Do you

all know what a stoker is?" He shielded his eyes from the spotlight, leaning forward to spot any raised hands. "You . . ." He pointed to a muscular, middle-aged man with a crew cut, who Jeff guessed was either a fireman or policeman.

"Someone who's stoked! Like me!" he responded like a good sport.

"No, actually that's a stok*ee*!" said Meltz with a burst of laughter. "Now, let me tell you what a stok*er* is, guys."

Jeff cringed again. Drawing from his experience as a preacher's kid, Jeff sized him up immediately. This was one of those concerned Christian guys who would reach his arm around you and breathe your first name in a warm, relational tone— even if he'd just read it off your nametag.

"You see," Meltz continued, using broad, exaggerated gestures, "during the early part of the last century, before the advent of modern marine engines, mighty ships like this one were fueled by coal. And the coal-fired engine required the employment of a very specialized, very dangerous profession. This was a crew of men whose job it was to stand in the mouth of the furnaces for fourteen hours a day and make sure the fires burned as hot as humanly possible. Often over five hundred degrees. These men were called stokers, because that's what they did all day long."

He paused dramatically, his arm extended in midair.

"And that's exactly what I'm going to make out of every one of you! Stokers. Ladies included. I want you to become intimately aware of the state of the fire that is burning, or maybe flickering, between you and your mate. And dedicated to working without ceasing to keep it as hot and as bright as humanly— and maybe divinely—possible. When you do that, you'll find yourself onboard for an awesome journey to places beyond your wildest imagination!"

The rest of the session had proceeded remarkably close to Jeff's expectations. Breaking up into small groups, reviewing the thick seminar book's Table of Contents, the writing down of personal goals and wishes on small bits of paper—folding them tightly and storing them securely in a purse or wallet.

Jeff felt like he was submerged in something he'd navigated his whole life: *Christian cool*. A fairly cheesy, if well-intentioned, alternate reality where everyone smiled broadly every moment of the day, every joke was *darn* funny, and every acronym spelled out a potentially life-changing insight.

He didn't actually despise or even disregard these characteristics. But after a lifetime in the pews, he simply felt jaded. Too familiar with their conventions to muster any personal investment.

And then came the question. Out of the blue, an earnest, overweight man in his forties stood up and asked something that brought the joy-juggernaut to a sudden stop.

"I'm sorry, but before I can even begin to take in what's being taught here, I have to settle a question that's been dogging me for the last few years. I've been told my marriage can't be blessed because I made a bad mistake at one point in the past and then moved on."

Meltz's charm offensive came to a screeching halt. He cocked his head, tried to mask a twinge of agitation, and began to visibly search his memory banks, raising his eyebrows and clenching his facial muscles.

"Man, that is such a loaded question that I'm not sure I should tackle it here," Meltz said slowly, clearly scrambling mentally as he spoke. "Can we maybe meet after—"

"If it's all right with you, I'd like to field this one," said Alan Rockaway, standing up.

Meltz looked at him and nodded, not saying anything.

Jeff's father walked forward, causing his son to flinch even more intensely than before. Alan took the microphone from Meltz's hand, then turned with a sudden brightness in his countenance.

With Meltz at his side, Alan said, "I think Jenny and I have special insight on that. I really do." He turned to the man who still stood with an open, questioning look on his face. "So you've been told that because you married the wrong person a long time ago, maybe before coming to know God, and then divorced and remarried the right person, that your life can't matter because you're out of His will?"

"Yeah, that's basically it," the man replied, easing back into his seat.

"Well, that's just nonsense!" Alan barked. "Let me set your mind at rest. The biggest thing I learned when I went through this very same valley was not how much I need a pass from God. What you really need to learn now is how to forgive yourself. Bottom line."

"I've tried, but I'm just not sure—"

"Listen," Alan interrupted, leaning forward and giving the man his warmest smile. "God is the God of second chances. That's what the Cross is all about—a grace so powerful and even *aggressive* that it swept into the world to give the human race another chance at reaching its true potential. Life like God wanted it—not our sad, dingy version of it. He doesn't expect us to sit and wallow in our old mistakes. The Cross of Christ gives us the strength and direction to get up and, with His power, to reverse our past. To do something about it. Take action. Sometimes it's hard. Sometimes, as I've learned from personal experience, it's incredibly painful. We become encrusted in our old patterns. Sometimes our lives grow up over those mistakes, the way skin sometimes does over a partially healed scar. And that makes the truest, deepest healing doubly painful, because it requires everything that grew up over the mistake to be torn away. But I promise you, the result is worth it. It's literally the difference between wallowing in death and stepping out in what the Bible calls 'newness of life.'"

Alan paused, his gaze fixed on the questioner.

He continued, "Please, everyone, pray this with me: Jesus, You forgave me, so I forgive myself."

"Jesus, You forgave me, so I forgive myself," came the echo on cue.

"Due to the grace You provided, my life is worth another chance."

"Due to the grace You provided, my life is worth another chance."

"Good. So was mine. And so was my family's."

Alan said this with the briefest of glances at Jeff, who was still crouching behind his camera lens.

The apparatus concealed a face streaked with tears.

RESCUED

5

The next several days of the cruise unfolded like one of those dreams from which people long not to awaken. The skies remained a deep blue, the daytime breezes wafted a slight autumn chill across the decks, and the cool nights dazzled with millions of stars and acres of shipboard lights. The ports of call—San Juan, Aruba, St. Thomas, and Dominica—offered the couples exotic, breathtaking getaways from the ship.

Best of all, the attendees' morale soared close to that of third graders on the last day of school. The Summit Chapel folks were downright ebullient, quickly becoming the cruise's most boisterous passengers.

Despite the somewhat rocky start, the retreat's teachings proved effective. Couples who had boarded the ship barely aware of each other soon found themselves throwing their flame's "dying embers into the wind," as Dr. Meltz described it, alternately laughing, crying, letting go of resentments, and sharing needs they'd kept cooped up for years.

"God's up to something!" Pastor Alan kept shouting from the podium between sessions. "If your marriage isn't improving by the hour, we may just have to issue you another mate!"

After his first day's delicate admissions, everyone laughed very, very heartily at that.

The only person, it seemed, not joining in the laughter and fun was, again, Jeff Rockaway. Every day found him increasingly grateful for his camera's ability to conceal his growing malaise.

Even Alan, caught up in the whirlwind of the journey, did not fully realize what was happening until the eighth night at sea, the eve of their Barbados boarding.

Left alone at the railing for the first time, after Jenny had gone to their cabin for a nap, Alan caught sight of his son lurking in a corner, filming him surreptitiously. It struck him as strange, sad, and wrong.

"Jeff," he called, holding his hand before his face like a stalked movie star. "Turn that thing off and come over here and talk to me."

For a moment, the question seemed to hover in the air between them.

Finally the red light blinked off, and the lens lowered to reveal features clouded with equal measures of confusion and wariness.

"Please, son. Come here," Alan repeated.

The camera seemed to fall like dead weight to the young man's side. He walked slowly over to his dad.

"Jenny's the most intuitive person I've ever known. Being a woman and all." Alan sighed, hoping the obvious yet unintended inference about his first wife, Jeff's mother, had gone unnoted. "And she tells me that you're not exactly having as much fun as the rest of us."

"It's all right," Jeff said.

"No, it's not all right. I asked you to come and I hoped it would be a great time for everybody. I'm sorry if it's been hard for you."

Jeff shrugged for the second time. "I should have known,

Dad. I mean, I don't have anything against Jenny. It's just . . . it's just weird being here and videotaping you 'making your marriage all it could be,' you know, 'working on your love'"—he made air quotes with both hands as he spoke the two phrases— "when you never did that for—"

"Your mother?" Alan interrupted sharply. "Hey, you have no idea how long and how hard I worked on my relationship with your mother. I'm sorry this is *weird* for you. But you can't just write off twenty years of my praying for a good marriage like it was nothing."

"You never took her on one of *these*."

"You know why? Because your mother would never have gone on one of *these*. She would have scoffed in my face. Said something like, 'I don't need somebody to shrink-wrap and market my marriage back to me.' Some derisive bit of genius like that."

"Fine. It's still strange, okay?"

"Granted." Alan sighed and looked back out over the railing. "So, do you want to quit?"

"No." His tone made it clear he hadn't set aside his anger. "I'm *not* a quitter. Tomorrow's our last port. The thing's almost over. Maybe I'll let someone else do the postproduction, I don't know. But I'm sticking with it to the end."

"Good. Well, Barbados ought to be fun," Alan offered, trying his hardest. "You wanna come on the submarine with us?"

"Yeah," Jeff jeered. "Like I haven't been in close enough quarters with all of you!"

Alan took a deep, exasperated breath. *Couldn't resist one last dig . . .*

"You can just stay on the pier, then, film us going under and surfacing. It'll probably work out for the best. I'll take my own video camera with me, and if you're lucky, I'll let you use some of my dive footage."

"Oh, right," Jeff snorted. "If I'm really, really lucky." He turned to face the sea.

"Come on, son. It was just a little joke. How about losing the attitude? It doesn't suit you." With that, Alan walked off across the crowded deck, back to his cabin, and to Jenny, who by now was probably waiting for him.

If I'm lucky, Jeff thought, leaning over the rail, *maybe the submarine can just stay down there for a long, long while.*

LATER THAT NIGHT—HIGH ABOVE THE SHIP

"Hello?"

"Mom, it's Jeff."

"Son? Is everything okay?"

"Yeah, everything's fine. You wouldn't believe what I'm looking at right now. Right this second I'm looking out over a solid blue horizon from three hundred forty-eight feet above the surface of the ocean. I'm so high that even the ship's bridge is about seventy-five feet below me. I can see the eastern coast of Barbados over twenty miles away."

"I don't understand. You're higher than the captain's bridge?"

"That's right. I'm at the very top of the radio mast."

"You sneaked up on your own? Oh, Jeff, you promised—"

The young man laughed. "Don't worry. I made friends with the communications officer back when I made the arrangements for the uplink. When I told him I was taping a documentary and needed some good master shots, he took me up here. He's a film buff, and he knew just what I was talking about. He sneaked me in."

"So you're legal."

"Sort of."

"Please get down, Jeff. I'm getting vertigo just listening to you talk. You know you and your brother are all I have left. I've missed you so much these last few days, and it's really come home to me. You and Greg are *it*. I'm not sure I'd survive if anything happened to one of you."

"Relax, Mom. I didn't call you to spook you. I called because

I'm having some serious second thoughts about what I came here to do."

"What? You're going to scrap having a good time?"

"No, I'm thinking of scrapping the whole stinking video project and doing something else. Instead of some lame, cutesy documentary about how Dad's flock got their marriages stoked up, I'm thinking of throwing together a totally extreme, in-your-face, MTV-style short on hypocrisy within the Christian world. What do you think?"

There was a long pause. When her voice returned, its lilt was laced with irony and even humor. "I could narrate it myself, son, you know that. But why? What changed your mind so quickly?"

"Mom," he said with a sigh. "It's so bizarre being on this cruise. I don't know what I was thinking. I mean, they're all here—not just Jenny, but Old Man Newman, that Stepford lady Carrie Knowles—all the same people who stopped talking to us, along with their kids, when Dad moved out."

"I understand. But still, they're good people, Jeff. Maybe not the bravest, or the most loving, but then, they were confused when things came apart between me and your father. They didn't know what to say, how to act. And I decided not to make them have to choose sides. I purposely made it easier for them."

Jeff's voice now quivered. "Do you realize how horrible those days were for me and Greg? Until then we were the most popular guys in the whole youth group. Preacher's sons—you know how it was. Everybody wanted to be our friend, all the girls liked us. We were invited to every party, every sleepover, every outing. Life was awesome. And then one day, not only did we lose our dad, our family, but our whole world. Nobody would look us in the eye. No one talked to us the same way. For the longest time I felt like I'd done something wrong, like I'd failed somehow. And then *bam*. We were going to another church, and it was all gone for good."

"I know, Jeff," Terri replied, her own voice beginning to quiver. "I know . . ."

"I thought I'd gotten over it. But now, seeing those same

faces and those same awkward looks, hearing the same lame greetings, it's all come back. And I don't think I want to put up with it again."

"Jeff, you're strong. You may not realize it, but you're the strongest person I know. And I know that not only can you take it, but you have the strength to put all this aside and film the documentary you promised your father."

"Why? Why do these people deserve this?"

"I can't speak for everyone, son. But let me tell you one good reason why your father deserves it. He wasn't always . . . well, you know, what he's become. He started out the most dedicated and inspired Christian guy I'd ever known. Which was why I married him. Let me tell you a story I don't think he ever told you . . ."

6

CARROLLTON, TEXAS—*EIGHTEEN YEARS EARLIER*

The Rockaway family had just moved to Carrollton, then a quiet suburb of Dallas, where Alan had assumed his first pastorate.

On one tranquil Tuesday morning, Terri looked over the bulge of her pregnant stomach to the sight of a disheveled-looking man standing in the front doorway. It stood open so the screen door would allow early breezes into the house.

One room away, on the small house's dining room table, Alan was busy at the keyboard of a second-generation PC, drafting his very first word-processed sermon.

Terri couldn't help but recoil at the visitor's appearance but realized that retreating to let her husband answer the door was already out of the question. The odd visitor had seen her.

She approached the door with a faint smile.

"Hello . . ."

"Ma'am, I won't trouble you," the man said with a strong Southern accent. "I'm just here to see the reverend." Terri stiffened, for his bloodshot eyes, swaying body, and the smell of alcohol indicated he'd been drinking.

"Honey, there's someone here to see you," she called over her shoulder.

Her husband quickly appeared. "Hello, Kyle," Alan said, a certain reserve creeping into his voice.

"Pastor, I was wondering if you'd step outside for a second."

The statement sounded very much like a barfly's fighting challenge, so Terri stayed put at the screen door and watched as her husband nodded and stepped outside with the man.

"I'm just wondering, Pastor," the man spat out as soon as the two had reached the front yard, "if it's true you're fixin' to tear up my marriage bond and marry my wife."

"Kyle, I'm not going to marry Susan. I'm just performing the ceremony."

"Please don't get smart with me. You may have noticed I'm not in a good mood."

"I *have* noticed," Alan responded. "In fact, your temper is probably the reason you're no longer Susan's husband. You and I both know you hit that poor girl many, many times, even threatening her life. I did not make the decision lightly to perform Susan's wedding. Yet in your case, I thought her divorce was not only justified but imperative. I don't want to be rude, and I wish there was a loving way to say this, but she had to divorce you to protect her own life."

"I wish you hadn't said that," Terri heard the visitor say, just before his arm lashed out and the sharp *smack* of a fist against facial bone rang across the yard. Alan's shattered glasses flew off into her petunias. Her husband stumbled backward, nearly losing his footing.

"You see, Kyle—that didn't exactly disprove my point," Alan muttered. He caught his wife's terrified expression as she stood frozen in the doorway, her mouth open, and nodded her away, silently warning her not to intervene. Meanwhile, blood started trickling from his nose, and a bruise was already beginning to shine on his cheekbone.

"Preacher, I couldn't care less about your point!" the man

shouted and then struck Alan again, this time knocking him to the ground.

Terri could not contain herself any longer. She yelled, "Stop!" and marched out onto the lawn.

Alan glanced up at her from his spot on the ground and said softly, "No, Terri. Stop. Jesus loves . . ."

Frustrated and amazed, she glared at him, knowing what he was telling her to do.

"Jesus loves you, Kyle," Alan finished, looking up at his attacker.

With clenched fists the man looked down at Alan, then at Terri, and moved back a step. He frowned, tottering on his feet, and glanced around him like someone who had no clue what to do next.

Alan rose slowly and plucked his mangled glasses from the flower bed.

The two men stood silent for a moment, Alan contemplating his lenses, wiping the blood from his nose, the drunken visitor glancing wildly around.

"You know what else I'm going to do, Pastor Rockaway?" the man said.

Without looking up, Alan chuckled at his lone lens. "No, Kyle. What else are you going to do?"

"I'm going to move my membership!"

Alan laughed out loud.

"Kyle, I imagine the deacons and I will be okay with that."

"Mom, I've heard that story a dozen times."

"I'm sure you have, Jeff. But did you ever hear what came next? The second part your father and I never told you . . ."

Three hours later, long after Kyle had left the scene, while Alan spent the remaining afternoon being cared after by his wife, a police cruiser pulled up. It was now dusk, an unusually fiery and beautiful sunset extending across the horizon.

It turned out that Kyle had not been content to revel in his pummeling of the hapless pastor. He had promptly sought out his ex-wife's new residence, produced a semiautomatic rifle, and proceeded to take the people he loved most in the world as hostages. At that moment he was surrounded by a sizable contingent of the metropolitan S.W.A.T. team.

And Kyle was asking for Pastor Rockaway.

"Don't you dare!" Terri warned him. "You did your part, honey. I mean, look at you."

It was then that Alan had turned and flashed her a grin she would eventually come to resent—even as she admired its idealistic bravado.

"I didn't tell him."

"What? That Jesus loves him?"

"No. That *I* love him."

"Don't go, Alan, please. I mean it."

He smiled, kissed her warmly, and started to leave.

"We've got a baby on the way!" she called a moment later as he climbed into the cruiser with the police officer. "Don't you leave our child fatherless!"

He raised his hand out the open window, waved, and the car sped away.

Five minutes later, outside the hostage site, Alan crouched at the front line of a scene ripped from the movies—behind the roof of one of ten police cars parked around the front of a modest clapboard house. On every side of him, police officers kneeled, gripping either a handgun or a rifle. Looking to his left and right, the young pastor counted a dozen or more guns aimed straight at the home's sagging and torn screen door.

Alan held a bullhorn in his hand, and as he pressed the button to speak, deep down he felt the surge of knowing a man's life depended on him.

"Kyle, Pastor Rockaway speaking. I understand you wanted to talk with me."

No response.

"I'm here to tell you something," he continued, "just in case you missed it. I was too busy worrying about my glasses, a silly little thing like that, to really tune in. Jesus loves you, Kyle. In spite of everything you've done, He loves you. But something else. I love you, too. Broken glasses and bruised face and all. I love you like a brother. And right now I'll do everything I can to help you with this situation you're in."

Again, no response.

Alan stood, his free arm held wide. "Listen, Kyle. Why don't we start with you letting your wife and girl go. Just let them leave the house, and I'll come in to replace them. Just don't shoot anyone, okay?"

"No!" a S.W.A.T. team member nearby hissed. "You're going to get yourself killed."

Alan turned to him, a look of peace and resignation on his face. "This isn't my choice," Alan said to the officer. "It's God's. He's been telling me to do this, and I believe He's going to see me through."

Ten seconds later, the small, terrified face of a two-year-old girl appeared in the doorway. Just behind her shone the tear-stained face of her mother. Both of them sprinted from the front porch toward the parked police cars.

Alan stepped out from behind the cruiser, both arms held high. "Kyle, I'm coming in!" he shouted, unaided by the bull-horn. "You see, I'm unarmed. No games."

"Stop!" said the S.W.A.T. captain. "You don't have to go in there. He made the mistake of sending out his hostages without having another. We can take him now."

"This is a distraught father who can still make something of his life," Alan said. "Nobody's going to *take* him. Besides, I gave him my word. I'm going in."

Alan began to make his way forward.

"Stop right there!" the captain ordered. "Do not go any far-ther."

Alan turned to face the captain, arms still high above his head. "I told you—I gave my word, and I'm going to keep it. This man is a member of my church, at least for now, and he needs my help. He's *asked* for my help."

He took his second, then third step forward. He could feel each gun barrel behind him, aimed on the porch.

"Then you're going in at your own risk," the captain warned, "meaning you've forfeited your right to protection. I'll give you ten minutes with him. Ten minutes and then we storm the place."

Alan flashed him a conciliatory smile but did not say a word. He continued walking. Time seemed to slow, until finally he had reached the steps. He climbed them and crossed the small porch. As he approached, the screen door parted and a pale arm extended from its shadow, beckoning him inside.

Kyle no longer resembled the aggressive, bellowing creature of that morning. His eyes were now filled with a fear Alan had not seen on a man's face before. His body was trembling, the former haughty expression replaced by one of dejection.

"You're right to be scared," Alan said, wading into the trashed remains of Kyle's ex-wife's kitchen. "They're talking about breaking in any second. It's time to give yourself up."

"It's too late," Kyle muttered. "Too late now. It's all over."

"No, it's not," Alan countered sharply. "Think of your little girl. Do the right thing, stay alive for her."

"In prison? What kind of daddy is that?"

"It's a daddy she can visit, call on the phone, write letters to. And come to know again, someday, when you get out. Instead of visiting a gravestone once a year."

Kyle sighed and shook his head sadly.

"Look," Alan said. "We'll go out together. I'll go first and shield you—"

"I heard them shout at you," Kyle interrupted. "They're mad at you; they're not going to cut us any slack."

"That may be true, but they're not going to shoot—not if you put down the rifle and follow right behind me, and when we get down the steps we'll kneel together with our hands up. Trust me, it'll be all right."

"No way! They'll shoot me for sure."

Alan tried to make his voice as soothing and calming as possible. "No, my friend. Once they see you're not a threat, they will hold their fire."

Kyle stood utterly still for a moment before speaking again.

"What is it?" Alan asked.

Finally the man replied, "Can . . . can we pray first?"

"Of course," Alan said, feeling a little sheepish that he, the pastor, had not thought of this—and also a bit impatient at the inopportune timing. Nevertheless, he reached out his hand to the shaking shoulder before him. He squeezed and shut his eyes.

"Dear Jesus, my brother Kyle has made some very poor choices today. All of us do, as You know, except that these are liable to carry some major consequences. And yet Kyle loves You and desires to follow You, don't you, Kyle?"

"I sure do," Kyle answered.

"We want to ask Your forgiveness right now, through the blood of Your Son," Alan continued. "We ask that You wash us both clean of the sins that stand between us and Your presence. And then we beg You for Your protection. We ask You to set up a hedge of angelic protection around the two of us as we step out that door. Will You please do that for us, dear God? In Jesus' name, *amen*."

A highly charged silence followed the prayer's end. The ominous destiny of the moment awaiting them loomed heavily, with an almost tangible weight.

"One more thing," Alan said. "I've changed my mind. And I want you to change yours. Don't move your membership. So long as you repent of all this, turn your life around, and want to still follow Christ, there's a place for you on our rolls. Understand?"

Kyle did not reply, for tears were running down his cheeks. He nodded mutely.

Alan then turned his gaze toward the front window and the situation outside. The late-afternoon sunlight was streaming into the house, glinting off the police cars surrounding the place. A great calm settled upon him, and Alan felt that, in a way he hadn't experienced before, he had just arrived as a pastor.

He had just come into his own as a shepherd of men.

Terri, who had arrived just a few minutes earlier, strained to see the screen door open a split second before any of the S.W.A.T. members poised in front of her. She heard her husband's voice and noticed that it seemed to embody more strength and authority than she'd ever heard it convey up till now.

"Don't shoot!" Alan called. "Please. I'm coming out first, and Kyle with me. Unarmed."

She saw the policemen's faces turn toward their captain, looking for his direction. It occurred to her that her husband's fate was being sealed in that delicate exchange—a subtle reading of one man's expression by more than a dozen policemen. The twitch of a cheek. The narrowing of eyelids. A slight head motion.

She turned back to Alan. She strained to take in every aspect of his appearance and found that she could not focus her gaze on his figure. She looked down and blinked her eyes to try to clear them. When she looked back, he was already at the bottom step and kneeling, Kyle beside him.

She blinked again. It looked as if the two were praying instead of obeying the commands of the S.W.A.T. captain, who had now approached and stood shouting over them, his M-16 rifle trained intently on Kyle.

She frowned, for she still could not gain a clear view of her husband. There seemed to be a glow about him, his face appearing radiant somehow.

Terri moved back to the perimeter's far edge, where Kyle's ex-wife stood on her tiptoes, trying to maintain her sight of what was happening. The little girl stood grasping her mother's legs.

Then the S.W.A.T. captain barked an order, and Terri turned to see the other officers rise up with their guns leveled on the kneeling men. She heard Kyle whimper as two larger officers fell on him and handcuffed his wrists behind his back. The sight of him buried under so much retribution caused her hostility toward the man to melt away. Instead of a combative, wife-abusing loser, she saw a lost church member, a precious soul for whom her husband had just bought some time, time in which to try and reclaim his presence on this earth.

She stepped out across the yard and ran toward Alan. He was pushing himself up from one knee when she reached him.

"So, Reverend Rockaway. You sure do work hard to retain your church members," she said with a wry smile, hands on her hips. Then she threw her arms around him.

"Hey, every single one is precious," he said, shaking his head at the whole experience.

PEARL OF THE SEAS—TOP OF THE RADIO MAST

"So, Mom, what's your point? That Dad is Superman?"

"Come on. You have to admit it's a pretty impressive story. One that says a lot about him."

"Yeah. I guess you're right. It's more than I'd ever dream Dad was capable of doing. I'm just curious what the moral is. I mean, given what else has happened between you two."

"The story's not over, Jeff."

"What? What could you possibly add to that ending?"

"Kyle, the man the story's all about? He's Kyle Jeffrey."

The line fell silent. Seconds passed before Jeff said at last, "Kyle *Jeffrey*? You mean Tia's dad? My favorite—"

"Your favorite soccer coach. That's right. Your dad kept in touch with him in prison. In fact, he never did leave the church rolls. Even when we moved to Denver, he treated Kyle like a member of Summit. Your dad wrote letters to him every week, prayed for him, counseled him, even informed him of the breakup of Susan's engagement. A few years later he remarried them about halfway through his stretch in prison. Kyle did nine years, and after he got out, your dad got him a job up here in Denver."

"Does that mean Tia's that little girl?"

"She has no memory of it, and they certainly don't talk about it today. That's why you never learned the second half of the story."

"I can't believe this, Mom. I mean, Kyle is the coolest, most together, greatest Christian dad I've ever—"

"Apart from your dad."

"Apart from what my dad *used* to be."

"Well, just remember that it's never too late for any of us to turn around. God's doing something inside even the heart you've most wanted to spit on."

"All right, Mom." Jeff sighed so loudly that his mother could hear it over the phone. "I won't derail the video project. I'll hold my nose and get the job done."

"Good. I'm so glad to hear that, honey."

"But there's a price."

"What's that?"

"You have to watch the outtakes. Every bad Hawaiian shirt, every pair of low-rider shorts with plumber's cleavage, every pair of black socks with leisure shoes. You have to watch every frame."

"If you film it, Jeff, I'll gladly watch every frame . . ."

And then her voice was gone.

RESCUED

7

BARBADOS—S.S. *PEARL OF THE SEAS*

The day dawned with no portent—calm and warm, just like the eight before it. The Couples Cruise participants took their breakfast together in the ship's cavernous Grand Buffet Room, feasting on copious servings of delicacies such as lobster frittatas, blueberry-stuffed pears, and crab enchiladas. Afterward they hurried into the theater that would, later in the day, host movies and a Broadway-style musical revue. But for now they were to hear Dr. Meltz introduce his idea of "jumping out of the fire and into the furnace"—in other words, how to maintain the cruise's good feelings after everyone had returned to their ordinary lives. The cruise was nearing an end, and everyone could tell their teacher was preparing them for it.

Later that morning, they had a light lunch (at least by cruise standards) and then disembarked into Bridgetown, Barbados. Half the group would spend the afternoon wandering the streets and shops of the *Bajan* capital, while the others boarded a small ferry for a quick jaunt to the boarding pier and the ultimate in sight-seeing excursions: a ninety-minute submarine ride amid the undersea wonders of the Caribbean.

NEWPORT, RHODE ISLAND—THAT SAME MOMENT

A full continent to the north, the dockside offices of Newport, Rhode Island's New England Shipwerks rang with a GPS-triggered alarm sent from the *Aqua Libre*'s navigational computer. Dan Scholberg, vice-president of the elite yacht maker, froze in place, frowned, and ran over to his desktop computer.

The sound of pounded keys and of Scholberg's cursing blended almost at once.

Then it stopped, and the rest of the ten-person office staff gathered breathless behind his shoulders.

"I don't believe it . . ." one female voice said, almost in a whisper.

Scholberg sprang from his seat, hands grasping for the cell phone at his waist, and rushed from the room.

Outside, on a deck overlooking the mast-studded, deep-blue water of Narragansett Bay, he bent over in distress and spoke into his flip-top phone.

"Brad, it's me, Dan. Look, there's been a disaster aboard the *Libre*. Or at least there's about to be. Best I can tell, it's the navigation system's speed preferences. Something's happened to Marshall, and it looks like he forgot to adjust the factory settings . . . Well, that's the thing, Brad. I can't get to him, and the boat's about to crash into the western coast of Barbados!"

Pausing to hear his response, Scholberg stood straight again and stared at the sky.

"No, I don't know anybody in Barbados, but I know someone who can help," he said in a rush. "Remember our man in St. Kitts, the one who handled the Gucciano flap? He's got connections all over the Caribbean. I'm pretty sure he has one or two with the Barbados Navy."

Now Scholberg turned briefly toward the office windows behind him and scowled suspiciously.

"Oh, I'm sure a half million would handle it just fine. Yeah, just an extra five or six hours and we'll know what we've got on our hands. If someone could intercept, he could make it so the authorities couldn't tell a thing, except that Marshall Rhodes wasn't at the helm. It might do the job. But who's gonna call the client? Oh, man—I want that job like I want a bullet through the head . . . Okay, but let's wait until this all shakes out before we tell him. For all he knows, the only thing we're sailing into Barbados is some other client's boat."

NEW JERUSALEM—MOUNT OF OLIVES

The young woman named Lydia and her mysterious new friend had now wandered up to the Mount of Olives and entered under the marble overhang of a vast and glorious building.

"In the Days of Mist this was called the Basilica of the Agony," her companion said, looking up around him. "It was built to honor Jesus' suffering just before His arrest and Crucifixion. And of course for worship."

She followed his gaze along the towering marble surfaces. It truly was a magnificent edifice, its once time-worn and moldering walls now renewed and glowing with splendor like the rest of the city surrounding it. Of course, the old worship sanctuaries were no longer necessary, as worship had now taken on a whole new dimension. Such renovated structures now served as testaments to their former purpose.

Sensing a break in the man's story, Lydia said, "I know you asked me to be patient and listen, but I'm having a hard time seeing how this . . . this disaster story is shaping up, how it has any bearing on me—here in this place, and my need to understand what I saw. Also, I don't even know your name."

"I see," the man said slowly. "First of all, please call me 'Storyteller.' That is my name now, given to me by Most High. Secondly, I know the direction of this story is not exactly clear to you yet. However, please trust me when I say my story is both important and utterly germane to your present needs. In fact, allow me to repeat something for you. I am not a stranger who happened to wander along as you began to experience distress. I was sent to you. I am sent quite often to help those such as yourself who have encountered the Pit without a full understanding."

"Well, that is reassuring," replied Lydia weakly.

"Here, let's duck inside the basilica," Storyteller said. "I didn't lead you here by accident, you know. You are not the only one who needs to hear this story today."

They stepped into what passes for shadow in the bright light of New Jerusalem, and made their way into the sanctuary, known for many years as the Church for All Nations. Along with the rest of the Holy City's former church buildings, its public seating areas were jammed with pilgrims, were redolent with the scent of incense, and echoed faintly with songs of praise.

Storyteller steered her toward the outer vestibule, separated from the main hall by large marble columns. Suddenly he disappeared through a narrow doorway. Alarmed, Lydia rushed forward to catch up.

Moving quickly down a long, arched corridor, he stopped, turned, and waited for her. "I'm sorry, I did not mean to leave you behind. It's just that the others have been waiting on us." He turned to his right, where a beam of light indicated another passage.

She caught up with him, and together they entered a small room, lit with dazzling shapes of red and blue from a row of stained-glass windows set high in the stone walls. She focused and was taken aback, for there in the center of the kaleidoscope sat a large group of people on deeply cushioned chairs.

They turned in unison and smiled at her.

"I had to leave quickly when I received the summons to help you," Storyteller continued. "But we are all here for the same purpose; everyone in this room needs to hear the story."

"Hello, Lydia," they all said as one.

"You all know my name . . ." she said in amazement, then took an open seat in the front.

"Again, we are all meant to be here," Storyteller repeated.

"You, Lydia, were the twenty-third pilgrim to have a similar reaction, just this morning. And here are the other twenty-two."

He turned to the group.

"Friends, I had only reached the beginning of the story with Lydia, just as the collision took place. So you will have the privilege of hearing most of it again. Perhaps it will help answer some of your lingering questions."

And he picked up the tale, his face beaming with confidence that somehow, sometime, it would circle back to address the bewilderment etched upon their faces.

8

BARBADOS—UNDERWATER EXCURSIONS BOARDING PIER

Descending the conning tower, Alan shifted his thoughts to his son behind the camera. He wanted more than anything to wave Jeff down, to invite him on the dive after all, letting him know that yesterday's unpleasantness was forgiven and forgotten, that he wanted Jeff to feel like his son and not some hired hand.

But he couldn't. Not only was he being watched by thousands of people who paid his bills, but the person filming the image for them was the very one he wanted to reach out and wrap in a big paternal bear hug.

Wouldn't work. It just isn't possible . . .

With an inner ache, Alan let the matter go. Instead, he turned back to the entrance of the sub and into the main compartment, where he allowed himself to take in his surroundings like a true tourist. To his surprise, the sub was far smaller than its military counterpart. The walls and interior surfaces were white, its floor taken up by two rows of seats facing the oversized bubble-shaped windows that formed both outer walls. Beyond these flickered the green luminosity of seawater. At one end, a passage led to the captain's compartment, a modestly proportioned enclosed sphere where a middle-aged man in marine uniform sat flipping toggle switches.

Alan had expected to suffer a twinge of claustrophobia, but the chamber's open and airy feel dispelled such a sensation altogether. He smiled as he moved forward. He did not even have to bend when he made his way to his seat. The voice of the captain greeted them from a speaker overhead, extolling the underwater adventure awaiting them. Already, just beyond Alan's window, a huge grouper weaved its way through downcast shafts of sunlight and seemed to glance inside, curious at the strange occupants within the strange object.

Alan's countenance brightened by the pleasantness of the conditions, and he stepped over to Jenny's side and took his place, craning his neck in the manner of all newcomers.

Then he thought again of his son, up top and waiting all alone with his camera in hand.

At that very same moment, Marshall Rhodes and his errant yacht were attracting some increasingly frantic attention in quarters not far from Alan and the others.

Two miles away at Willoughby Fort, the old British garrison at the head of Bridgetown Harbor that housed the Barbados Coast Guard, radar operators officially determined that the motor yacht bearing down on their waters had not altered its course by a single degree in several hundred miles. An analysis of its signal ID had produced its name, the S.S. *Aqua Libre*, along with its intended destination, hundreds of miles to the west.

An alert was sounded. The *H.M.B.S. Triumphant*, Barbados's primary Coast Guard cutter—outfitted with powerful engines in order to interdict Caribbean drug-runners—was dispatched on an intercept course and even now plowed through coastal waters at full throttle, three miles away.

UNDERWATER EXCURSIONS BOARDING PIER—FIVE MINUTES LATER

Jeff stood on the pier, thinking of the previous day's dark wish and watching the sub's spine disappear below the surface, when he heard a sharp shout, followed by an abrupt rumble. The deck around him fell under a swift shadow. His ears filled with the most awful of sounds: a deafening, splintering crash that would change his life forever.

The deck hurled upward beneath his feet. He felt himself catapulted into the air, and for a split second he feared he might land in the water. He struck something hard—he couldn't tell what—and was left lying flat on his back. The angle on which he struck had prevented him from suffering serious injury.

Dazed, he rolled over and looked up. The scene around him had turned strangely quiet and still, with the exception of churned-up seawater and a large yacht whose hull stood bobbing up and down in the water, turbulence around it the only sign of its now halted momentum.

Jeff leaped to his feet, his mind screaming with the realization that the intruding vessel, listing badly to one side, was floating right over where he had last seen the sub.

He peered down to where he thought the sub would lie. The water was clear and the bottom fairly visible, forty or fifty feet down. Yet he could see nothing. Nothing but impossibly clear turquoise waters which, in other circumstances, he might have marveled at. And through the commotion of the waves he got glimpses of pale coral sand.

The sub wasn't there. He formed a visor with his hands against the sun's glare and stared harder. His breathing seemed to develop a hitch. The world around him started spinning and his knees suddenly lost their strength. He could feel his eyes stinging with tears. He couldn't help it—his father was down there! And no matter how deeply he resented the man, this was still his dad, the dominant face in his personal Mount Rushmore.

He looked around him. The pier operator stood off to the

side, yelling into a cell phone for help while wrestling with a wet suit and scuba gear. Overhead, a fast-moving dot in the sky revealed a helicopter approaching from up the coast. Then a gray hull came into view, some type of military ship bearing a flag with a trident at its center.

That was when Jeff noticed the satellite phone, the one his father had used, lying on the deck by his feet.

He should do the right thing, he realized. He should contact the church back in Denver, the people who loved his dad the most and who no doubt had witnessed through his camera what had happened. He should check in with them, tell them what he knew.

He snatched up the phone and pressed redial. After several seconds of strange grinding and beeping noises, Summit Chapel's control booth tech came on, his voice high and strained.

"Sound booth? Tom, this is Jeff! Jeff Rockaway from, you know, the scene!"

"Jeff! Hold on—let me plug you into the speaker system. Will you give everybody a report? Some kind of explanation of what's going on?"

Jeff spoke the only words his anguished mind could form.

"Tom . . . everyone! Some boat just came out of nowhere and—it must have crashed into them! It hit the sub! I can't even see them!"

INSIDE THE SUBMARINE

Only five of the sub's passengers, peering out the vessel's left-side window, had any advance warning of the impending collision.

Their foreknowledge lasted only 2.6 seconds.

What they saw was a deep, black keel moving just below the surface's undulating mirrors, rushing toward them at a dizzying rate. Since none of them were boat people, the object appeared as nothing more than a large dark blade, thrown straight at them.

The two closest, and most in position to react, did not have time to do so. One of them started to cry out, but her shouting was buried in the cataclysmic roar of impact.

No one who experienced the sudden disaster could fathom the shocking abruptness of the event, how it could begin and end before their brains had a chance to process it. For those who lived through the horrific few seconds, there was no prelude. No understanding of Marshall Rhodes' coronary thrombosis, the yacht's long, out-of-control approach, the reactions of local officials or faraway businessmen. Nothing.

Just an abrupt roar of propellers and an ear-splitting crash out of nowhere.

And screams, loud and echoing. A pitching to the right, as violent and merciless as the impact of a freight train—a lurch that hurled one row of passengers onto the other, and the first row against the windows.

There were groans of metal shearing apart, the roar's sudden end as the yacht's hull sensors slammed its motors to a complete halt, a loud popping noise, and the hissing sound of air escaping from just above their heads.

The flicker of cabin lights blinked out, leaving a strangely monochromatic twilight.

And then they rolled again, a fury of horror and chaos that tossed shrieking passengers on top of one another like loose coins in a dryer.

Finally the momentum's jarring stopped, once more sending passengers crashing into walls or the human barriers around them.

All of these things, in less time than it takes to inhale a deep breath.

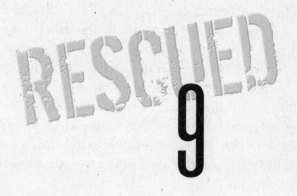

9

Raw sensations slammed first into Alan's brain. *Terror*—more merciless and savage than he had ever endured. *Pain*—ribbons of agony throbbing across his body, his head, his shoulder, his left ankle. *Constriction*—his torso wedged in, preventing him from moving his shoulders, his legs. The weight of other bodies pressing down hard on his head, his hips, his arms.

He could hardly breathe. Hardly move. Barely think rationally. From every side came a groan, then two, then three more. He heard sounds of suffering so awful they sounded inhuman, like the howling of a bitter wind through old rafters, or the eerie mewing of feral cats. The mere sound of them made him shudder violently.

A dark ridge of horror, of bottomless fear, seemed to hover at the edge of his consciousness, an approaching storm front on a brooding horizon. He found it nearly impossible to do anything but fight off this encroaching doom, to keep it at bay.

Then a specific impression came to mind. He fought to process it clearly.

Alan felt the object, then recognized its shape, lodged between his left ear and his shoulder. *A leather-sandaled foot.* His own right leg was draped over the lap of someone. He strained to see who it was through the gloom, then recognized Carrie Knowles. He tried not to look directly at the horrific scene about him, but even peripheral vision showed him a tangled mass of limbs and torsos that reminded him oddly, perversely, of those panoramas of hell by that medieval Dutch painter . . . *Bosch, wasn't that the name? Hieronymus Bosch?* Hundreds of bodies piled on top of one another in a twisted, snarling mass of human misery . . .

Alan closed his eyes, trying not to recall all the sobering newscasts he'd seen in his life. *Bus crash kills family on a mission trip* . . . *Schoolchildren drowned on capsized ferry* . . . *Missionaries speared to death* . . . He'd never chosen to dwell on such news because it confirmed a hard truth: that sometimes God's people suffer agonizing deaths. Even good people—those up to good deeds, worthy causes.

Happens all the time, he thought, attempting to be rational amidst the horror. The world wouldn't stop turning; in fact, most of his fellow American Christians would hardly give it more than a few minutes' pause. Maybe a quick prayer. Maybe a cringe and the thought, *Thank the Lord it wasn't me. But at least they're in heaven now.*

Something inside him wanted to scream out, "I can't die now, Lord Jesus! Not today! I'm only forty-seven years old! I'm finally happy. I'm the father of two boys who need me, the husband of my beloved Jenny, the shepherd of six thousand people who need me, too. No, this can't be the end!"

It just couldn't be today, not like this. This wasn't how it was supposed to happen, the story of his life he'd played out countless times in his head. In his version, he would live—live to be an old and vibrant man, close to his sons and grandchildren, still active in ministry, preaching and writing, still romantic . . .

No, he told himself again. *I won't let it be today.*

He shook his head, focused his attention back to the disaster before him. The sub's interior was now quiet except for the moaning, one female voice sobbing, the sounds of air bubbles pouring out above them.

Jenny! Where is she?

He looked down and in the dim light saw the top of her head. "Honey! Are you hurt?"

"Yeah," she whispered. "I'm hurt . . . but not bad. Can you reach down and pull me free?"

"I'm not sure. I'll try."

He raised one foot as far as the window pressing against him would allow—about eight inches. He tried raising the other but found he couldn't. His left arm was pinned beneath a heavy torso, his right against the wall by his own weight.

He breathed deeply, trying to fight back another wave of panic and claustrophobia, and looked around. Bloodied and maimed bodies, unrecognizable, were doing the same as he was—slowly extricating themselves, one inch, one limb at a time.

Finally Alan felt enough wiggle room to free his arms. He reached up, grabbed something, and pulled himself up. Then Carrie moved, Jenny pushed away, and the whole tangle seemed to loosen at once. He sighed in relief. Beside him, he saw Hal sliding back into his seat, with Audrey clinging to him. Next to them was Carrie, straightening up with a deep, almost masculine groan. It seemed the victims had found their own spaces again and were pulling themselves into a ragged form of order.

"What happened?" a young woman said. "Some kind of explosion?"

"More like collision," someone else replied. "I saw a wake and a hull. A boat hit us."

"Where's the captain?"

Everyone turned toward the forward end of the craft. Instead of the open bubble compartment they had seen upon entering, a blank white wall now blocked passage.

"Must be an emergency closure," Hal said, "to seal off the front section from any leaks or whatever's going on back here."

"Guys," said Alan, attempting to sound reassuring, "I'm sure they've got in place a whole series of rescue routines. If we can just hang on, we'll be fine."

Carrie's husband looked at Alan. "That is, if the oxygen holds out. That bubbling sound above us is the sub losing air. And we're losing it fast."

The *S.S. Aqua Libre*'s collision with the submarine instantly reshaped the sub from a fully functional modern vessel, complete with an array of safety systems, into a twelve-ton mass of crumpled steel, vinyl, and human cargo settling down to a sandy sea bottom.

By the time it struck the ocean floor, both of its redundant electrical systems were crippled, rendering all communications and onboard systems useless. The aft-mounted antenna that transmitted voice data to the tender boat now lay twisted into something resembling a small octopus. Even worse was the state of the sub's oxygen tanks, sitting on top of the cabin compartment. They had been sheared off by the impact and were leaking cubic yards of their reserves by the second.

Consequently the sub's shell, which minutes earlier had promised safety and fun-filled sight-seeing, was now a tiny prison whose ability to support human life numbered in the minutes.

UNDERWATER EXCURSIONS BOARDING PIER—ON THE SURFACE

"I'm not totally sure what happened," Jeff panted into the satellite phone, "because the pier I'm standing on was thrown upward by this . . . this bow wave that came through and pitched me across the deck. But I heard something—an impact. And now the water's so churned up that I can't see the sub. It's just . . ."

"Jeff?" It was the voice of Larry Collins, sounding distant and fuzzy through the earpiece. "I know this is an incredibly difficult time for you—"

"I don't know what to do! I can't just stand here, but what do I do? Jump in the water and swim after something I can't see? The pier operator is about to dive in with scuba gear. Maybe I could help him . . ."

"Jeff, could you, would you be willing to pick up the camera and record what's happening for us here in Denver? You have no idea what state our people are in right now."

Jeff glanced around and spotted his camera several feet away, lying on its side on the pier. It had apparently slid there when the deck had been jolted. The decking around it looked to be dry.

"Yeah, if it's working," Jeff answered. "I'll shoot from under the overhang out of the sun. The picture will be better, too."

He picked up the camera, walked under the tin roof shelter that stood on the pier, open on all but one side, and switched it on. Everything seemed to be in working order. An amber light in the viewfinder indicated the camera's microwave relay, which beamed a line-of-sight signal back to the ship and its powerful satellite uplink.

"Okay, then," said Jeff. "We're going live!"

DENVER—SUMMIT CHAPEL SANCTUARY

The auditorium flooded with bright blue, its wide screen filled once more with a jittery yet vivid shot of the Barbados coastline.

"They're somewhere down there, under the boat that hit 'em," Jeff said, the strain clearly audible in his voice as he aimed the lens. "Maybe you guys can see something I don't."

The view swerved with nauseating swiftness in the opposite direction, across the expanse of water, finally stopping when a ship came into focus: gray, sleek, traveling fast, trailing a variety of flags from its forward masts.

"It looks like we're getting some help!" Jeff said. "I think it's the Barbados Coast Guard."

ABOARD H.M.B.S. TRIUMPHANT

Captain Ronald Soares was scanning the accident scene through his binoculars when his cell phone chirped. Without lowering the binoculars he reached down, flipped it open, and held it to his ear.

"Soares."

"Ronnie, it's Johnny Stillman. Remember me?"

" 'Course I remember you. But I'm kind of busy right now. Need to call you back."

"I know. You're busy with a wreck off the coast of Bridge-town. Some yacht that lost control."

"That's right."

"Well, that's exactly what I'm calling you about. I'm calling on behalf of the yacht's owners. And they . . . they need some help from a well-placed friend. They'd be very grateful."

"How grateful?"

"A half million times over, U.S. money. Plus that gambling thing that's been hanging over you—that would be forgotten. They'd express their gratitude immediately. In one of the West Indies finest institutions. In your name, of course."

"What do they want?"

"Is the yacht still floating?"

"Yeah. I'm watching it right now."

"Well, they want it on the bottom. Simple, really. Are there any other witnesses around?"

"There's a pier nearby. Let me check." He scanned the board-ing pier with a quick pass of the binoculars. Its exposed surfaces stood vacant; its shelter was shrouded in shadow. He blinked his eyes, looked again and lingered on it for a while, and, seeing no signs of activity, said, "No, I don't see any witnesses," into his cell phone. "We passed the sub's tender boat over a mile away, headed back to the cruise ship. It's already there by now. So it's just my men and me out here."

"Good," said Stillman. "Now, we need you to sound the alarm that you've spotted heavy guns being armed on board the yacht, aimed at the city. Drug-runners trying to save their hides at any cost. Put a couple of fifties under her bow, real quick. Sink her."

"And what's the *real* story?" asked Soares.

"The boat was being ferried, and the captain either dropped dead or jumped ship. No one's sure. But their autopilot safety system also failed. They're not anxious to face the liability. That's all. If you provide a cover story that it was taken over by narco traffickers, it'll save their hides. And the water will save the cover."

"Fine. I want a call back and that account number within thirty minutes. Understand?"

Stillman hung up.

Soares looked around the scene. The only thing in his sight line was an empty pier. No other boats meant no other witnesses—except for his own men, and he'd handle them.

He pointed ahead and shouted, "Drug-runners on board! Arming for attack! Prepare to fire into the bow!"

Instantly the *Triumphant*'s single 50-caliber cannon whirred down into position, centered on the *Aqua Libre*'s bow, and waited for the signal.

RESCUED

10

Still holding the camera, Jeff stood from his crouch in the shelter's corner and kicked the tin of the shelter's only wall. The strength of the blow caused the camera on his shoulder to shudder. He winced, remembering a church full of anxious onlookers.

"Sorry, everybody," he said into the microphone, "but I want to do something! I can't just stand here watching!"

"Even though we're far away back here in Denver, we're all with you," said Larry Collins into his earpiece. "And we're all praying. That's something you could do with us."

"I don't want to pray!" Jeff barked. "I want to get in the water and *do* something! It's just . . . I don't know what that would accomplish." He turned quickly to get the attention of the pier operator, now in head-to-toe scuba gear, just as the man leaped into the sea.

"Well, I'm sure he can do more than I could," Jeff said to Larry and the others watching. "I've been hearing him yell into his phone, and it sounds like all kinds of emergency procedures have begun. The pier operator just jumped in, on his way to save everyone in the sub."

Jeff pointed the camera into the depths, adjusting the zoom, barely in time to catch the scuba diver's blurry outline as he swam away from the pier toward where the crippled yacht lay, the receding shape blending in with a lighter patch of . . .

"There's the sub!" Jeff cried. "I thought that was a sandbar or something, but it's the sub! Just below where the boat is."

Again he adjusted the lens, this time zooming in all the way onto nothing more than a pale, oblong shape shimmering beneath the waves.

INSIDE THE SUBMARINE

With a sinking feeling in his heart, Alan stared into the circle of widened eyes and blood-splattered, traumatized faces ringing the darkened interior of the sub. "I just think . . ." he began, his voice trailing off. He could tell he wasn't up to the task confronting him; he felt an enormous lack of courage, of wisdom. *Come on*, he admonished himself, *don't fail now* . . . "I think this could be our finest hour," he said at last, his voice now coming back to him. "I say we make it a tribute to who we are. Let's . . ." He gritted his teeth to fight a sudden shaking inside him. "Let's show the world what we're made of."

"I agree," said Carrie Knowles. "Why don't we pray?"

Alan nodded. He fought back a sob at the sight of Hal and, to Hal's right, a passenger he did not know, too injured to bow her head in the usual manner, merely closing her eyes instead.

"Lord," Alan prayed, "at a time like this we don't know what to do except come to You. We ask You to enter this place." He took another deep breath. "We beg You to bless our rescue from this . . . this *horror*. Please anoint and help those people trying to save us. Please make whatever happened today a testimony that will glorify You, something that will draw people to You. We ask this in Jesus' name. Amen." Alan let out a loud sigh.

Everyone opened their eyes.

"Look!" a man exclaimed.

Every head jerked up toward the source of the words.

A church member whom Alan did not know was turned around in his seat, waving out one of the bubble windows. Along with most of the others, Alan was forced to crane his neck sideways for a fleeting glimpse, yet it was enough of a look to tell him all he needed to know.

A diver!

An absurd sight—a body covered in light blue rubber, with mask and fins and a metal tank attached, a gloved hand waving wildly in the window. Not the most human-looking of saviors perhaps, but still the most welcome sight Alan had ever seen. All around him were the sounds of cheering, crying, outright calls of relief.

"What's he doing?" Jenny said. From where she was sitting she had a difficult time seeing what was taking place.

"He's writing something!" said the man just inside the window in question. "He's got one of those magnetic writing pads and he's scribbling a message."

"What is it?" Carrie said.

"Just a sec . . ." the man said. After a short pause, he said, "Here it is! The message says, 'Hang on. Help on the way!'"

Another loud cheer went up inside the sub. Despite his feelings of despair, Alan couldn't help but rejoice along with the others. He turned back to look Jenny in the eyes and was not surprised to glimpse tears. She raised a hand and pursed her lips for him as if to blow him a kiss.

"There's more!" the man closest to the window announced. "The diver erased the first message and is writing another. Here it is: 'Rescue under way. Stay calm. Breathe slow.'"

Carrie's husband leaned forward, gave Alan a knowing look. "See? I told you we were losing oxygen," he whispered.

Alan nodded in reply.

But maybe it didn't matter. Alan clapped his hands together, the way he did to call elder meetings to order, and said, "Isn't God good?"

Several emphatic "Amens" affirmed his statement. Finally he was getting somewhere.

"Thank you, Lord," said an older woman in the corner. Alan looked her way and allowed himself the longest eye contact and smile he had exchanged with this woman in years. He hated this part—here was one of those church members whose presence at Summit Chapel predated him by decades. One of his life's most familiar faces, always there, smiling, beaming that ethereal Christian glow.

Only, he couldn't remember her name.

He hated even to think of it, to imagine what she must think of him, a pastor who couldn't place the name of one of his church's most loyal and lifelong members.

The name was something old-fashioned, he remembered. *Ethel? Viola? Thelma?* She *would* have to be here, on this trip. She'd beamed at him from four decks and a dozen buffet lines. In his guilt she seemed to be mocking his foolishness, his bad memory, his mixed-up priorities. For wasn't memorizing members' names one of the pastor's preeminent tasks? Hadn't he read that somewhere?

When he got back home, he promised himself he'd look up her name and commit it to memory. Maybe confess to her his ignorance and explain to her that his reticence had always been his fault, not—

Just outside the window facing him, no more than two feet away, stared the magnified eyes of the diver behind his mask. No longer peering in and waving, the man was now reaching for something just beneath the sub, barely out of sight.

"I think he's opening some kind of valve," Alan said. "Hopefully a reserve oxygen tank."

"It won't be long now!" Hal Newman declared.

"That's right," Alan chimed in while feeling regret for his lack of faith earlier. "Any minute now and we'll be rescued." From the beginning of this terror, he should have believed everything would turn out all right. "God heard our prayer . . ."

UNDERWATER EXCURSIONS BOARDING PIER—ON THE SURFACE

BOOM!

The first blast shocked Jeff Rockaway so badly that he stumbled backward, almost falling off the pier into the water. The noise thundered from the *Triumphant*'s cannon with the deafening suddenness of a thunderclap roaring out of a blue sky.

Jeff about dropped his camera in the process, then quickly recovered it. He wanted to see. *Had to see.* He wanted *them* to see, too, he realized—the church members back home.

"Did y'all hear that?" he shouted into the camera's mike.

"Yes, but what was it?" Collins replied.

"It came from the Coast Guard ship and—"

BOOM!

Another one! This time Jeff captured on tape the cannon jerking back and ejecting white smoke into the wind. He swung the camera to follow the gun's probable trajectory . . .

. . . and landed on the yacht just as the second round shattered a large hole in the front of the listing boat's waterline.

"They're firing on the yacht!" Jeff shouted. "I don't understand. There's no one there. Look—I'm zooming in. You can see for yourself. The bridge, pilot compartment, all the decks are empty. It's like a ghost ship. So why is it such a threat—"

BOOM!

A third round exploded, and another breach tore into the yacht's hull just a few feet from the previous ones. The yacht lurched in the water, then dipped noticeably forward.

"They're trying to *sink* it!"

Jeff pointed the lens at the bow of the *Aqua Libre*, proving his point. Yes, it was true, but he could not bring himself to think it, let alone narrate what was happening to the audience watching through his camera.

BOOM! This one was the deathblow, forming a perfect triangle in the hull's most vulnerable point. The yacht pitched sharply forward, its doom certain.

"No!" screamed Jeff. "No! You can't! Look below! Look *below*!"

He turned the camera, zooming in on the attacking ship's foredeck, focusing on someone holding a pair of binoculars turning toward him, then stopping—looking straight at him!

The man with the binoculars dropped them to his chest and motioned furiously to a sailor near him, who went into action, obviously responding to an order.

Jeff swung the camera back to the terrible sight of the sinking yacht, which, even before the attack, was already severely weakened by its impact with the sub. He watched as it groaned apart into three large chunks.

Jeff stood in stunned silence.

"Oh my—" He stopped, remembering the large group listening to him.

As though pulled apart by invisible cables, the three portions of yacht now collapsed into the water with great splashes, shattering even more and tossing a heap of debris into the depths.

Jeff shouted in dismay, "They sank it! Right over them!"

"What do you mean, Jeff?" asked Collins in the earpiece.

"Didn't you see, Larry? Weren't you guys watching or listening? That's what I was yelling about!"

"What was?"

"They're under there! Right under it! The yacht's breaking up right over the sub!"

Alan barely had time to see the diver jerk his head around, apparently alarmed by a sudden dimming of light at the surface. They both saw it at once—the doomed rescue diver and the terrified passenger staring from each side of the safety glass—a forest of debris, billowing outward and descending fast on top of them.

Alan cried out in renewed alarm.

The faces turned swiftly toward him and the sight filling the bubble window.

"What is it?" shouted several at once.

"It's . . ." Alan started to explain, when he was interrupted by a *thump* on the window. The mass of swirling debris had engulfed the diver, who appeared to be crying for help directly into Alan's face, reaching out desperately toward the window.

The man slid from view, leaving only an arm, then a hand clawing a bloody streak across the glass—a grisly sight that immediately melted off into the darkening water.

The sub jolted viciously, as if it had been picked up by a large, angry hand. It began to roll, not once, not twice . . .

And the tumble of human flesh, again tossed about like chum in a fisherman's hold, escalated into an infernal nightmare.

11

DENVER—SUMMIT CHAPEL

The fifteen hundred worshipers, who an hour earlier had formed such a happy cross-section of American society, now lay prone and scattered across Summit Chapel's rows and aisles like the survivors of some great disaster. The image looming on their giant screen—that of the *Aqua Libre* breaking apart and foundering into the deep—launched another terrible shock wave through their terrified ranks. Another communal gasp of horror wrenched itself from scores of throats, sending their anguished cries to echo off the thick beams overhead.

Somehow the huge image on their church's screen showed them what Jeff's tiny viewfinder had mercifully obscured from him . . .

. . . a large, dark shroud of decimated yacht matter had just floated down upon the stricken submarine. Its shell was now invisible to the surface, completely buried under a mountain of splintered steel, fiberglass, and wood.

And billowing above the scene, like a deadly stingray, waved an enormous slick of marine fuel.

"Jeff, can you hear me?" Larry Collins called out into his ear-piece, his cry to young Rockaway magnified as well by the sanctuary's bank of speakers. "Jeff! Please talk to us!"

The screen's view remained fixed on the patch of churned-up water. Only the sounds of sea gulls and satellite static reached their ears.

"You just saw it," said Jeff at last, now in an exhausted monotone. "You just saw them die. There's no way out . . . Who's gonna rescue them now?"

INSIDE THE SUBMARINE

Not only was the craft engulfed in the underwater avalanche of debris, but its initial contact with the cloud sent it tumbling along the sea bottom as capriciously as a toy kicked by an impetuous toddler.

As he hung on with all his strength, every terrified thought and sensation of doom Alan had just discarded came hurtling back. The death tube imprisoning him had rolled completely over. He heard great crunching noises of tearing metal and shattering glass, which slapped shock waves through the vessel's outer skin. His ears filled with screams of terror, of agony.

Of death.

His hands lost their hold on Jenny, just as his spirit lost its grip on hope.

Again, the entire episode lasted only a few seconds in real time, yet to the frantic passengers trapped within, it seemed to stretch into an eternity's worth of torment.

Finally the sub came to rest once again, nearly forty feet away from its previous perch.

Straining his neck for the smallest gleam of light, he peered out the nearest bubble window for a glimpse of the surface. His anguished stretch was, in fact, rewarded by a distant trace of refracted sunlight. But suspended in that glow, drifting slowly down, sank the severed head of the boarding pier operator, his mask shorn away, his exposed face frozen in panic.

A few feet away, Alan could see Hal Newman clutch his chest and hear him groaning loudly. Audrey, grabbing on to him, began screaming uncontrollably. The old man thrashed violently, gasping for air, and then suddenly his body went limp. His wife of forty-nine years pulled him to her chest and cradled his head. At the sight of his eyes rolled back in his head, she uttered a moan so heartbreaking that Alan was sure it was the most miserable sound he'd ever heard.

UNDERWATER EXCURSIONS BOARDING PIER—ON THE SURFACE

"Murderers! Stinking murderers!" Jeff screamed. "I'll show them! I'll show the world what they did!"

Jeff had lost all ability to restrain himself. Alone on the pier, sweating in the midday sun, enraged by the *Triumphant*'s indifference to the sub's fate, he abandoned himself to fury. Then realizing his video feed to America was his greatest weapon, the young man tightened his desperate grip on the camera as an uninterrupted record of what was taking place. For even now, bathed in rage, he could see them—strangers in foreign uniforms—cringing at the sheer incrimination his camera threatened.

Get a grip! he admonished himself. *Maybe they're still alive . . .* Jeff knew then that he needed to take action. Do *something*. Maybe he could go down there himself. But what about the debris field? What about half a yacht lying right on top of the sub?

He rubbed the sweat from his face with a brisk fling of his wrist. He'd deal with the dangers when he got down there. He rushed up to where the pier operator kept his supplies in the wheelhouse, the place where he stowed a stack of manuals and clipboards. Jeff reached in and pulled out the stack he'd seen the man frantically paging through before slipping into his wet suit.

Safety Systems. Emergency Procedures. Sea Rescue Guide.

He'd heard the operator ranting those words into his own radio handset. Jeff figured the man was now dead. No one could have survived the deadly rain of toxic fuel and crushing debris that had fallen upon his father's sub.

The sounds of helicopters grew louder, undoubtedly broadcasting the news to the world. And the Coast Guard cutter he might have counted on for assistance had just become his biggest obstacle.

It was up to him now to do something. Maybe he could finish what the pier operator had started in his dive. His father was counting on him; he just knew it.

"Larry, I have to put the camera down for a while," Jeff said into the mic. "I may have found a way to help them."

"That's fine, Jeff," replied Larry Collins. "You may know this already, but we're now coming up with other ways to follow this thing."

"What do you mean?"

"Look around. Do you see aircraft? Helicopters?"

"Yeah—they just showed up."

"Well, they're carrying cameras, too. The cable networks are carrying it live—breaking news. So go ahead and do what you have to, but please check in with us every so often. Let us know what you're doing. I have a feeling most of us back here at Summit Chapel aren't going anywhere."

"Great. Keep praying, and I'll be in touch."

Jeff lowered the camera to the deck, closed the uplink case, and returned to the safety manual.

That was when he noticed, out of the corner of his eye, the approaching prow of the *H.M.B.S. Triumphant.* Suddenly, observing the growing size and menacing girth of the vessel, his anger became tinged with a stab of fear. Had his shouts and gestures been noticed? Had he incurred some commander's wrath? He could see a pair of sailors' heads above the railing—they appeared to be still engrossed in the site of the yacht's sinking, not him.

The ship swung around at the last minute, avoiding a

head-on collision with the pier on which Jeff was standing, then pulled up alongside. Just as quickly a tall black officer appeared at the rail, holding a bullhorn.

"Hullo there!" he bellowed. "Are you in need of assistance?"

Jeff shook his head vigorously.

"Are you a member of the submarine crew?" the officer asked.

He shook his head again.

"Are you a member of the press? We saw your camera."

"I'm *not* a journalist," Jeff explained loudly. "Just a private citizen recording what I see. But you should know—it's being simulcast by satellite to the United States."

"Then prepare to come aboard. We will escort you to safety."

Jeff paused. He wasn't going anywhere, and yet the officer's voice seemed not to be asking but telling. His anger returned.

"My father's down there! There was a damaged submarine right under that boat you blew up! It went down on top of him, so I'm not going anywhere!"

There was a long pause. He could see the officer's eyes studying him from behind the bullhorn's curve.

"I repeat," the officer said, "please allow us to escort you to safety. We must secure this area for rescue operations to begin. Surely you can see that."

For the first time in his life, Jeff felt the strength of an unshakable resolve surge within him. He looked down. The camera. His witness.

He picked it up, flipped open the uplink case, lifted the camera to his shoulder, and switched on the power.

"I'm staying right here!"

DENVER—SUMMIT CHAPEL

The worshipers had been watching the scene unfold from the circling aerial perspective of a Global News Network helicopter. Jeff was but a distant, solitary figure gesturing wildly across the water to a ship full of gray-suited sailors.

Then another image blinked on.

Jumpier, grainier, this scene was being shot from the surface. It was unmistakable who was holding the camera. Jeff's voice sounded higher and more desperate than it had all morning.

"I'm filming live back to the States!" he shouted. "I have the uplink right here, and fifteen hundred people are watching you right now! I filmed you firing on an unarmed yacht and sending it down on top of seventy-five helpless passengers!"

"Sir, please understand . . ." The officer's tone had changed—friendlier. Maybe *too* friendly. "The *S.S. Aqua Libre* was commandeered by traffickers, drug-runners preparing to attack. They needed to be stopped!"

"That's a lie!" Jeff shouted. "I've been here the whole time, and there were no guns on that boat! I didn't even see a person on deck."

The camera view zoomed up to the lead officer's face, framing it in a shaky closeup. The man lowered his bullhorn and glared straight into the lens, appearing to contemplate a grave decision.

He raised it again.

"Sir, I repeat. You're only placing yourself in danger and slowing our rescue operation by staying here. Please let us carry you to safety!"

The camera shook with Jeff's response.

"There are seventy-five American citizens below the surface. I am their sole witness. And if you take me away, you'll have the U.S. government to deal with!"

The officer turned away and raised a cell phone to his ear.

FORWARD DECK OF THE *H.M.B.S. TRIUMPHANT*

"Soares here. I'm in the middle of something. There's a spectator we didn't see until it was too late. We think he filmed the yacht going down."

"No kidding, Ronnie. I'm watching you on TV. International, not local. Thank goodness they just got there and weren't around five minutes ago. Look, I'm calling to tell you, you've done your part. My people are satisfied, and the yacht's down on the bottom. The water's already done its job. Whatever this kid recorded won't amount to a hill of beans unless you keep pushing it. So let it go. The crunch is over."

"Roger. And you've got my password?"

"It's coming. In ten minutes."

"It better, or I send a diver down there to confirm we made a mistake."

The lieutenant lowered the phone and walked away from the rail, waving disgustedly at the boarding pier. He had bigger issues to face—like seventy-five Americans dying on his watch.

Fifteen yards away in the boarding pier's wheelhouse, Jeff glanced from the safety manual to an LED display mounted in the instrument panel before him.

He gasped as he looked at the tiny letters above the largest counter. CABIN OXYGEN REMAINING. And beside it the words PASSENGER SURVIVAL MARGIN. The first counter's digits were spinning rapidly, like an altimeter during free fall. The second reading was counting down faster than a stopwatch.

Jeff picked up the camera and pointed the lens at the second number.

"Everybody," he said into the mic, "do you understand what this means? It means you need to pray like you never have before!"

It read, *44 min. 38 sec.*

RESCUED

12

UNDERWATER EXCURSIONS SUBMARINE—SEA
BOTTOM, ALONG THE BARBADOS COAST

The sub's interior had now deteriorated from uncomfortable wreck to blackened death chamber. Rather than terrified cries, Alan now heard deep, guttural moans from every side, their sounds so diverse that he couldn't tell whether any of them came from Jenny. He could not see her or make out her voice. Or even feel her presence. Somehow that knowledge frightened him more than any other.

A world without her . . .

"Jenny!" he called, but his voice only trickled out as a hoarse whimper, the sound trapped amid the crush of bodies.

Something about the utterings around him pierced him with the certainty that people he couldn't see—quite possibly folks he knew and loved—were dying. Yet he could hardly move to do anything about it. This time the storm front of encroaching panic moved closer, much closer. He could now smell it, just as he'd sniffed the fishy ocean breeze on the boat ride over. It was so close that he could sense it was actually not a storm but rather a bottomless abyss, one that beckoned him to a horror with the implacable pull of a Pacific riptide.

"Jenny," he called again, "where are you?" *I desperately need your calm. Please don't leave me now* . . .

Fresh.

It was the first and only word that had entered his mind upon seeing Jenny's face for the first time, bright and vibrant, up there onstage and singing her heart out. Fresh, not as an alternative to beautiful, although Jenny was certainly that—a fiery-eyed blond beauty with glowing skin—but fresh as in pure, passionate, *unjaded.*

That first sight of her had been completely innocent, devoid of any fleshly desire or ill-intention. He was but an impartial observer, admiring the splendor of God's creation. Alan had even prided himself, while walking away from her, on the nuances of admiring a woman's beauty without going so far as to picture anything inappropriate. Being pastor of a large church gave him many occasions to observe such nuances.

Later sightings, however, would begin to incite unfavorable comparisons in his mind.

Such as the fact that Jenny seemed to be everything his wife was not.

All that had once been youthful and inspiring about Terri, his college bride, had in Alan's mind become a brittle shell of opinions and competencies hardening around her by the day. Years of being a pastor's wife might have given Terri a hard-won wisdom, a street-smart canniness. He would grant her that. But they had not done much for her appeal as a spouse.

Bottom line, he knew that Terri did not view him through the same gauzy-filmed halo everyone else in his life saw. And he knew she was entitled; after all, she had climbed with him from starry-eyed seminary student to the celebrated pastor he was today. She had witnessed firsthand the ascent, so its lofty destination held no great awe for her. Yet it did not make what he interpreted as her caustic remarks, her thinly veiled sarcasm, or her jaundiced view of the church and its foibles any easier to endure.

It did not make Terri the kind of spouse he had always dreamed God would give him as he arrived at the pinnacle of his career.

On the day he saw Jenny for the third time, Alan had ventured a single, split-second appraisal of his wife. And the reaction he had felt was regret. Regret that so much success, parenthood, and life experience had not given Terri more of the "inner beauty" he preached so often about and now viewed up on that stage when Jenny entered his field of vision.

She was standing behind a keyboard stand, playing and singing with her eyes closed, wearing such a look of ecstasy and abandon that he felt transported back to the very first days of his Christian life. Alan had begun as a minister to the post-Christian generation, to the faithless and wounded refugees of evangelical fervor, so he was far more familiar with disillusionment and jadedness than the kind of unspoiled beauty that blossomed around Jenny.

Within ten seconds of seeing her that third time, Alan Rockaway had been transformed. He'd seen nothing less than a glimpse of heaven in her unforced smile, her casual grace, her . . . well, freshness.

And yet, smitten though he was, like most men, he was familiar with romances of the eyebrows, more vivid in the mind than anything else. Still, Alan had no idea that the third time he saw Jenny would prove the initial step on a journey that would change his life forever.

"Jenny?"

Now Alan heard a groan that sounded vaguely like her, and he knew. She was seriously hurt. She was probably within an arm's length of him, yet he couldn't reach her, did not know her precise location.

He felt a liquid drip on his forehead and travel down his

cheek. He knew it was blood. He flexed his arms and pushed against the crush, then felt a tinge of guilt for pushing so hard, so mercilessly. *This is humanity*, he reminded himself. Bodies hemming him in, perhaps some of them dead or injured, the forms of the precious people he pastored.

"Please, everybody," he said, louder now. "We have to try and work together, give each other space to breathe. I'm sure the rolling has stopped for good now." Then in a softer, higher pitch, he said, "Jenny, I'm trying, honey. I'm coming for you."

That moan again.

"Hang on, honey, please?"

Again came the agonizing, interminable process of untangling limbs. This time Alan felt a weight on top of him and realized it was not moving. He wanted to push it away with all his strength, but something, he did not know what, was blocking him.

He reached around and felt the smooth skin and telltale contours of a nose, a mouth. Smooth skin, a delicate nose. A woman. Then he shuddered, for it occurred to him that she had not flinched, or reacted at all, to the intrusion of his fingers.

With a sudden start he realized that the features, the hair, were Jenny's.

Now he pulled with no regard to anyone beside or above. He had found her, and he wasn't about to let go. He sheltered her neck and slid her to his side. As he grasped her, her head fell forward against his shoulder.

Alan leaned back and then realized why the disentanglement had taken so long this time.

The sub had landed upside down.

Their seats, which had once faced opposite each other in two rows, now hung above them, twisted and bent. Their only place to sit was on the sub's rounded ceiling, lined with electrical conduits and light panels.

With his shoulder still cradling Jenny, he nudged an inert body away from them and settled down into a narrow sitting position.

A small flame lit up the gloom; someone close by had a cigarette lighter. In the glow he did not recognize the lighter's owner, but she appeared to be a woman in her twenties.

He looked to the side, inhaled sharply, and almost leaped away from his spot. The limp body beside him bore the craggy features and lean limbs of Hal Newman.

"Hal!" he blurted. "Anyone—isn't there a medical kit somewhere in here? I thought I saw one. It's Hal. We have to move fast!"

He saw someone move slowly toward him. Hal's wife, Audrey, her face ravaged by fear, her body trembling, kept moving toward Alan, crawling over others' legs and feet.

"Come over here, dear. We'll do everything we can," Alan heard himself say. Jenny was stirring beside him, coming to consciousness in the dim flicker. He reached over and cupped her face. "Honey, please wake up . . ."

But as he moved his fingers he saw he had smeared her cheek with blood. Her own, he knew.

Without warning, a square plastic shape landed in his lap. He reached down, turned it over, and read the words *Portable Defibrillator.*

"Good," Alan said through clenched teeth.

Now all he had to do was figure out how to use it—in near darkness, in terrifying and cramped conditions.

It doesn't matter, he told himself. *I'm going to do this, because it has to be done.* Opening the case caused the attached power light to turn red. He yanked the twin paddles from their foam pockets. He'd seen enough ER dramas on television to know he should never let the paddles touch, at least not while they held a charge. A whining hum filled his ears.

"Can someone remove Hal's shirt?"

He saw a woman lean forward in reply and recognized Carrie Knowles. "I've had some medical training, Pastor," she said. "Let me help you."

More than willing, Alan handed her the paddles. Carrie took them and glanced down.

"There ought to be a tube of conductive jelly somewhere in that case. Without it we stand a good chance of burning his chest."

"Here," he said and slid the case over to her.

Carrie tore open Hal's shirt and smeared twin globs of the blue gel across his upper chest.

A beep sounded.

"That's the ready signal," Carrie murmured. She carefully set the paddles down, then punched Hal's chest with both her fists.

"Why'd you do that?" Alan asked sharply.

"That's what surgeons do to get the heart ready for the charge," she answered. "Now it's your turn." She grabbed the paddles and lowered them to Hal's chest in the correct position, then turned to Alan. "Okay, now you take the paddles and hold them real tight," she instructed. "All you have to do is push down and with your fingers hit the buttons on each side, see?"

Alan did as he was told. A loud clamping sound rang out, and the paddles seemed to jump backward, taking Hal's chest with them.

"Let go!" Carrie shouted.

Alan released the buttons, and Hal's torso fell back again.

Then, without the paddles near him, his body flew back upright again! Hal's face, less than two inches away, contorted in terror. The man's eyes flew open.

"No! No!" he cried. "Don't! Please!"

Hal's mouth had moved along with the words, but the voice was barely recognizable as his own. It was high, unnaturally loud, and drenched in fear. Audrey scrambled back in alarm and struck her head against the sub's wall. She groaned, reaching for her husband. But he was not in a state to recognize even her.

His bulging eyes and twitching face betrayed a state of horror so overwhelming that his features hardly seemed human. His cold fingers clenched Alan's upper arm and squeezed, *hard*.

"No!" he screamed again. He then collapsed into Audrey's arms and fell lifeless once more.

"Here," Carrie said as she reached down to the case and

flipped a toggle one setting higher. "Let's try the next voltage."

Audrey laid the man back down for another try. Alan raised the paddles and lowered them to her husband's chest. He glanced at Carrie, who gave him a nod. He pressed down and hit the buttons. Again the upward jerk, the fall backward.

At first nothing, until just seconds later Hal bent forward violently. "No! No!" he screamed.

Audrey turned to Alan. "Please, don't torture him!" she begged. Sobbing, her eyes were filled with fright. "Please let him go! He's asking you to stop!"

"But I thought you'd want me to . . ." Alan said, his voice trailing off.

"Why—just so he can come back and suffocate down here with the rest of us! No. Not like this."

"Pastor, you can't just let him die," Carrie said in a low but determined tone.

Alan turned away in confusion. Beside him, Jenny's eyes were growing wider by the second. She was returning, at least in stages.

"No! Don't!" Hal shouted again, this time even more powerfully.

"He's in arrhythmia!" Carrie said. "He won't stop until you revive him completely!"

"No . . ." Audrey said. "Please don't do this!"

The defibrillator case beeped again, prepared for the next level.

"Now!" Carrie yelled.

"Please . . ." Audrey pleaded.

Alan turned to Audrey. "But don't you think he's asking us to save him?"

"No, I don't!" she insisted. "I think he's asking you to *stop*! You're torturing him!"

"If you don't do it now, the charge will be lost!" Carrie cried. "You have to do it now!"

"Please!" said Audrey.

Hal's fingers tightened their grip on Alan's arm. "No!" he

screamed through gritted teeth, as though he was following their disagreement and stating his position. Exhausted, Alan handed the paddles to Carrie.

Then it hit Alan. Something in Hal's voice told him the man was reacting to something else, somewhere far from here. The "No's" were not directed at them. They were gasps of horror at something or someone *there*—on the other side.

He nodded to Carrie. "Go ahead. Jolt him again." Immediately Carrie lowered the paddles and pressed the buttons, felt the body rise up with the electrical charge, then relaxed her fingers and felt it fall back down again.

"No . . ." The voice was drifting away.

"I love you," Audrey said in the darkness. "Good-bye, honey. I'll see you soon."

A sharp rattle came from the body, then the sound of a fading exhaled breath.

Full of dread, Alan wondered if Audrey's words were not truer than she even knew—for all of them.

RESCUED

13

BARBADOS—UNDERWATER EXCURSIONS BOARDING PIER

The digits continued to dwindle in front of Jeff Rockaway, in his camera's viewfinder, and also on the large screen of a distraught church body over three thousand miles away.

37 min. 16 sec.

Without warning they disappeared from the video feed, which panned to the patch of water, now calm, where the submarine had last been seen.

"I'm sorry, everybody," said Jeff, "but I don't know what else to show you. Or what I can do. Even if I could swim down there without oxygen, I'd have to fight my way through all that junk. And even then, I wouldn't know where to begin . . ."

"Pray," Larry offered. "Pray for a miracle."

"Is there a way to reach up there and grab God by the collar, shake Him into doing something?" Sheer frustration filled Jeff's voice.

"Sure there is," Larry said. "But you better be prepared when

He does. Because He might just shake you around in the process. In all seriousness, Jeff, God is for us, not against us. There is power in prayer!"

"I'm ready," Jeff declared. "Anything but this sitting here and waiting. Talk to you later, man. I'm all narrated out."

With that, the young man fell to his knees on the rough deck. An unknowing observer might have thought he was merely exhausted, but the way he pounded his fists against his thighs would have been much harder to interpret.

His cries to God, however, were impossible to mistake.

INSIDE THE SUBMARINE

It took the other submarine passengers a moment to recognize the sounds they had just heard and realize the fact that Hal Newman, founding member and pillar of Summit Chapel, had just died.

A chorus of groans, sounds of dismay and anguish, rose up in the blackness.

Alan, who had spent the previous moment whispering softly into Jenny's ear, now turned toward the tumult.

"You know what?" he began. "Right before descending, I thought about having a small word with you all, urging you to think about our time underwater as a metaphor for baptism, a time for reflection, of reevaluation, for reckoning with ourselves and the lives waiting for us up on the surface. I never got the chance."

"It's never too late, Pastor." The voice was small, quavering, spoken by the saintly woman whose name Alan could never remember.

"Well, listen, my friends," he said after a long moment. "We all know the situation is dire. Before this last incident, we had every reason to expect we'd be rescued in a matter of minutes. Now . . ."

He felt he had nothing left to breathe into his words, so simply let the last statement drift off into the void.

"But the thing is," he finally continued, "if in fact these are our last minutes here on earth, how do we want to spend them? Panicking? Grumbling? Or showing one another the respect of a little love and grace? Or even of making our farewells to the people we love?" He stopped abruptly and reached into his pocket. "I just remembered *this*," he said. "My mini video camera. I was going to use it to add to Jeff's footage for the documentary later. What do you all say to making a little documentary of our own? A video to remember, for those we leave behind?"

He held it up and turned on the power. A tiny beam of light shone out from the camera's tip. He'd forgotten about its built-in illumination.

"Here. They'll even be able to see us. At least a little bit. Who wants to go first?"

"I will."

It was a young woman's voice, an unfamiliar one. To gain a better look, Alan moved the camera and aimed the light in the direction of the voice, which turned out to be that of the cigarette lighter's owner.

"I'm sorry, but have we met before?" Alan asked.

She shook her head, her eyes downcast. "No. I'm not with your church or anything. I'm just a tourist, actually. Is it still okay if I say something?"

"Of course," Alan said. He felt awkward, realizing that he had limited time before the camera's battery went dead, though of course they all had limited time . . . period. Even so, it felt wrong to reserve this privilege only for those here from his church.

The young woman continued, "I've been a party girl for as long as I can remember, so I've got too many people to count whom I need to ask forgiveness from. Or make amends, any of those things."

Then her voice took a turn.

"Instead, I want a word with . . . my only child, wherever he or she may be. Darling," she continued quickly, "they tell me you were as perfect a baby as my doctors had ever seen. Only, it was my fault. And I'm so, so sorry. I was as low as I'd ever gotten, messed up on a whole bunch of different drugs even while I had you inside me. I know a lot of folks think a pregnant woman stupid enough to take an overdose at nine months along doesn't care about her baby. But I did care, honey. I cared. I was just too lost and too imprisoned to do anything about it. I don't know if that makes sense. But maybe, who knows, we can talk about it together, sometime soon. I . . . I know this sounds silly, but I said a prayer along with the preacher on the satellite last night. It was to give my life to Jesus Christ. And once I surrendered to Him, I felt something so wonderful, unlike I've never known. I knew God had saved me from my pathetic life. So who knows, maybe I'll see you soon. Either way, I'm sorry, baby. And Jesus. I'm sorry. I really am sorry. Okay?"

At the final word, her voice cracked for good, and Alan knew she was done.

He turned off the light and immediately felt a tug at his shoulder.

"I'll go next." The voice belonged to Audrey Newman. Instead of the plaintive cry of a few minutes before, she now sounded monotone. "I dread this more than anything, but I'll bet I also need it more than any of you."

Alan pushed the Record button, swinging the camera's light to center on Audrey's tear-stained features. She wiped her eyes, and then a serene, determined expression came over the seventy-year-old face.

"Laurie, this is your mother. I don't mean that the way I always used to say it—*this is your mother*—right before scolding you. I mean it as . . . good-bye. Forgive me . . ." her voice caught. "I mean, I have more serious things to ask you to forgive me for, but I mean forgive my *state*. Your father just passed away a few moments ago, and I am still . . . And yet, I need to say this. Would you please forgive me?" Audrey took a long, shaky breath. "I am so ashamed at the way I failed to protect you, my precious girl. You know what I'm talking about."

Audrey paused, and except for the slight quivering of her lips and the blinking of her eyelids, one might have thought she had just frozen in place.

"I looked the other way those nights," she resumed, "when—when Dad's brother, your uncle—came into your room and did . . ." Her voice faltered to a stop. "I wish I could tell you how long and hard I tortured myself, telling myself I was unworthy to be your mother. I knew what was happening, Laurie. I lied that time you came to me, so brave, and told me what I already knew. I'm so sorry for not standing up for you. I'm so ashamed of having talked you out of pressing your case. I know you don't understand. This is not an excuse, but I can only tell you that I was scared out of my mind. I was frightened that your father would take out his rage on me. Maybe even kill his brother."

Alan reminded himself to draw a breath. The shock of Audrey's words was so powerful that he actually felt like he had been struck across the chest by a heavy object.

"And, Ted, my beloved son, I ask for your forgiveness, too. I pulled away from you when you decided to leave us and become a missionary. Of course I knew that it was a good thing, a great thing even, for you to be doing with your life. But I only thought of myself, and how I'd be missing my grandchildren growing up, and you growing older, my beloved boy. And so instead of just working through the pain, I retreated. And of course caused you infinite pain in the process. I am so sorry, Ted."

She paused again and wiped at her eyes.

"I don't deserve your forgiveness, my dears, but here, in my last hour on earth, I ask you anyway. For your sake, not mine, I hope you can forgive my weakness. My terrible failure to stand up for the most precious things God ever gave me. I love you both so much . . ."

Alan hit the Pause button, and the light went out.

In the moment that followed, Alan felt even more trapped than before—sitting here in the warm, damp darkness, anticipating death, hearing words and disclosures that had never been spoken before.

Why now? Alan thought. *Did this disaster have to get even harder?*

He was a pastor. He took a deep breath and resolved to address the situation.

"Audrey," he said, "have you asked for forgiveness of all these things?"

"Oh yes, I have," she said. "I've begged God to forgive me probably a million times over."

"Then they're forgiven, Audrey. They were dropped at the bottom of the ocean a very long time ago." He noted the irony, but no one commented. He looked around, more than ready for the next confessor. "Jenny?"

He turned to her but was not surprised to see her shake her head no—not yet. She was still fighting her way out of the fog of her injury.

"Anyone?"

The shock of Audrey's confession still hung over the passengers. They were too stunned to speak. Then he felt a tentative tug at his arm.

Jenny did want to speak.

RESCUED

14

Jenny's voice sounded timid, like that of a schoolgirl. Those around her in the crippled sub knew it was all the strength she could muster just then. They had heard her lift up a worship chorus like a woman three times her size; they knew the power she usually carried inside her petite frame.

"I don't have children to speak to," she breathed, "but I do have parents whom I haven't spoken to, and who haven't spoken to me, in years. I'd like to explain some things to them that I've been too proud to talk about until now."

In the dark she squeezed Alan's arm and ventured on, gaining strength as she proceeded.

"When I first saw Alan Rockaway, it wasn't like most people's experience—sitting in a pew, watching a tall, handsome guy all lit up by spotlights. I saw a man in a parking lot, bent forward in the passenger seat of his car, being harangued. To this day I don't know what he and Terri were arguing about, or should I say what Terri was incensed about, because she was doing the talking, and he was mostly hanging his head. I needed to walk by them on my way to the church office, but I couldn't. It was just too embarrassing. I sat until long after it was over, after they both had left, separately.

"What I'm saying, Mom and Dad, is that I saw a man in pain. A good man, with so much to offer the world it'd make your head spin. But a man wrestling with everything inside him, over what to do with a marriage costing him dearly."

DENVER—FIVE YEARS EARLIER

Despite her knowledge of how troubled his marriage truly was, Jenny Rodeham had never intended to pursue a romantic relationship with Alan Rockaway. She looked at him and concluded he was a man not so much in need of romance and affection but of things much more basic: respect, affirmation, support. And she didn't think it took a wife to help provide a dose of those.

Only a friend.

So, one day at worship team practice, she walked up and introduced herself to her pastor, in the bashful and halting way many people in large, impersonal churches introduce themselves to their spiritual shepherds.

Pastors inevitably develop an ability to size up potential "problem persons," and Alan only needed the briefest, sweeping glance across those flawless cheekbones and bottomless eyes to know his safest bet was to give this one a wide berth.

Not because of her apparent issues, however. Because of *his*.

Jenny, for her part, was oblivious. She had no idea how utterly beguiling her reticence and obvious embarrassment could be. And she could be forgiven for that ignorance, because Jenny naturally possessed one of the most unaffected, naturally humble personalities ever given to a person, let alone a beautiful woman. Sadly, numerous men had tried over the years to turn that sweetness against her. To their disappointment, they had all discovered that in addition to all of this, she was also, paradoxically, keenly discerning of human character.

As a result, by the time she told Alan how his recent sermon series on the book of Romans had changed her life, Alan was already enchanted, despite himself. The sight of her singing onstage had been enough. But now, up close and personal, being the careful pastor he had always been, he reacted to his enchantment by overcompensating badly in the other direction.

He rebuffed even her most basic overtures of friendship. He concluded their first conversation by cocking his head back, gaze locked over her shoulder, nodding once, and pretending he'd just been called away by an urgent matter. After a perfunctory two-second smile and a quick "Thank you, it's great meeting you," he was gone.

On several later occasions, when he saw her walking down a long hallway alone, he took to turning on his heels and disappearing into another room, a janitor's closet, or on one memorable occasion, into a ladies' Bible class—fortunately in the back of the room.

Jenny, of course, was confused. Because her discerning nature continued to whisper to her of Alan's pastoral gifts, she refused to believe the worst interpretation—that he was simply rude. She knew better. And as almost all of the six thousand–plus Summit Chapel members would have told her, there wasn't a rude or chilly bone in Alan Rockaway's body.

Because he was married, and because he was a respected pastor, however, she failed to admit what she might otherwise have sensed in a heartbeat—that his cool demeanor meant exactly the opposite. Because she did not intend to violate Alan's wedding vows, she did not guess his true conflict on the matter for a single moment.

She did not realize what Alan had recognized in her within the very first instant they met. A walking, breathing, flesh-and-blood rebuttal to every flaw he felt his wife possessed.

And in Alan's opinion, Terri Rockaway possessed more than her share.

THE SUBMARINE

"So, Mom and Dad," said Jenny as she fought to breathe, "I just beg you to accept what I'm saying. I didn't pursue a married man. And I didn't end a marriage. Despite all that, what I *did* do, I prayed about for weeks. Months, even. But you have to realize that God made it clear, through a series of events, that He meant for Alan and me to be together. He created us for each other's company. We're not perfect, you know. Alan taught me, and so many others, that Christians aren't perfect. We're just forgiven, with all the same weaknesses and shortcomings as non-believers. I wish I had time to tell you the whole story of what really happened. Alan and I fought against this knowledge for so long that at one point I considered moving away or going to another church just to spare him the trouble of struggling against it all the time."

The last five words drifted off into a breathy whisper. Alan slowly closed his eyes in resignation. Clearly she was reaching some kind of barrier. An end to her strength.

He reached up to caress her face and hugged her tighter, just a little, as tightly as he dared.

"Jenny, it's all right. You don't have to do this anymore. We don't. You just need to hold on. Hold on for me, sweetheart? Will you?"

Her eyes opened slightly, and her lips seemed to form the faintest hint of a smile.

"Your folks know what kind of girl they raised," he said. "What kind of woman you grew into. In their hearts, they know. And God knows."

She nodded slowly.

"Jenny, think of the good things," he whispered into her ear. "Think of how we started. Cairo. Remember Egypt?"

"We'll always have Cairo," she whispered back, and Alan thought he heard a sound that, given the weak lung power behind it, might have been a chuckle.

He echoed her chuckle once, loudly, for her. It was their

private joke, their secret allusion to the famous *Casablanca* line.

The city where they had fallen in love was not quite as romantic, but it was theirs. And it was a memory impossible to forget.

"That's right, honey," Alan said with a smile. "We'll always have Cairo."

15

CAIRO, EGYPT—*FIVE YEARS EARLIER*

"Isn't this awesome?"

Turned toward Alan in a halo of spotlighted glory, Michael East shouted back with a wide grin, his voice barely audible over a thunder of voices. And awesome it was—the evening was a triumph. The Nasser Memorial Soccer Stadium surged with exuberant faces and upraised hands that massed around the stage, the air ablaze with light, throbbing with the roar of a worship chorus lofted in unison from fifty thousand throats.

There are indeed Christians in Egypt!

Alan shook his head in amazement and repeated the statement to himself, looking out from backstage over a horizon of heads thrown back in ecstatic worship. He knew it was true, yet how spectacular a confirmation.

He was actually answering the cynical, flippant question he had posed months earlier when first approached with the prospect of addressing the Third Annual Egyptian Believers Rally. *"Do we really exist in Egypt? Are we allowed?"* He had intended it first as rhetorical questions, for of course he knew that Egyptian Christians existed in great number, most within the Ethiopian Coptic branch. Yet given all he'd heard about religious tensions and Muslim persecution in the country, the prospect had always seemed unlikely. He had never pictured having spiritual brothers and sisters in Egypt, and he'd had trouble visualizing it until just before stepping out on this stage.

Yes, there were Christians in Egypt; he had just finished speaking to them for a half hour, and during all thirty minutes the vast throng had stood transfixed, every face raptly fixed on his as he spoke through an interpreter about the incredible grace of Jesus Christ.

Now he stood backstage, hardly able to move as the veil of sweat and wonder poured out from his body. More than the sound, more than the blazing light or the sweltering heat, he felt an overpowering sense of family and oneness wash over him.

And there she was, up there singing right next to Michael. Jenny, the constant attendant of his dreams, tantalizing protagonist of his every waking fantasy, looking more ethereal and beautiful than he'd ever seen her. Her upper body was bent back as she held a long, high note, her blond hair thrown into an aura of backlit splendor. He could hardly bear to look at her. Her very silhouette seared itself onto his vision like a lightning bolt. And he swore to himself that the attraction he felt was far more than visual. It was her passion, her utter sincerity in throwing caution to the wind, lifting her praise before these strange, dark faces.

He tried to steer his thoughts back into a worthier direction, but just then the very act of picturing his wife assaulted his joy like a gong striking an intrusively dark and mournful note.

DENVER—SEVEN MONTHS BEFORE CAIRO

"Terri, didn't you tell me a while ago that you've always wanted to see the pyramids?"

It was 9:30 P.M. at the Rockaway residence, a little late for just having gotten their two boys off to bed, but nevertheless their "peace hour," the quiet period before retiring themselves. It was also the time when they usually had most of their talks.

Terri looked aside from the sink, where she was rinsing off the evening's plates in preparation for a late-night dishwasher run.

Tired, out of humor, and now curious, Terri knew that his questions were rarely this vague unless they concerned something fairly important. The rest of the time, her husband was as direct as lightning.

"I think so, yes," she replied. "At least until I heard about all those tourists getting slaughtered over there."

"That was a decade ago. They've tightened security quite a bit since then."

Drying her hands, she turned around at his approach.

"How would you know about that, may I ask? You been doing some studying?"

"Yeah," he admitted, walking up behind her and stopping short. In years past he might have tiptoed up behind her, reached around and held her close, kissing her on the neck in hopes of starting something while she stood giggling and making false protests, both of them hoping neither boy would pad down the stairs.

But no more. Not these days.

He could not even imagine how such an overture would have been greeted. Certainly not well. How long had it been since she'd showed, even in the remotest way, an interest in marital relations? The image of the last time hovered in his mind, sometime between last Christmas and Thanksgiving. And even that had been a cursory ritual, a taking care of things.

"So? Are you going to tell me why?" Terri asked, facing him now and folding the towel.

"Because we're going there, that's why."

"We're going to Egypt?"

"Sure."

"What about Yellowstone? We were planning on doing that this summer."

"We can still go to Yellowstone," he said, "because I'm not talking about a vacation. I'm talking about a three-day speaking invitation I just received from a group of pastors in Egypt, scheduled for April. We're going international."

Terri took a breath and nodded, trying to buy herself a few seconds to figure out why his announcement had provoked only a deep sense of reserve.

"*You're* going international, you mean," she finally said.

"If you go with me, it'll be *us*," he insisted.

"Is there a good reason to go over there?" she asked.

"Well, yeah. It'll be the first time any foreign group has known enough about me to send an invitation. I'll be the main speaker, and it'll be the beginning of a huge leap in my visibility."

Terri sighed and closed her eyes. "No, I mean is there a good reason for the *believers* over there? Is there a cause, a specific kingdom need?"

"Oh," Alan said, realizing at once how shallow and ambitious her correction had made him sound. "Well, I think the need in Egypt is pretty much a constant. There's been persecution and, in spite of it, underground growth there for decades."

"Right."

She knew he hated her sarcasm, but she did not feel, at moments like this, capable of suppressing it.

"There are oppressed minorities and unsafe places to preach right here in Denver," she noted. "You don't have to travel halfway around the world and spend tens of thousands of dollars to find those in Egypt, of all places."

"Yes, but they've asked me. It was *their* idea, not mine."

"But my thesis—that's right when my review committee will be meeting and scheduling my defense."

He groaned, turned away in frustration. It was true—Terri had invested four years of hard work, late-night commutes, and mind-numbing Saturdays at the library working on her master's degree. Her one-way ticket to what—significance?

Significance without him. He'd never told her—although he was quite sure that she'd sensed it—but he resented her quest for meaning apart from him and his ministry.

Or even, for that matter, apart from their God. The whole master's thing was all for *her* and her emotional emancipation, he thought.

We could have been partners, he muttered inwardly. *Succeeding together, not apart.*

"Look. I really need you to go with me, Terri. It'll look bad if you don't."

She chuckled bitterly and glanced away—at city streets through their oversized windows. "You almost had me, Alan. Until that last sentence. You know, there was a time when you would have asked me whether I thought you should go in the first place. You would have asked for my counsel. We would have prayed about it together. And then you would have asked me to go because you *wanted* me to. Because you needed me with you during a challenging time. Now you just tell me it'll look bad if I don't go with you. You used to cringe and snicker under your breath at preachers who said things like that."

Alan shook his head while running fingers through his hair.

"Please, Terri, we could both say things about how neither of us is as great or as pure of heart as we used to be. But let's not go down that road, okay? I'm just asking if you're going to come with me to Egypt."

"So it's already a done deal?"

"I've already accepted, yes. It never even occurred to me that you would object to it."

"Well, the strange thing is—" she shook her head and seemed to search the ceiling with her eyes—"I don't know why, but it feels very wrong for some reason. I really feel like I shouldn't go and that you shouldn't, either. I don't feel it's safe somehow. I'm serious. Don't go."

"Not safe—how? Not safe physically, or in some other way?"

"Maybe in *every* way."

"We've been given full assurance by the Egyptian government that we'll be kept completely safe during the whole perfor—I mean, the whole service."

"Maybe I don't mean us, or your entourage. Maybe I mean—"

"What?"

"Please don't make me say it," she said with a twinge of pleading in her voice.

"Well, then, how can I respond to you?"

"Me," she whispered. "I mean *me*. Safe. Emotionally."

"Oh, so now I'm some sort of emotional batterer? When did *that* happen?"

"Don't attack me, Alan. It's just a sense that I have. Stronger than anything I've felt in a long time."

"That's because it's been a long time since I wanted something this much."

"Now, Alan, that's going too far," she said, her voice rising. "I've never wished you ill or resisted you out of spite."

"No, but you've never really gotten behind my ministry, either. I've got janitors at the office who believe in what I'm doing a hundred times more than you do!"

A certainty began to grow in her—this was the moment when a mere low point in their marriage could well explode into a full-blown crisis.

She closed her eyes, wishing the whole conversation would just go away. It became suddenly obvious to her that her husband was goading her, verbally pushing her into saying something from which they, as a couple, could never recover. The physical sensation was as alarming as if it were actually happening.

And yet more urgent than either of those was her sense that only danger awaited them in Egypt. It felt like a succession of sirens going off inside her. The first one was the physical threat, the fact that Egypt teemed with armed militants committed to murdering any Christian who stepped foot on their soil, let alone staged a massive rally. Then there were the more vague threats that, combined with Alan's ego, his ambition, his response just now to her objection all caused a distinct unease in her spirit.

But the most potent of threats for her, which she hardly

dared to think about, was by far the state of their marriage. Somehow it seemed too delicate, too fragile, to survive the tensions of the trip. As it was, it would take many months of intricate surgery to stitch matters back together again with Alan. And Egypt loomed like the very opposite of a safe place.

She opened her eyes and was confronted with Alan's expression, close and clenched in an irritation so palpable it almost seemed like hatred.

He wanted an answer to his last provocation, and somehow she was overwhelmed by an urge to lash out.

"Your staff is caught up in a cult of personality, Alan," she heard herself say, aghast at her own brashness. "And the most frightening thing is that you're getting caught up in it yourself."

That was it. They had turned the corner. *I've just made myself an enemy*, she thought.

Alan's expression now turned into full-blown rage. "You make up these names for it because it's completely foreign to you," he hissed. "But here in the real world, it's called support. It's called *loyalty*."

He started for the front door, then spun back around.

"You stay here at home with what's important to you," he said in a flat, emotionless tone. "Don't wait for a postcard."

16

HIGH ABOVE WYOMING—SEVEN MONTHS BEFORE CAIRO

A Citation Excel business jet, streaking across the sky at thirty-five thousand feet over the Wind River mountain range of Wyoming, broke through thin strata of cirrus clouds with its nose aimed southeast on its way to Denver.

Inside its pale gray cabin, lined with leather and burnished walnut, were only two passengers. Jenny, who sat holding a stenographer's notebook, and opposite, forty-eight-year-old Martin Dexter, a superstar plaintiff's attorney with his legs splayed in a graceless angle at odds with the elegance of his shiny tailored slacks.

"I'm through," Dexter said. "No more brief left in me," he quipped with a chuckle at his own whimsy. "Draft on if you'd like, but I'm drafted out."

"I wouldn't dare draft another word without you," Jenny replied, closing her notebook.

"Oh, please. You'll do just fine without me. In fact, the

writing would probably improve if you took over."

"Thanks," said Jenny, averting her eyes and inwardly praying the man's flattery was not about to turn more intentional. She yawned and stretched her arms, then realized the gesture only accentuated her figure before the probing eyes of her notoriously lecherous boss. She lowered herself back onto the armrests and shifted her shoulders forward.

"Kick back, Jenny. Relax," he said, slouching even more in his seat. "Come on. Let down your hair—literally."

As much as she didn't like the direction of his suggestions, Jenny had to admit that after a five-hour deposition sandwiched between five more of air travel, she did long to release her hair from its tight, head-hugging clip. After a moment's consideration, she reached back, removed it, and shook the tresses free.

"I don't think I've ever seen you with your hair loose," Dexter said. "I'm not sure anyone in the firm has, either."

"Oh? You mean my hairstyle has been a topic of discussion?"

"For a few of us, sure." He leaned his chin on an elbow, playing coy. "At least the half dozen or so who've busted their chins trying to ask you out, or even get a little closer to you. I think they consider you a bit tightly wound."

"Martin, are you telling me this as my supervisor?" She felt her voice rise along with her discomfort. "Is my demeanor becoming a job issue?"

He reached out and gently touched her forearm. "No, Jenny. Nothing like that. I'm just making chitchat, that's all. To get to know each other a little on a personal level, and I don't mean that as a euphemism for something else. But you have been known for being a bit on the frosty side."

She breathed out slowly, staring at the curve of the plane's fuselage. "I don't mean to be. It really isn't intentional."

"That's too bad. Because a lot of people think you might be an interesting person to know. Me included. May I ask, are you dating anyone at the moment?"

"Yes, you may." She waited awhile before giving a reply. "I'm not attached, and I'm not looking. At least, not in the usual, desperate way people usually associate with women over thirty. I mean, I'm not going to turn down Mr. Right if he happens to walk into my life. But I'm not holding my breath, either."

"I understand."

"Really?" she said dubiously. "Because your reputation is that of someone with a slightly less . . ."

Dexter let out a self-conscious, boisterous laugh. "At a loss for words, are we? Well, say no more, Jenny. I know well my reputation."

"And, may I ask, is it deserved?"

"Probably," he said. "And what about yours—is it deserved?"

"Definitely. I'm just not one of those women who sits around pining for a man."

"What turns you on, then? I don't mean that in the inappropriate sense; I mean you don't strike me as someone who lacks inner fire. Not a passive individual."

She shook her head, then looked him in the eyes. "You really want to know?"

"Yeah. I do."

"My passion is my faith. Church. Especially singing with the praise and worship team, which is most Sunday mornings."

"Oh . . ." He drew out the word into one long, rising syllable of genuine surprise. "Now I really understand."

"Please. I'd rather not be patronized as just another—"

"No—it's fine. It's not for me, but I know others who have gotten honestly turned on to religion, and it's done a lot for them. Can't knock it."

"Maybe you'd like to come to a service sometime? To Summit Chapel? You might have heard of it—one of the biggest, most progressive churches in Colorado. I think you'd like it."

"Is this a date, or just some kind of holy invitation?"

"Neither. I honestly think you'd appreciate it."

He made a face that indicated he'd consider the proposition and turned his attention toward the jet's window.

Jenny remembered that she needed to check her Blackberry for the messages she'd uploaded after leaving Seattle. She took the device from her purse, pushed a few buttons and read for a moment, then gave one of those half frowns, half smiles that revealed the arrival of a pleasant surprise.

"What is it?" Dexter asked. "Mr. Right finally show up?"

"No, not that," she said, her eyes still glued to the small screen. "I've just been invited to Egypt."

"Oh? So maybe he did show up after all? I hear the Nile can be mighty romantic."

"Hardly," she said, her eyes distant, processing. "It came from my pastor."

CAIRO

Here Alan was, on the night of his greatest spiritual triumph— four hundred people had come forward, making professions of faith only minutes before being whisked away to a vast underground room for counseling and prayer—and standing alone. With a perennial temptation before him.

He gazed forward, drinking in Jenny's lithe form, a testimony not only to unabashed worship but unburdened youth, to lack of pretension, free from the burdens and affectations of age.

Officially, the decision to bring Jenny to Egypt with the worship team had been Michael's. At least, that was what any reasonable inquiry would reveal. But the impetus had all rested solidly with Alan. Three or four indirect comments and one broad recommendation to his budget committee and the deed was done. Though he hadn't bothered to examine his motives too closely, he knew this wasn't done out of an outright wish to cheat on his wife.

Perhaps just an invisible reprisal on his part. A gesture of defiance, thrown in the face of her infuriating attitude. After all, he told himself, Jenny could edify him more by her mere proximity than Terri could do in a year of spousal drudgery.

He could feel the danger like a fierce tingle up and down his spine. By having her here, in this frame of mind, he had just tiptoed right to the very brink of marital disaster—he knew it even as he toyed with the reality of his actions like a light he could turn on and off.

He frowned and peered forward—some glassy projectile was flying through the air toward her. It was moving fast and level, as though hurled from a strong and angry hand. Somehow, its path left a trail of smoke over the heads of spectators.

He did not see it strike Jenny but saw her recoil violently and fall to the stage. The object then slid several feet, twirling to a stop in a pool of light.

Seeing Jenny lying there motionless, Alan felt his mouth drop open and his knees start to buckle.

The projectile was a Coca-Cola bottle. The smaller variety, the kind he drank from as a kid. Except it was filled with an amber liquid, and a filthy rag clogged its neck, trailing a rag strip.

The strip was on fire . . .

A Molotov cocktail!

The world went gray, sluggish, hazy. A host of alarms struck him at once. Dim shouts, even screams, echoed distantly from the stadium ahead. Hoarse cries from backstage rang out all around him, followed by the pounding of panicked footsteps. He looked forward into the crowd and saw something that would forever chill him to the core: an approaching wave of human limbs and torsos, rising and leaping from the rear of the crowd.

He turned back to the limp form onstage and realized Jenny was unconscious. The Coke bottle had not shattered but spread its deadly contents on the floor around her. The rag fuse stubbornly nurtured its guttering flame. Within seconds it could burn into the neck and explode! And worse, Jenny would soon be trampled by worshipers desperately scrambling away.

Someone from behind him shouted, "Muslims! The machete men! *Machete men!*"

The chaos grew overwhelming, and Alan realized he was facing upstream against a fierce human tide. Just as he was about to rush the stage toward Jenny, he felt hands grasping his arms. A dark-suited Egyptian man he'd met earlier in the evening, one of many security personnel who had hovered over the group since their arrival, panted, "You must come with me, Pastor!" His voice was thick with fear. "Now! An attack is under way!"

"But I can't—not without Jenny!" Alan said, pointing behind them.

"Who?" The man spun around, following Alan's gaze.

"Jenny. She's over there on the stage, unconscious. I won't leave without her!"

"The Molotov!" the man shouted. "It will explode!"

"I don't care!"

The Egyptian gave a quick nod, a determined look in his eyes. A second later they were both shoulder to shoulder, shoving their way against the stampede. The fifty feet to where Jenny lay stretched interminable and perilous.

Finally they reached her. Jenny was not completely unconscious but groggy, stunned, and disoriented. Ignoring the Egyptian, Alan immediately bent down to pick her up. The Egyptian turned to him, pistol in hand, and told Alan to follow him *quickly*. Even as her weight sank against his arms, Alan took off behind their protector, trying not to think about the thrill of holding her shuddering through every inch of his body.

They were running with the flow now, except that the threat had only intensified. The screams had grown louder, nearer, more bloodcurdling. Alan would not look back, but he could hear the snarls and grunts of men attacking innocent people in the audience.

And the heart-wrenching sounds of the dying—worship choruses still warm upon their lips and hearts.

RESCUED 17

CAIRO, EGYPT

Alan's world narrowed into a blur of frantic breathing, furious sprinting, and bodies careening on every side. Jenny became a burden in his arms, yet he bore the weight not only with resolution but with gratitude. He gritted his teeth and focused on following close behind the Egyptian security man before him.

Even with a storm of terror erupting all around them, he couldn't deny the warm feeling of finally touching her, of holding her. And of being the one there to protect her, to grasp her against himself and keep her safe.

He looked up from the security man's back and saw that they were now flying down concrete steps, down toward a street exit. Raising a cell phone to his lips, the man screamed instructions in Arabic. The steps ended and swept them into a frenzied street scene just ahead. The security man didn't hesitate but plunged into a mass of bodies crowding the sidewalk. Alan followed tight behind him, holding Jenny and watching helplessly, when an Arab man wearing a suit similar to the Egyptian's leaped high in the air and waved his hand over the crowd.

Alan heard a screech of brakes. The black minivan that had brought him to the stadium pulled up to the curb and jerked to a stop. The side door slid open, guarded by the driver who waved them over. As Alan hurried to carry Jenny to the van and gently set her down inside, he noticed that this man was also brandishing a revolver, waving it about like a flag as he urged them onward. He quickly took a seat next to Jenny, whose limp form leaned heavily into his shoulder, and then the two Egyptian security men climbed in the vehicle up front, slamming the doors shut as they raced away.

Swirling red flashed ahead—a portable police light handed from the driver to the other security officer, lifted through the passenger window to the rooftop.

He looked to the side window and saw a woman, one around Jenny's age, peering into the van with a look of mortal fear twisting her features. Next to her, too close, pressed the face of a man furiously mouthing some inaudible malediction. Alan glanced away from the panicked tableau. The van alternately sped ahead, then without warning slammed on its brakes in a maddening spasm of escape. Their driver, a young Arab whose body was too engaged in the moment's frenzy to even sit in his seat, was now standing on his brakes and shouting into his windshield words Alan could not understand.

They made a sharp turn, and ahead of them loomed a sight Alan would never forget. A line of seven black-clad hooded men holding machetes. The thugs instantly closed ranks to block the van's passage.

The Egyptian shoved his revolver out the van's window, and the weapon jerked backward from a tongue of flame. After a second shot, the van accelerated forward. One of the machete men near the center collapsed to the street. The others ran aside to avoid being run over.

As they rushed past the group, several machetes struck the van with hollow thuds. Alan saw one pair of maddened eyes, then another, and looked down at Jenny.

Turning away from their hate-filled stares, Alan felt himself hyperventilating as the van sped away, leaving the scene behind. He couldn't believe he'd just witnessed a man get killed, no more than ten yards away!

Soon they were heading into the thick traffic of downtown Cairo. Alan leaned forward to look out the front windshield. Ahead of them stretched no apparent lanes, only a freely interweaving flow of automotive anarchy. The van entered the fray. He caught his breath when a child no more than ten, clothed in nothing but rags, darted in front of them. The driver did not slow down but swerved and punched his horn. The angry blasts of others' horns seemed to replace turn signals as the only means to prevent the vehicles from crashing into one another. A woman holding a baby ran before them, giving them a sharp yet practiced look. They passed an old man holding up packs of cigarettes in a string from one arm. The grizzled senior seemed oblivious to the noise or the danger—he remained intent on plying his trade.

"Why are all these people in the street?" Alan asked.

"There are no crosswalks in Egypt," the driver answered over his shoulder. "You just jump in and keep moving, with your foot ready to brake."

He made another quick turn, then said, "By the way, I just heard that the other members of your party are safe. But you two are leaders. We will take you somewhere very safe. Many are dying, and many more will fall in the hour ahead. This is no riot; it is an organized massacre. And the killers will be looking for both of you."

Alan nodded. Jenny, apparently provoked by the gunfire, began to stir and struggled to raise her head.

"It's Alan," he whispered into her mass of tousled hair.

She looked up and gave him the bleariest of smiles, not seeming at all surprised to see him there next to her.

"They threw it at me," she whispered. "At first I didn't recognize it."

"I know, Jenny. I know. I saw it too."

They turned to the right, hard, driving Alan into his armrest, making him flex to shield Jenny from the pressure. They were moving down a narrow street now, empty and darkened by the growing shadows of night. The van accelerated in a furious whine, abruptly turning again, this time to the left. Alan flinched and tightened his grip around Jenny once more.

A tinny voice came through the Egyptian's cell phone, which functioned as a walkie-talkie. The man ignored it and pointed to another side street. They swerved and proceeded on, then suddenly slowed in the middle of a lane surrounded by nondescript buildings. The Egyptian muttered something into his handset and then jumped outside. The van stopped and its side door flew open.

"Please, come!" he said, glancing feverishly from side to side, his pistol at the ready.

As quickly as he could, Alan helped Jenny exit the vehicle.

"Come with me," the Egyptian repeated.

With Alan still supporting Jenny, the three of them crossed the street and entered a building. Inside, a low, dark entryway led to a surprisingly elegant marble-floored hall harboring the intricate grillwork of an antique elevator. The Egyptian punched a call button, then turned to Alan and held an index finger to his lips, his other hand holding his gun pointed at the ceiling.

The elevator door slid open and they squeezed into its narrow interior. As they ascended, Alan felt a sense of relief, as though gaining altitude offered more safety than any walls at ground level.

"Are you hurt?" Alan asked Jenny while they continued rising in the elevator.

She shook her head. "A little. It was just so—" she stared blankly, trying to find the words—"sudden, so shocking. Out of nowhere. I saw it for a split second, and then I fell and everything went black. Oh, Alan," she whispered, "I've never been more afraid . . ."

"It's going to be all right, Jenny, I promise. We've left it all far behind."

The elevator stopped and the doors opened. They walked swiftly down another hallway, where they approached a large black door. The Egyptian produced a key, and soon they were all inside, the door locked behind them. The man motioned to a leather sofa in the center of a darkened living room. The lights were kept off, although at the other end of the room a tall patio window offered enough light for them to see because of the glowing city outside and a near-full moon.

"This is one of the *Mukhabarat* safe houses," the Egyptian said.

"Mukh *what?*" Alan asked as he helped Jenny to the sofa.

"Our secret police. That is who I work for. But understand—you are not out of danger. I am a Copt, a fellow Christian. There are only a few in our ranks, and we fought hard to be assigned your protection. Others in the Mukhabarat are cooperating with the Islamic militants. They have even become assassins on their side. So no one knows you are here except me and the one who assisted in escorting you to the building, and he is trustworthy. Still, do not open the door for anyone but me. There is a peep-hole in the door. Do not turn on lights, speak loudly, or call attention to yourselves. I will inform the Embassy of the United States, and I will come for you when all is safe. It is the most I can do. You must understand that the whole city is stirred up by this. We cannot be too careful."

"Thank you, my friend," Alan replied. "And what is your name? Or what may I call you?"

The man took a break from his careful glances around the room and faced Alan squarely.

"My name is Ahmir. If something should happen to me, and my Coptic colleague must come in my place, he will introduce himself as my friend, not as an officer. Now, does your wife require medical attention?"

Alan inhaled sharply, pondering whether to correct the man. He realized that his overwhelming concern for Jenny, his insistence on saving her, maybe even the manner of his holding her, had all contributed to the assumption that they were man and wife.

In an instant he decided not to correct the man. Perhaps the impression was the Egyptian's only reason for leaving the two alone in a safe house like this one, Alan couldn't tell. But something deeper, and stronger, had also risen within him and compelled him not to speak.

It felt right, somehow, to think of it this way. Natural and comforting.

"I think I'll be all right, thanks," Jenny replied.

Alan wasn't sure if she felt as he did or if she simply hadn't heard the words *your wife*.

Ahmir nodded. "I believe there is fruit and water in the refrigerator. Otherwise, you have my sincere apologies for what happened today. I must go now. May God keep you. You will be in my prayers."

He strode from the room and out the door, turning and locking it with his key before walking away.

RESCUED

18

CAIRO

A profound silence fell over the room. Alan stood still for a long moment, basking in the peace and all it represented. They were safe for now. Safe, hidden, and anonymous in an out-of-the-way place even he could not find again if he had to. He closed his eyes and sighed, trying to ignore the latent afterimages of violence and terror still writhing in his mind.

He blew out slowly, then breathed in. The apartment held the stuffiness of a room left vacant for months. He looked around and moved toward the window.

"I think it would be okay if we opened this," he said. He flipped the latch and pulled the glass to one side. A warm breeze blew into the room, laden with a brew of foreign scents.

"You smell that?" he said. "Cairo's unique aroma."

"Our bus driver told me this morning on the way in," she said, her voice weak and shallow, "that it's a combination of rotting trash, various spices, car-exhaust fumes, and the smoke from those nargileh pipes."

Alan laughed, a little too eagerly perhaps, but he was suddenly overjoyed to hear her speak. And she did have a point; her list had described the smell perfectly.

He turned to her, then looked down. Jenny lay on the sofa neither asleep nor fully awake, her arms wrapped around herself. She needed a blanket, he realized. Finding one did not prove difficult in the westernized apartment. He discovered a light throw in a side closet, returned, and draped it over her.

It struck him as ironic—he had covered her up ostensibly to shield her from the breeze wafting in from the window, and yet, as much as she may have needed the added warmth, he needed the blanket there to spare him the sight of her lithe body.

"It's quite a view," she said.

"Yes, it is. Although you can't see much of it from back here."

"I'm okay."

"Would you like it better if I moved the sofa closer to the window?"

She shrugged briefly. "Sure, why not."

He bent down and, with her still lying on it, carefully pushed each end of the sofa across the floor until it was directly up to the window.

"Oh, wow. Thank you," she said, looking out over the vast cityscape of downtown Cairo.

"Glad to do it." He pointed to a broad body of shining water curving through a mass of glass buildings in the night. "Look, there's the Nile."

"The city is so much more modern than I expected," she said. "I was picturing nothing but minarets and domes."

"Me too," he said, smiling. "And I didn't expect it to be so big."

"Or beautiful. The lights spread out all the way to the horizon, don't they?"

"They certainly do."

"Thank you, Alan," she said, after a long pause, in a softer tone.

"You thanked me already—"

"No, not for that," she interrupted. "Thank you for saving my life. You came back for me. I remember. I was down on that stage, feeling more vulnerable than I ever have before, trying to shake my head free of, free from . . ."

"I know."

"And then you came. I didn't recognize the first face that bent down toward me. But when yours appeared, well, I can't tell you what a relief that was."

Alan didn't answer but simply nodded and sat down on the carpeted floor, leaning up against the sofa near where she was resting her head. Facing out toward the countless lights arrayed below the window, he sighed deeply.

"I was through," he said flatly.

"Through with *what?*"

"Through avoiding you. Through treating you like I was indifferent toward you. Like you meant nothing to me."

"So it hasn't been just my imagination," she whispered, almost to herself.

"Of course not. I haven't been very subtle about it."

"Why?" she asked. "Why have you been doing this? I've really wondered if you found me . . . annoying or repulsive in some way."

"Oh, please," he said. "Surely you know."

"No. I'm afraid I missed it."

Alan stared out the window over the city, troubled at being forced to say it.

"I don't know if I'm ready to say it out loud, Jenny. There's too much at stake."

The two watched silently while the side curtains billowed from a sudden gust of wind.

"Let's just say for now," he continued, "that it's the opposite of annoyance or repulsiveness."

There was utter quiet for a minute or two. Finally her voice returned.

"Oh . . ." She shook her head slowly, a bewildered frown marking her features. "How strange . . . I never considered *that.*"

"It's probably because you thought better of me."

"That's true," she answered. "Maybe I did."

"So maybe we should just stop talking and enjoy the view."

They both nodded and turned back to the foreign city outside the window.

Cairo seemed alive at this hour of night. Distant avenues teemed with brake lights, vehicles in a hurry, and tiny bodies shuffling to-and-fro.

"The driver said it's on account of the heat," she commented. "Everyone comes out at night."

"Yeah. Including murderers."

She reached over impulsively and placed her hand on top of his—his right hand, which rested on the sofa's leather cushion. "It's not your fault, you know. You were great tonight. The Spirit of God was moving in that place."

"Yeah, but they came to hear Alan Rockaway, and instead some of them got a horrible death."

"They got a word from the Lord, and then an eternity with Him," she countered.

"Surely you don't mean that what happened tonight was a good thing."

"Of course not," she said, pulling herself up to a half-sitting position. "But I do think that, overall, tonight was a—a victory over evil. And I think you were the reason why. The earthly one, at least. You and the word God gave you to speak. You were magnificent. I've never heard you speak so boldly, so on-target, with such inspiration."

"Thank you," he said, smiling wearily, as though such praise was an effort for him to accept.

"Tell me, Alan," she said, obviously regaining her strength, "where is Terri? What's the real story behind her not being here?"

"She was—"

"And I don't want the public story," Jenny interrupted.

Alan chuckled and closed his eyes. "I didn't think you

would," he sighed. "Where do I start? College? Ordination day? Last week?"

"Start with why she treats you the way she does." Then, seeing his surprised reaction, Jenny continued, "I've heard her speak to you. It's not hard to miss, Alan. Your wife's voice isn't exactly a mousy one."

He chuckled again, but then a pained expression overtook the amusement. "Terri treats me the way she does because she is not the mate God had in mind for me, that's why."

Alan's mouth fell open as soon as the words left his lips. He was as shocked as Jenny at what he had just said. It was as if some alter ego had spoken through him.

He felt obliged to explain himself. "You see, Terri and I started dating in my junior year of college. I was attracted to her self-confidence, her poise, her ability to stand on her own two feet. For some reason, I found that just as attractive as the physical part. She challenged me. She expected great things, and she made me want to succeed."

"And you did, didn't you?"

"Yeah, I suppose. But that's the thing—she sort of expected success all along, yet now that it's come our way, she's not satisfied with any of it. Nothing seems to please her. I can't quite measure up. Funny, but I can disappoint her just as much by leaving my socks lying on the bedroom floor as I would have by failing to grow the third largest church in Colorado."

"And this explains why she's not here tonight?"

"It does, actually. She considers this frivolous. An ego-stroking exercise that has nothing to do with my ministry. My *real* ministry, that is, which to her extends to about a fifty-mile radius of our church parking lot. Which is why, even though I would have done anything for her to see me handle that crowd tonight, tackling language and cultural barriers yet still managing to impart God's power—she would have had no use for it. I measured up tonight, but . . ."

He felt his voice trail off, felt a trembling enter his speech, and realized he was beginning to weep. The emotion and the tears were complete intruders; he had no idea where they'd come from. His surprise was as great as his sadness.

He felt the hand upon his again and shivered from the intimacy of the touch.

"It wasn't enough," he continued. "It wasn't her kind of thing. It was an adventure, a thrill and a tragedy all mixed together, and she wouldn't have any of it. If only she could have been here with me . . ."

Again he found himself unable to finish the sentence. Probably because, near the end of his words, he'd become flooded with a sense too momentous and undeniable for words. He hadn't truly wanted her to come. Not like she was now.

It's over.

His long-drawn-out attempt to justify his existence, his ministry, to Terri . . .

"It's over."

He spoke the words out loud, low and resolute. Then again.

"It's over, Jenny. I'm through trying to measure up for her. God knows who I am."

"We do too, Alan. Your church knows."

"Yeah."

"*I* know."

The tears flowed freely all of a sudden, coursing unchecked down his face. He buried his face in his hands while his lungs heaved with great, gulping shudders. He sensed with utter certainty that a dam decades in the making had just been breached.

"You've been fighting a battle that's consumed more of your strength than you even know, Alan. It's been the Enemy's way of siphoning off your true godly power. Keeping you distracted. Always half engaged in a conflict few of us knew about. And you know how God always works. You've preached it yourself. You taught it to me."

"You mean through paradox," he said, wiping his eyes. "Strength through weakness."

"Exactly. Victory through surrender."

"I *do* surrender, Jenny. I surrender my marriage to God. I

surrender my foolish war to win a struggle that couldn't be won. That should never have started in the first place."

"I just can't imagine that God would have chosen a mate for you who belittles you and your ministry that way."

"He wouldn't. He didn't. I surrender it, Jenny. God help me—I'm in dangerous waters, but I just know I can't go on this way. Even if it's wrong, I will just rest in His grace . . ."

Alan curled into a ball, and suddenly their two postures were now reversed. He was the afflicted, stricken figure in shock and sorrow, and she the stronger one. The one strong enough to reach down, hold his hand and his pain in her hands, and comfort him.

RESCUED
19

*INSIDE THE SUBMARINE—18 MIN. 32 SEC. AND
COUNTING . . .*

Alan Rockaway opened his eyes and was instantly whisked from
Cairo—the night he and Jenny first discovered the affection that
would change everything—back to the grim present: inside a
crippled, damp, and dark submarine losing its ability to support
the lives within it.

It occurred to him that while their life together had begun
with Jenny reaching down to hold his hand as he sobbed, now it
seemed destined to end with him reaching down to hold her as
she lay dying.

"Honey, please . . . you've got to hang on," he pleaded softly
into her ear. "I can't face life without you. Please . . ."

He looked up at the ring of stricken faces around him and
realized that this most tender of moments was playing itself out
in front of many spectators.

"Cairo is where it all began," he explained. "That night in the
Egyptian secret police safe house, where Jenny and I clung to

each other for reassurance, for hope. It might sound tawdry to some of you who remember that I was married at the time, but what happened between us was not of a physical nature. It was far, far deeper than that."

He breathed deeply, as much to quell the emotion rising within as to propel the words to come.

"It was spiritual, I'm telling you. It was ordained. Anointed, even. I wept like I'd never wept before, and I told Jenny exactly how empty, how depleted I felt. How completely unworthy I was of all God had brought my way. Here I was, the pastor of a church numbering, back then, over four thousand people, the center of a never-ending whirlwind, and my fondest hope was for the earth to open up and swallow me whole. But Jenny didn't just listen to me say this. She healed me. She held my hand and told me words that reached down to the innermost core of my soul."

He stopped and exhaled loudly, like a runner pausing after a victorious finish. He did not glance into the eyes of his listeners to gauge their reactions. He seemed to speak for himself, for his own purposes.

"Then Jenny opened her innermost thoughts to me. She shared about how a horrible experience just after college, something she still would not name, had made her wary of men, keeping them at arm's length for years. She was losing hope of ever overcoming the fear of entering into a close relationship with a man. Of course, even as she was saying this, it was happening . . ."

CAIRO—LATER THAT NIGHT

Though it had begun in violence, terror, and disorientation, that night seemed in its deepest hours to refashion itself and blossom into the single most memorable evening of Alan's and Jenny's lives. A delicate chrysalis of time, enhanced and made exquisite in part because of its crazed beginnings.

Indeed, Alan and Jenny did not express their burgeoning love in any physical manner other than Jenny offering her hand from the sofa, to alternately caress Alan's face or grip his hand during his most vulnerable confessions. Alan remained on the floor, too exhausted to move, too afraid of what might happen if he joined her on the sofa, and then, eventually, too enamored of their window's view and the casual affection of their postures to even want to move.

The dark apartment, which had first struck them as forbidding and vaguely threatening, seemed, over time, to soften and cradle them like a private penthouse, perched as it was high above the din of nighttime Cairo. The manic intensity of their arrival mellowed into a fatigue-drunk languor, an unfamiliar vulnerability.

Over the ensuing hours they wept, both of them, several times. They laughed even more frequently. They told each other their stories, in a manner far more intimate and awestruck than the usual first-date routine. They allowed the night's cooler breezes to blow into the apartment unchecked, once causing a wayward curtain to swipe an end table and send a decorative vase shattering to the floor. They laughed and let the mess remain.

They speculated as to when their Egyptian friend would return and end this perilous idyll. Alan even spun a whimsical story of them being stranded, unable to either leave or contact any help from the outside for weeks.

They both chuckled at that, for by that point if either had possessed the energy or alertness to act on the feelings between them, far greater intimacy might have resulted.

At last they watched a gorgeous Egyptian dawn set the eastern horizon aglow in clouds of lavender and pink.

Then they fell asleep.

The knocking began on the apartment's door at ten o'clock the following morning. After a futile minute of increasingly assertive blows, the key turned in the lock. The door swung silently open, nudged ajar by the nose of a handgun silencer. The figure crept inside and moved to the center of the room where he saw the pair—one lying on the sofa, the other in front of it on the floor. Suddenly taken by alarm, the man leaped over to them and with his free hand felt Jenny's neck for a pulse.

Instantly Jenny jumped, nearly knocking the gun from the man's other hand, almost causing it to go off accidentally. Just as quickly Alan sprang up, his eyes flying open.

"Greetings in the name of our Lord and Savior Jesus Christ," the man said with a thick accent. "I'm sorry to say, my friend Ahmir went to be with the Lord last night. His last words were to inform me of your whereabouts and to ask that I come for you. Do not fear—all is now calm. I have come to escort you out of here."

"And still I resisted," Alan further explained to his captive audience in the sub. "I clung to the notion that changes like this weren't done—certainly not by pastors. No matter what, you stayed with the one you married. And you sure didn't expect God to somehow just up and bring you the answer out of the clear blue. Instead, my old way of thinking told me that you stick with your mistakes even if they end up killing you, if nothing else to show how persevering and long-suffering you are. You embrace your worst immature mistakes and reconcile yourself to a life of second best, or what might have been."

He paused, then said, "And God brought me Jenny."

As if reminded of her by the speaking of her name, Alan pulled her limp form closer to himself, joined his hands across her waist, and held her tightly. He was not looking at her, but the tears in his eyes and the quaking in his voice told his listeners that he was speaking to delay the moment of realization, the inevitable need to admit the truth of what was happening.

Jenny Rockaway was dying.

20

DENVER—SUMMIT CHAPEL

Five TV network news trucks—their brightly plastered channel numbers, call letters, and logos, their microwave masts extended high like great robot arms—had taken up positions just outside the church building. Camera crew and anchors' faces all stared through windowpanes in hopes of glimpsing the grieving worshipers inside.

When the live remotes began, and more and more camera lights and reporters lined the sidewalk out front, Larry Collins ordered the window shades be shut.

Even that measure failed to shelter the shell-shocked people from the outside world's invasion.

Three minutes later, the control-booth manager waved Larry aside and pointed at a small monitor wedged in between the consoles. The image was a familiar one: turquoise ocean, bright sunshine, scattered pieces of yacht. But now the accident had its own logo and news-media title.

CNN Breaking News: Tragedy in the Caribbean!

Feverishly, Larry weighed the pros and cons. Then he nodded upward to the giant screen. The technician hit the button to transfer the signal through the main projector.

A woman's voice, somber and urgent, suddenly echoed through the sanctuary: "With every passing minute, the survivors of this collision at sea—if there are any survivors—are losing alarming amounts of their remaining oxygen. The surrounding wreckage has made it impossible to ascertain, so far, just how much oxygen is left, or the precise condition of any survivors. Barbados authorities are working to bring in divers to try and effect a rescue. But even if these heroic folks arrive soon, they will have to fight through all the treacherous debris covering the stricken vessel—the remains of the yacht that sank it in the first place."

The CNN camera broke away from the woman, and another of their cameras zoomed in on Jeff, who looked much as they'd seen him last, only now from an aerial perspective. He was still kneeling on a pitching deck, facing a patch of floating white shards.

"Meanwhile, a poignant human story is emerging," the woman went on, her face reappearing on the screen. "The lone figure you just saw on the tourist submarine boarding pier is that of Jeff Rockaway from Denver, a videographer and the seventeen-year-old son of the clergyman who's trapped below the waves with several dozen of his parishioners. Spectators report that the young man has refused all offers of help or evacuation and insists on simply remaining on the pier, watching and recording the accident scene and, some say, praying for his father's safe return."

The sea breeze suddenly blew the correspondent's hair into her eyes. She held it back with her free hand, tightened her grip on the microphone, and forged ahead with her live report.

"This poignant vigil," she said, "is the only tangible sign of the human cargo still trapped under the ocean here, and of the human toll that will ensue if help does not arrive very, very soon . . ."

BARBADOS—INSIDE THE SUBMARINE

Alan Rockaway's rambling monologue was growing more desperate and pathetic with every passing second.

"After we returned home," he muttered, hardly pausing for a breath, "we didn't take any action. We knew we could walk away from it—no one really knew we'd been alone together that night. We talked about it privately on the flight back and decided that if what we felt was real, from God and not just the by-product of a highly charged adventure, then it could survive some time apart. So we went back to our lives, hard as that was, to test our feelings. I tried my hardest to rediscover the spark that had once flickered between Terri and me. And Jenny went back to being the bright light of the worship team, as well as the best paralegal in Denver.

"Problem was, Terri had not handled my twelve hours of unexplained absence very well. It wasn't jealousy so much but panic and frustration over why no one could tell her where her husband was. When she heard of the attack and that I was missing, she started bombarding the United States Embassy with demands. She was about to call a press conference to air her panic and frustration when she finally received the phone call telling her I was okay. What complicated matters was when she heard why Egyptian police had been reluctant to give any information—they'd been under the impression that I was in hiding with my wife in Cairo. As you can imagine, Terri was expecting some answers when I came home, and that didn't make for a tender reunion. I told her . . ."

A faint gasp came from Jenny as she slowly raised a trembling hand up to Alan's lips. Her eyes were barely open, yet enough to convey a look of tenderness and pity.

"I told Terri the truth about where I was those twelve hours, but that nothing happened. I didn't tell her all of it, though. I didn't tell her that Jenny Rodeham had brought me back to life again."

JENNY'S DENVER APARTMENT BUILDING—SOON
AFTER RETURNING FROM CAIRO

The feeling that someone was watching her—not just casually looking but intensely *watching* her—burst through Jenny's nervous system at her third step into her building's common area.

It was the eleventh night following her return from Egypt.

The lobby was filled with people that night, as it often was: elderly grandparents playing with toddlers, a young couple necking in a corner, a few men in suits sitting at the edge of their seats in deep conversation, and other silhouettes milling about in the background.

Often she would feel a bystander trail his eyes across her face and body as she charged across the foyer toward the elevators.

But tonight was different somehow. It came to her first as a faint tickle on the nape of the neck. Then she felt eyes upon her back, an attention both willful and intense. Heat flushed through her face, and her heart began to race. Jenny narrowed her eyelids and tried to sense whether the scrutiny was merely curious or malicious in nature. She turned the corner toward the elevator bay at a tight angle in order to gain a peek at the watcher but saw only a darkly clad male figure in the process of standing up.

He was coming for her, she was certain of it. But then she reminded herself to *get real*. As a single woman, she knew she sometimes contrived these solitary mental dramas simply to stay alert, not to mention ward off loneliness and boredom.

And then there was Jenny's sinister, deeply felt justification for paranoia. The one she never skirted too close to, even in her mind. She banished even the suggestion from her thoughts.

More recently, there had been the trauma suffered in Cairo. Those electrifying few moments on the stage between realizing that death was headed her way and feeling herself awaken in Alan's arms. Surely she'd been more on edge since returning home.

She punched the elevator button extra hard and waited impatiently for the door to slide open. Footsteps approached, and someone walked up and stood close beside her. Her fear erupted once again.

She turned and sighed deeply, for the smile that greeted her came from the well-dressed lady in her fifties whom Jenny had seen around the complex many times. She grinned and turned back to face the elevator.

Then more steps approached. Heavier ones. A larger silhouette moved behind them both. *Should I turn again?* she wondered. It appeared she would soon share an elevator with whoever it was. A small, enclosed space. The very thought overwhelmed her. That was the last place she wanted to be caught facing a potential attacker!

An idea came to her. She shook her head, shrugged, and sighed loudly as if to broadcast that she'd grown impatient waiting for the elevator. Then she turned abruptly for the stairs. The elevator light dinged on behind her as she reached the stairwell door, but she decided to ignore it.

She was on the fourth turn, taking the steps two at a time, inwardly congratulating herself on her clever escape and trying her best to write the whole thing off as a good excuse for a little exercise, when a door swung open on the floor beneath her. She glanced down and caught sight of someone, then heard the same solid footsteps.

It was him! She knew it. And it was no coincidence.

Now it all came back, the paralyzing fear, stronger than she'd known since that hateful night in her past. Her mind groped for a course of action. She dug in her purse and took out her cell phone, flipped it open, and started speaking in a loud voice.

"Hey, sweetheart!" she nearly shouted. "I'm here, just twenty seconds away, on the stairs. Yeah, come on out and meet me. I can't wait to see you!"

She heard a male voice calling upward but had missed the words during her pretend message.

"Sure. Come on down," she continued loudly. "I don't know if I can wait that long . . ."

She grimaced at how foolish she sounded, but it was the best she could do. She was grateful for even the idea of doing this much.

Finally she reached her floor. A long hallway greeted her. She decided to sprint toward her last left turn before the man following made it to the landing behind her. As she took off running for her apartment, about halfway down the hall she no longer felt the attention at her back but fear itself like a strong wind blowing her forward, lifting her feet.

The stairwell door opened behind her with a metallic clang just as she hit the wall, unable to slow herself, and threw herself sideways out of sight.

Now what should she do? Should she run for her apartment door and try to lock herself in? Or would that give her away? Should she make her stand right here, try to defend herself out in the open?

She struggled to analyze the situation the way she had been taught. The odds of her unlocking her door and making it inside without him seeing her were not good.

She clenched her jaw and decided that she'd fight it out right here—make the jerk pay, whoever he was, for putting her through all this.

She breathed in and tried to remember what the self-defense instructor at the community college had told her. *"Relax your body. Picture your attacker and what he wants to do to you. Channel your rage . . ."*

The next moment exploded like a grenade.

Jenny tossed down her purse. The footsteps were growing closer. She saw a shadow turn the corner.

Jenny screamed as loudly as her lungs would allow. Her eyes wildly scanned the space beyond the hallway intersection. She saw nothing . . .

. . . except that, ever so cautiously, the person began to come into her view.

She didn't wait a second longer. Hopping forward two long steps, Jenny took advantage of her standing position by confronting her stalker with a leaping scissors kick, making contact under the man's chin. Her foot struck bone. She saw his neck snap backward, followed by a spray of blood piercing the air. The body fell limp upon the hard hallway floor.

Adrenaline coursed through her. Enraged at having to take such desperate action in her own housing complex, she shoved the heel of her hand into the stalker's cringing face. She pressed into soft flesh.

"Don't move, you . . ." she began.

But the words were unnecessary. The stalker was not about to move an inch. He was unconscious.

Then Jenny grew absolutely still.

"Oh no!" It was more a scream than a shout of recognition.

Alan's familiar face was smeared with blood.

21

"What have I done?" Jenny screamed.

On her knees, she tried to cradle his head, which lolled about. She checked his pulse. Thankfully he was breathing, his heart still beating. While caressing his cheek she allowed full vent to her anguish. "God, please, I pray he's not hurt badly," she pleaded to the hallway's ceiling. "I couldn't bear it. I just couldn't . . ." She looked down and saw that his eyelids were struggling to open.

"Oh, Alan! I'm so sorry. I thought you were—"

His eyes opened completely, then his whole face wrenched into a grimace of delayed pain.

"What did you do to me?"

"Uh . . . that was a scissors kick," she said, cringing.

"What—were you trying to kill me?" he said through a mouthful of crimson.

"I'm so sorry. I thought someone was stalking me. You should know better than to shadow a vulnerable single woman."

"Vulnerable, my foot," he said, holding his jaw.

"Well, why didn't you just call me or something? Never mind—let me help you up."

She half carried him down the hall to her door. Once inside, she led him to the sofa, where she lowered him on one end.

"Is this because I haven't called?" he finally asked, the corner of one eye squinting at her.

"No. It's because I was raped."

Alan froze, his eyes wide. Then his fingers rose slowly to where hers were wiping blood from his chin with a tissue she got from her purse. He grasped her hand and squeezed tightly.

"Years ago, I mean," she said. "Actually, it was nine years, four months, and seven days ago. It's the thing I alluded to in Cairo. I . . . I didn't mean to tell you like this."

"And I didn't mean not to call."

"It's been almost two weeks since Cairo, and you're back to giving me the same old treatment. The averted glances, turning away, the awkward silences when I walk in—"

"I tried, but I failed."

"Tried *what*?"

"Tried to forget about what happened between us. Tried to live without you. Tried to return to my sorry marriage and my unhappy, second-rate life. Remember our decision? That if God really wanted us together, He'd make returning to our old ways impossible. Well, I gave it my best. The cost of this is so high; I had to be sure."

"And the best way you could think to convey this good news was stalking me through my apartment building?"

"I'm sorry. But think about it, Jenny. I'm the pastor of the third largest church in Colorado. There's not a place we could meet that's out of the way enough to ensure some church member—somebody we would never recognize, yet who'd recognize me in a heartbeat—wouldn't see us. Unless you count, maybe, the summit of Mount Evans. And even there, all bets are off."

"Why didn't you identify yourself in the stairwell?"

"I tried to, but you were talking so loudly on your cell phone, you couldn't hear me."

"So. You're here." Her nervous rush was starting to wear off, with a certain glum bluntness taking its place.

"Yeah, and can we back up a bit? To the R word?"

"I'd rather not. Look, Alan, it doesn't define me or rule me. I try not to think about it."

"Right. Except for when you're walking up to your apartment and you feel the need to kung-fu somebody into the hospital."

"I really am sorry, Alan. But I was abducted, taken away by car late one night after my shift at Starbucks. The guy was already in my car, hunched down in the backseat. He made me drive him out to the country. Inside I was freaking out, because I was sure he was going to kill me afterward. And by all indications, he intended to do exactly that. I waited until—until his moment of greatest vulnerability, then I kicked him in the face and managed to get away. I never ran so fast in all my life, and I used to run track in school. Later the guy was caught, and I testified at his trial, which was only slightly less frightening and traumatic than the rape itself. Since then, I've educated myself. Took some courses. I overcame, with the Lord's help. But one of my coping mechanisms is that I'm always on guard. I carry a gun, and like my personal alarm system, it's always locked and loaded."

"And the nifty little kick to the chin?"

"Jiujitsu. Two years of lessons. Anyway, if the fake cell-phone call hadn't worked, or the jiujitsu, then the gun would have come out. So, can we drop the subject now?"

"I'm sorry. But if I hadn't asked, wouldn't you think I didn't care?"

"I don't want you to care. Not about *that*. I don't want it to matter. I don't want it to . . ." She looked away, her eyes brimming with tears.

"What, Jenny?" he asked in a low tone.

"I don't want it to color how you see me. How you feel about me."

He took a deep breath.

"Well, Jenny, you don't have to worry about that one. Because the reason I followed you and jeopardized not only my ministry but my family to see you again is precisely *that*. I do want you. I want you as badly as I want my next breath."

"So?"

"So the problem is, wanting is the easy part. I want lots of things I can't—and shouldn't—have. The biggest question still hasn't been answered."

"And I can't answer it for you. You know that."

"I do, Jenny," he said tenderly.

"Are you sure it's *me* you want, and not just a way out of a troubled marriage?"

"That's a fair question." An expression of such melancholy came to his features that Jenny thought she could see every sad, unfulfilled second of the last decade or so pass through his eyes. "I'd have to say no, though. I'm not sure. Obviously we wouldn't be talking about this if my marriage was a happy one. Still, you're not the cause or way out of those problems. Just the light at the end of the tunnel."

"And are you sure it's not a midlife crisis you're dealing with?"

"I'm content with my midlife. Except for my marriage, that is."

"You're not out there pricing Porsches or Corvettes? Making passes at stewardesses?" she quipped.

"Hardly."

"Not just my feminine wiles?" She was teasing now, batting her eyelashes and playing with the bottom curl of her hair.

"On that one," he said with a wink, gladly sharing in the levity, "I'll take the Fifth."

"So again, what is it you want?"

"Promise not to laugh?"

"No, I don't. But I do promise to let you explain."

"I want God's best for me. Not the dregs of my worst adolescent choices."

"Oh please, Alan," she said, frowning and shaking her head.

"See, I told you you'd make fun of it."

"But that sounds like a bad line from an old college boyfriend," she said, smiling.

Alan shrugged. "It's what I believe. Would you believe me more if I was smoother? Better rehearsed?"

"As rehearsed as one of your sermons?"

"Sorry. It takes me three days to work out one of those."

"Really? You had me convinced that you delivered them off the cuff." Jenny turned serious then. "My psychologist would tell you that what we all want is a certain *feeling*. What kind of feeling are you after, Alan? And what makes you think you'll get it with me?"

He sighed heavily, then answered her while staring at the floor in concentration. "I'll tell you how you make me feel. When I think of you, I feel like the hero of an epic sort of story, instead of a poor shlub who's just trying to keep his head above water. When I see you, I feel a hundred happy, hopeful endings gallop through my mind. When I'm around you, I feel like the center of the universe." He stopped a moment. "Sappy, I know. I should be more eloquent than that, I suppose. But that's exactly the way I feel. The way I *want* to feel. And just like your shrink said, that's the bottom line, right?"

She smiled at his chivalrous imagery and buried her fingers in his hair.

"Yeah. I suppose so."

"Will you come with me? Will you go along for this ride?"

She sighed, a sad and apprehensive look in her eyes. "This is going to be rough, you know. You're sure it's the right thing?"

"I don't know," he said. "Sometimes I'm one hundred percent certain. Other times, I'm a basket case. But isn't faith just like that? My ultimate consolation is that, wrong or right, I'm covered by grace. I'm living in it more than ever. Grace and nothing else."

"Good. 'Cause you're going to need it."

"We both are, honey. You in this with me?"

She reached up, cupped his chin in both her hands, and kissed him long, warmly.

"I am."

BARBADOS—BACK IN THE SUBMARINE

Two, then three of Jenny's almost lifeless fingers traced a line across his mouth. Alan stopped speaking. He looked down at her and drank in the significance of who lay draped across him in that dark, anguished place.

"No, I did not tell Terri that Jenny had restored my sense of wonder, my love for life, my whole reason for living . . ." he took up his tale once more.

Jenny mouthed some words, but the toll upon her waning strength was agonizing to witness. It was impossible to read their meaning precisely, but from the look that passed between them, it was clear enough what they had meant.

"I love you, too, sweetheart," he whispered. "More than ever."

The fingertips hovered there, grazing the contour of his lips for a second longer.

Then they fell. And as they did, a groan came from the women nearby. Then another one, much louder this time, escaped Alan's mouth.

"No," he moaned. "No. No. God, this can't be . . ."

He lowered her face into the crook of his arm, reached out with his free hand, and cleared away a strand of blood-clotted hair from her forehead. Then his eyes squeezed shut, and he lay his face on her chest.

Those around him looked away. One man's hand reached out from the darkness and settled on Alan's heaving shoulder.

After a long, horrible moment, Norm Knowles leaned in to him, his face ashen.

"Pastor, I know you're in a terrible place right now, but

maybe you'd still like to say something. You know, to the camera, leave something for posterity?"

Alan looked up, disoriented, and nodded. He handed the camera to Norm. The light came on. Alan spoke then, a deadness in his eyes.

"Mr. and Mrs. Rodeham, she's gone. She's gone." Alan closed his eyes again, clearly trying to gather up his will. "I can tell you this: No one could have loved your precious daughter more than I did. Still do. It wouldn't be possible. I know you two have a different take on what God did in our lives. I struggle with it, too, but let's leave that aside for a moment. Please—this is all I ask. Grant yourselves the mercy of forgiving us, and at least recognize how much I adored her. How much every little thing about her, every curve of her face, every tone of her voice, her marvelous . . ."

The sentence ended.

He fell perfectly still.

Then, ever so gradually, his strength returned. His eyes opened, his head straightened, and his facial muscles regained their shape.

"Now, for my children. I have to start with Jeff . . ."

RESCUED

22

BARBADOS—INSIDE THE SUBMARINE

"Jeff, my firstborn . . ." Alan began. "My boy, you'll never know how much joy you brought me and your mother. And Greg, my little one, with your sweet face and that adorable stutter when you first learned to talk. Can you boys ever forgive me. . . ?"

Alan paused and leaned back as if he was examining the vessel's overturned condition. It was obvious, however, that he was merely braving the onset of more tears.

"Boys, I'll never forget the night your mom and I came into your room to tell you she and Daddy weren't going to live together anymore. Greg, you looked at me with those big eyes of yours and asked if we were going to send you off to an orphanage. It took you a full minute to ask your question, because all of a sudden after three years, your stutter was back. And, Jeff, you started to cry and then you corrected your brother. You told him nobody was going to an orphanage; we just weren't going to be a family anymore. Then you looked at me with an expression that said, 'Why does this have to be, Dad?' At that moment I felt the lowest a man could be."

Alan looked around. It seemed it was just now dawning on him that there were others here with him, listening to his every word.

"It broke my heart. I fear it broke both of yours, too. Please forgive me for causing you so much grief and confusion. You know, when I get to heaven I'm going to have a serious sit-down with God. And ask Him how something that turned out so wonderful in my own life had to be so painful for my boys."

A look of amazement came over him then. He began to speak again, only now in a completely altered tone. A lower, breathier voice that others in the vessel had not heard before.

"Terri, I have to say this. I need your forgiveness, too—for so many things. For starters, please forgive me for the hateful things I said to you during the divorce process. I thought everything should stay calm and civil, but facing your anger threw me into a rage. I know that doesn't make much sense, but that's what provoked me. The truth is, you were never a bad wife, or unsupportive, or beneath my calling. You challenged my preaching, my theology, and I didn't accept that from anybody. But in exchange, I told you that you'd failed as a wife and mother. And that was such a lie. I'm the one who failed."

He shut his eyes in weariness.

"I'm the one who failed, Terri. And now all I'm asking is your forgiveness."

He shot a piercing look at Norm. "Turn it off, Norm. Please, turn it off."

BOARDING PIER—ON THE SURFACE

Jeff glared at a circling helicopter overhead, squinting against the sunlight reflecting off the lens of a camera trained on him, when he turned abruptly away.

His cell phone was ringing.

He frowned, for he had asked Larry and the church to let him be for a while.

But a glance at the phone's Caller ID display revealed

another, more compelling source. He stiffened in surprise, quickly flipping open the phone.

"Mom."

"Jeff, sweetheart—are you okay?"

"No, I'm not."

"I'm sorry. I didn't know how else to start . . ."

"He's gone, Mom. He's underwater, they're running out of air, and I don't know if it's happened yet, but . . ."

"I know. And I'm sorry I haven't called until now. No one at the church informed me. I saw it on TV, just a minute ago while flipping through the channels, completely by accident. One click and there was my son, bigger than life, under one of those Breaking News color bars. I almost had a heart attack. Are you sure you're okay? You're not injured or anything?"

"Didn't you hear me?" he shouted, swept away by his grief. "I'm not the victim here! I'm not the one fighting for his life! *Dad* is!"

"Jeff, please . . ." Her voice started to tremble. "I loved your father for nineteen years. I'd still be married to him today if—"

"Then why can't you acknowledge what's happening to him?"

"I can, it's just awkward since he and I are no longer married. So while he matters a lot to me, he doesn't concern me nearly as much as my firstborn son, who last time I checked was still very much a part of my life. And *you're* the one I'm talking to, so I'm anxious to know if you're okay."

"Well, thanks for asking, but I'm not."

"I mean injured."

"I'm not physically maimed in any way, Mom. All right?"

A long pause.

"No, Jeff. I'm *not* satisfied. I can tell you're in an unbearable frame of mind right now. Not only that, but the man I thought God had chosen for me is on the verge of death. I'm not all right. But thanks for asking."

"I'm sorry," he said. "This is just . . . hellish. I'm not handling it very well."

"Nonsense, son. There's nothing to handle. This situation would get the best of anybody. You're doing better than most."

"Thanks," she heard him say, and with a mother's imagination wondered if she'd detected the husky timbre of crying in his reply. It had been so long since she had heard the sound, she couldn't be sure.

Another lull fell between them. It became somehow apparent that Jeff was working up the courage to ask a question. At length, he spoke.

"Mom, do you remember the night you and Dad came into our room and told me and Greg about you guys splitting up?"

"Of course I do. I'll never forget that night as long as I live."

"Dad said that you'd both agreed it was best. That you both thought you needed to live separately. That God had led you together to the decision."

"I remember."

"Mom, did you mean it? Did you agree with Dad that God wanted you guys apart?"

He could hear her sigh through the background static, from thousands of miles' distance between them.

"Mom? Did you agree?"

"No," she answered, almost in a whisper. "I didn't agree."

"I could tell, Mom. I never told you, but your face was so . . . I don't know, it just wasn't right. It was all flushed, and your eyes were sad and hollow like they always got after you guys had been fighting."

"I'm sorry, son. I can guarantee you—it was the most difficult moment of my life."

"So why'd you do it? Why did you lie?"

"Don't try to make me the bad guy in this, Jeff."

"All I want to know is *why*."

"It's a long story."

"Well, make it short, Mom. 'Cause right now I'm very—" an abrupt halt in his speech revealed that Jeff was fighting back tears—"*confused*. I'm facing losing my dad, and I don't know how to feel about him. I don't know what to think of him."

"You honor him, Jeff. With every bone in your body you spend the next minutes honoring your father. Honoring him with your actions, your words, with the way you carry yourself. Do you know that right now just about every news outlet in the world is carrying live footage of you talking to me? What you choose to do now will stay with you for the rest of your life. Maybe into eternity."

"How do I do that, Mom? I have no idea what to do except stay here and watch."

"I don't know. I truly don't, honey. But when it does come to you, you've just got to go for it. Obey it no matter what. Okay?"

"Okay."

He stood up from a crouching position and hid the gathering tears by holding his hand over his eyes and scanning the horizon.

"Mom, I still need to know. Why did you go along with it that night? Won't you tell me?"

He heard her breathing heavily on the other end of the line.

"I did it for you and Greg. I was angry, hurt, and devastated, but I knew that being an adult, I had the inner resources to bounce back someday. But you and your brother were just kids. Kids who loved your dad. And your dad loved you back. Whatever his faults, Alan loved being your father. He still does. I could tell he was shattered over what he felt he had to tell you. And nothing mattered more to me than sheltering you guys from as much pain and loss as I could. Preserving as much of that relationship for you as I possibly could. You're going to think this cheesy or sentimental, Jeff, but it's true—I did it as a gift to you and your brother."

"A gift," he repeated.

"Can you understand? I was your mom. I could absorb a little blame without ending our relationship. But your dad was another matter. I couldn't live with having done anything to hurt that bond."

Jeff began to weep in earnest. But he had forgotten all about the world's media trained on the forlorn figure on the pier.

RESCUED

23

NEW JERUSALEM

One of the listeners' arms waved high in the air. Storyteller realized he had waited too long before allowing more questions.

"Why are these people so afraid of passing into eternity?" the young man asked.

"Remember," he said, turning to include everyone, "we have all sorts of life stories represented in our group here. Some of you who passed over could easily provide the answer to this, while others of you did not live through a passage of your own. Some of you are so young that you never saw those days or lived through such times. So for you this is all a bit strange. But it also helps to understand what the Pit has to show us."

At the mention of the Pit, Lydia shuddered. She turned her head to gaze through the window nearest her.

"They feared passing for a great many reasons," Storyteller continued. "Remember, bodies back then were subject to pain, to physical suffering. It's hard to describe if you've never felt it, but it's the opposite of pleasure, and something people were anxious to have stop as soon as it started. Usually the body went through a great deal of this pain before giving up its spirit."

"What's *anxious*?" the same young man wanted to know.

"I'll finish this, then answer your question. Now, another reason why people feared what they called death is that they confused the end of that life with real death, which is spiritual and eternal. Not only that, but the exact outcome of their life's passage was unknown, and very few felt sure of what awaited them."

"But didn't they have God's Word to tell them what to expect?"

"Yes, but even so, many of them found it confusing. The Word doesn't spell out everything. For many things were seen in glimpses, or described in allegorical terms, word pictures that defied their precise understanding. Back in those days, remember, the world was in a state of war. And many of our enemy's allies caused people to doubt the truth of the Word. They told people that maybe it didn't mean what it said, that maybe it was telling stories, spinning far-fetched examples. Even some believers were unsure what they actually faced when they died. That, by the way, is what *anxious* means. Being unsure of something, and feeling fear as a result. Remember, too, that earthly existence was all they'd ever known. Imagine being told that in a minute or so you'd leave the only world you've ever known. The prospect of leaving it forever, to live in a dimension you've only read about in a book that most everyone around you makes fun of—that was frightening for those not firmly grounded in the faith."

"Is this a fright story?" asked another man, also young looking.

"You could say that," said Storyteller.

"I know what kind of story this is!" a young girl shouted. With her bright blue eyes and a tousled shock of white-blond hair, the girl eyed Storyteller expectantly. "It's a cliff-hanger rescue story."

"Where did you hear about that?" asked Storyteller.

"From another who lived in those times."

"Do you know what it means?"

"Something about a rescue at the last minute, and a very happy ending."

"Well, that's pretty close. To the meaning of cliff-hanger rescue, that is. But this story may turn out a little differently than that. It is a rescue all right, but, again, of a different sort."

"It's a God-in-the-machine story!" said an excited young listener sitting at Storyteller's feet.

"Very good. For the rest of you, 'God in the machine' used to be called by its name in the old language of Latin—*deus ex machina*. Do you know what's special about one of these stories?"

"Because it's a story where God comes down from heaven at the very end and judges everyone, makes everything all right?"

"That's correct, Jacob. The ancient Greeks, who first came up with dramatic plays, would lower their so-called gods in an elaborate contraption from high above the stage. Yet that's not the reason it's so special."

"Why, then?" the teenager asked.

"Because the whole history of the Former Years is one big deus ex machina. One big three-act drama in which God came down and won the victory all by Himself."

"So, was that the right answer?"

"No."

"What do you mean?"

"The story I'm telling you," Storyteller replied, "is not like any other you've ever heard."

"Does it have a happy ending?"

Storyteller paused and pursed his lips, silently considering how to answer.

"I promise you this: you won't have any trouble figuring out what kind of ending it is when the time comes."

INSIDE THE SUBMARINE

Carrie Knowles stared at the camera lens, gathering her strength to say good-bye to her children. Alan looked into her face, usually drawn into a prim mask, and saw a completely altered demeanor. Carrie's eyes, which had always sparkled above the smiles, now held sheer terror, and her cheeks hung loosely.

"I'm just grateful," she said flatly, "for a church that gave me a place to serve. For a pastor like Alan who encouraged us volunteers, even offering us a place of recognition."

She turned to her husband, Norm, and gave him a weak smile. "I thank God for an understanding husband who allowed me the time to give back to those less fortunate, or those less blessed with time than we had. I'm grateful for servant opportunities that made me a better person and taught me all I needed to know about how to live the Christian life. And made me a better mom, a better wife in the process. Norm, would you like to say something now?"

Norm blinked, as though not expecting to get the opportunity. He swallowed hard, and his roving eyes seemed to indicate he hadn't yet thought through what he might say. "Tony and Tom," he began, "I want you to know you've been the joy of my life. I'm proud of both of ya. I'm going to miss you guys something fierce—provided there's any missing allowed up there. I suppose I should thank the church, as well. For giving me a few hours' peace every day, a few hours while the little woman went to serve someone else. Bug someone else."

Carrie shook her head, reached forward, and clapped her husband's arm in a weak attempt at playfulness.

"Could I say something?" came the breathy voice of a woman.

Alan took the camera and aimed its light in the direction of the voice, which turned out to be that of the old woman whose name he could never remember.

"Pastor, I've already said my good-byes, and those I love know already how much I love them. See, the Lord told me this trip would be the beginning of a great adventure for me. I didn't understand at first exactly what He meant, but now I do. I just want to tell the people back at the church I love that right now, in my last moment, all is well with my soul. And I beg everyone watching to make sure, to do everything they have to, to know beyond a doubt that all's well with theirs, too."

She formed a delicate smile and then stopped speaking, and just at that precise moment in time, almost poetically, the light on the camera gradually dimmed and its tiny motor clicked to a stop.

The battery was dead.

RESCUED

24

Bleary-eyed and emotionally spent from nonstop CNN-watching, fourteen-year-old Greg Rockaway stepped into his mother's bedroom. He found it dark, except for the glow of her bedside TV, with his mother weeping before it. He went to her and wrapped an arm around her shoulders, leaned forward, and took in a jumpy, faded image he'd never seen before.

Bathed in a single beam of golden light, his father looked much younger, resembling a slightly older version of his brother, Jeff. The face was smooth, his light brown hair full and sporting the bushier unkempt cut Greg had only seen in movies from the 1970s. Alan wore loose high-cut shorts of some shiny fabric and a dark blue Adidas T-shirt that looked a lot like the badly faded, torn monstrosity his dad liked to wear while performing household chores such as washing the car or cleaning the gutters.

The camera panned over to reveal boulders and pine trees and, much farther in the background, a sweeping vista of rolling peaks and thick forest. It was a mountaintop, nearing the time of sunset. A dozen or so similarly dressed young people stood nearby on logs and rocks, smiling, nodding, and listening intently. Greg found his father's words indistinct. Having heard him speak for so long, the boy was far less intent on the message than on the appearance of the man.

The lens now lingered on an attractive young woman with thick brown hair pulled back in a ponytail, and a beaming smile that clearly showed she was in love with the man beside her.

"That's me," Terri said to her son, pointing at the TV, sniffling. "Back in 1979. Bass Lake, California, at one of the best camps in the world. Your father had proposed to me the night before. I was in heaven."

"Or so you thought," Greg said in a sympathetic tone.

"No, I really was. In many ways," she said. "This was your father at his very best. A good man, on fire for what he believed. There's no reason to attack him. No reason at all. Especially now."

"Why haven't you shown us this before?"

She turned to him wearing a wounded look, and Greg realized he'd overstepped his bounds. His mother usually tolerated a mild level of ill-concealed disdain for his father, although the limits of the boy's sarcasm were rigidly enforced.

She looked back at the screen. Hearing her breath quiver and seeing her chest shake, Greg figured out the answer to his question. He knew why she was watching things she had not seen, at least in his presence, for years.

She was saying good-bye.

His mother was letting go of a man she still loved from beneath a web of conflicted emotions. A man she had been given cause to grieve a long time ago, in another context.

Finally she pushed the remote forward, stabbing its Power button with her finger. Picking up another videotape, she held it before her face and stared at its label for several seconds. He leaned forward to read the words: *Summit Chapel—Sunday, March 12, 2004.*

Greg flinched. He knew the date well. It was the morning

after his father's terrible revelation. The first dawn of the grayer, sadder new world he still inhabited.

Slowly, reluctantly, Terri moved toward the TV as she pulled the video from its case.

"This one," she said haltingly, turning to him, "I've never seen before. And neither have you."

"I know," said Greg.

Terri slid the video in the VCR and pressed Play, then sat back down on the bed. Greg shifted himself closer to his mom, took a seat beside her, and gave her shoulders a squeeze.

The image flashed on. This was the Alan Rockaway that Greg knew, with his now-thinning hair perfectly groomed, smile radiating from a lean, tanned face, wearing an impeccably cut suit of contemporary styling. The pulpit, the stage, the expertly lit background all said Summit Chapel—his dad's latest, greatest achievement.

Yet somehow his dad did not look like himself. He held his shoulders stiffly. His usually loose and casual gestures were restrained, his arms nearly glued to his sides. His face, always a brimming reservoir of smiles and genial cheer, now appeared drawn and troubled.

Apparently the video had been edited by someone, cued so the preliminary praise and worship time was over, with Pastor Alan already launching into his message.

For once, Greg sat there and tuned in, intently.

"This radical grace I've been talking about doesn't mean a whole lot if it doesn't carry us through the 'kicks in the gut' that life sometimes tosses our way."

Greg nearly rolled his eyes, for it was one of his dad's most timeworn phrases, one that his church members often repeated along with condescending chuckles. For all his mastery of the sermon, their pastor still had several verbal ruts from which he could not seem to escape.

"And although this message is not about me," Alan continued, on-screen, *"I must confess I'm in the middle of one right now. I'm not going to elaborate and bore you with the details of my personal*

trials, because, for one thing, they're hardly any more weighty or serious than any of yours. All I'm going to ask for is your prayers. Would you pray for . . . Terri and me during this difficult time?"

He paused as though awaiting some kind of reply from the audience.

Obligingly—although perhaps with some degree of reluctance—the camera cut to the reaction of someone in the sanctuary. It was a middle-aged woman, expensively dressed. She was frowning, her head cocked in bewilderment. The face looked vaguely familiar to Greg.

"Phyllis North," his mother said. "I'm surprised she didn't already know."

Greg shot his mother a questioning glance, but Terri waved him off, replying with a look that said, "It's not worth it."

"I'm grateful for many things," Alan went on, "despite the extreme delicacy and difficulty of the decisions before me. You see, it may be a cliché, but it's no less true. God uses the low times to draw us closer. Make us stronger. To purify our hearts and their purposes."

"Oh please—are you going to exploit this, too?" Terri exclaimed, then put her hand over her mouth in a sob.

"Hey, it's nothing if it's not sermon material, right?" Greg commiserated. The insight might have sounded beyond the sophistication of most boys his age, but it was a lesson he'd learned long ago, when one of his innocent boyhood malapropisms had provided his dad fodder for a three-week series of sermons entitled *Purity of Heart*.

"I realize that my discretion, or maybe reticence, may provoke a slew of rumors in the days ahead," Alan said, his eyes fixed on the podium, yet clearly not reading from any prepared notes. "I know I can't stop that. And I know so many of you care about Terri and me and our boys, so in some ways I wouldn't want to stop you all from being concerned. All I ask is that while you sift through the things you hear, you reserve your judgment. If you've been here at Summit for a while, I trust you know a little of my heart. A man can't stand here and speak for hour after hour, Sunday after Sunday, without revealing the unvarnished truth of what kind of man *he is. Of his true heart. So if you've formed even a decent opinion of me during your time at Summit, please don't relinquish it without hearing from me. The time will come—soon, very soon—when I can be much more candid about some of the details. In fact, you'll be asked, as a church, to walk with me through some of the passages ahead. But until you hear it from me, please leaven what you hear with a heaping dose of the amazing grace we've been basking in from the Lord all these years. Please suspend that ingrained tendency we all have to cast judgment and wag our fingers, even as we've asked God to suspend His own in favor of mercy. Okay? Will you do that for me?"*

He cupped his hands behind his ears and cocked his head, as he usually did when awaiting a returned "Good morning!" or "Howdy!"

The "Okay" that washed back his way was far more subdued than any he'd ever accepted from his congregation. Rather than repeat himself, he gave a nod and a forced smile.

"All right, then. Thank you so much."

Alan now stared ahead, into the empty space between him and the huge void of the sanctuary's vault. He seemed to be holding back tears.

"Thank you . . ." he said again, and now his voice confirmed it. He portrayed the embodiment of forbearing courage, of emotional perseverance.

The scene disappeared, swallowed up into a lone white dot against a sheet of black.

Terri had clicked the video off.

"The few folks who bothered to talk to me after that day," she said, staring into the box of tissues clutched in her lap, "told me that my absence—and yours and Jeff's—from the front pew was all they needed to know. That said it all. And of course a handful of folks did leave the church over what Alan did. But when the leaders sided with him, the die was cast for most of the members. That chose their side for them."

"How long do you think it took before everybody in that church knew *everything*?"

"Oh, I imagine about four or five hours. For anybody remotely connected, that is."

"Why watch this, Mom? Isn't it torture?"

He knew why, yet he was more than ready for the ordeal to end.

"Sweetheart, up until that day I hadn't missed a day of church more than four times in my whole life. That's including measles and the day my grandma died. Almost half of those Sunday mornings had been spent watching your dad. Being his wife. It was who I was. I'd never had to even imagine being anybody else. But after that morning, it was all gone forever. Just like that. I know you can relate."

Greg nodded. Despite being teenage-cool, he could feel his face twist in the grip of tears' threshold.

"Yeah. It was *my* life, too."

"Right now your dad is facing the loss of all that for himself, son," she said, instantly regretting her candor as Greg's eyes finally let go a pair of large tears.

"Yeah," he said, "along with everything else."

RESCUED

25

Back at the wheelhouse, Jeff glanced in at the clock and reeled backward.

12 min. 32 sec.

Time and oxygen were running out, and fast. Thinking of his father and the others down in the mangled sub, he racked his brain trying to figure out what to do.

Come on . . . think!

His mind raced across a pitching deck of disparate images—the boarding pier's rescue manual pages, the operator's last words, even returning images of the wreck itself. The operator had been a professional, at least supposedly, trained in proper diving procedures, though even now Jeff could see the man's leg floating in a pool of blood not forty yards away.

So how was an amateur like him going to accomplish what the pro couldn't?

And yet something inside told him that he couldn't just sit here and do nothing.

Desperate for an idea, Jeff let his gaze linger on the wheel-house's control console—the engine gauge, two gleaming throttles, radar and sonar screens, and radio channel screen.

Bingo. The radio channel digits were blinking. He remembered seeing the operator punch in new numbers just before pulling on his scuba gear. Could this mean something?

He peered down. *Come on, Jeff. Concentrate. What was the last thing the operator said into his phone?*

The radio . . . reestablishing . . . signals . . .

Jeff's eyes widened. Could it be? He searched the console. There it was!

Sub Comlink. The power light glowed red. A toggle switch stuck out between two settings, Cockpit and Cabin, and was tuned to the former. *Could it be that simple?* He flipped the switch to Cabin, said a quick prayer.

"Dad?"

In the blackness of the sub, Alan Rockaway's whole body jerked in a spasm of shock. Where did his son just speak to him from?

He bent forward and cocked his head. Was he already dead? Hallucinating? Under the spell of some spewing chemical?

"Dad, can you hear me?"

Just as soon as the voice died away, a murmur of astonished voices flooded his ears, and he knew he hadn't been the only one to hear it.

Dumbfounded, he called, "Son . . . where are you?"

"It's coming from a speaker over here," said a man to Alan's right, "just above my head."

"Dad, it's Jeff! If you can hear me, please try to pick up. Look for some kind of handset. The manual I have says there's one in the sub—somewhere toward the middle."

The middle? Alan turned his head from side to side in the darkness, trying to decide which direction he should turn.

"Who was sitting around the midpoint?" he called out.

"Me, Pastor." It was the voice of Carrie Knowles.

"Can you feel anything around you, like a cord? It would be connected to a telephone."

"Yes. Here it is. Can someone help me?"

A loud thump announced the handset had been dropped against the vinyl flooring. Arms and hands were moving, grasping all about him. Alan reached out, and all he could think to say was, "I'm here, over here!"

Finally a hard, cold shape passed over his left hand. He grabbed it.

"Thanks, I got it!" he said. His index finger found the handset's Talk button. "Jeff. . . ?"

"Dad, is that you?"

A garbled flood of emotions poured through Alan's voice. "Yes, it's me! It's me, son!"

"Are you hurt?"

"I'm hurt something fierce, but not the way you're asking, Jeff. Jenny's gone. So is Hal Newman and about half a dozen others. It's very dark and cold down here. We're getting a little scared."

"I'm sorry, Dad. I'm so sorry. But please hang on; help is on the way. Choppers have been circling for a while now. You're on TV all over the world. There must be millions of people praying for you."

"Even Denver?"

"*Especially* Denver. The eleven-o'clock service turned into one big prayer rally, and it hasn't ended. Remember, I still had my camera on when you guys were hit," Jeff's words trembled out through the speaker.

"Jeff, if . . . if they don't reach us in time, be sure and retrieve my video camera. We've recorded some words."

"Oh no. Please. Don't talk like that. Besides, you don't have the oxygen to spare. Please do me a favor and everyone stay still, and don't talk any more than you have to. Because the thing is . . . well, your oxygen is running very low. Everyone hang on . . ."

ON THE SURFACE

Skimming over the waves at its top speed of thirty knots, a Kodiak boat sped recklessly toward the accident scene, six divers in full gear crouched along its sides. As it neared the site, the whine of its throttle lowered, the craft slowed abruptly and began to trace a tight circle into the target zone.

"They're here! They're here!" Jeff shouted joyously into the handset. Waving wildly, he caught the Kodiak pilot's attention and motioned to the precise spot of the collision.

"It's right there!" he yelled, pointing emphatically.

The pilot nodded and killed the motor. Before the boat's momentum had bled off entirely, the divers had already tumbled into the sea in full emergency mode—experts in action.

During their initial descent, the six divers swam through an undulating blue-green paradise of tropical water as clear as any on earth. But then the lead diver pointed downward. Once the other five caught up to him, they all stopped their kicking and hovered in place, watching.

Had they not been wearing masks and biting down on regulators, which forced their mouths in place, they would have been slack-jawed, mouths hanging open, too stunned to speak a word.

What awaited them, barely fifty feet below, was a great shadow of indeterminate composition, unlike anything they'd ever seen underwater. The submarine, buried under this pall of sludge, suspended wreckage, and surging air bubbles, was made visible only as occasional patches of white surrounded by a gloom as deep as night.

The mass seemed to be alive. The coastal currents and tides of Barbados tugged at the cloud's softer edges and plucked out various tongues and fingers of its brown skin like winds aloft dissolving a fraying cumulus.

As much to himself as to his fellow rescuers, the lead diver shrugged and swam on. Within seconds the dusky beams of invading sunlight disappeared. The shallows' soft teal quickly turned to limbs of amber and rust, curling outward as if beckoning the newcomer into a toxic netherworld. Again the lead diver paused. He waved at the swampy limb nearest him to test its solidity. Its edges did indeed float off into a soft feather of diminishing hue. But it did not disintegrate. In fact, the new fringe of escaping vapor appeared to rejoin its parent only a few seconds later.

Enough, the lead diver told himself. He pushed aside the pesky shape and swam boldly into the center of the mass. Shadow gave way to near darkness, light brown to blackness, poor visibility to shades of dense opacity. The diver switched on a flashlight fixed to his belt and held it out before him. Its powerful beam only illuminated a brackish crescent hardly five feet ahead.

He rotated to gain a bearing on his companions. Only two nearby beams shined brightly enough to reach his mask; he assumed the other three weren't far away but simply hidden in the murk.

Knowing that only a few minutes remained before several dozen people died of asphyxiation, he swam on, a wall of debris looming in his flashlight beam. He made an opening in the wall with a gloved hand and paddled through.

Then something struck his shoulder. He turned, and his light revealed a long fiberglass hunk of debris entangled in electric wire. He jerked back, and instead of water he felt something catch at his ankle. He noticed that waving his hand was no longer improving his view. The trapped fuel slick floated all around him now. He tried waving his hand even more vigorously, but this yielded nothing but the slightest brightening of the gloom surrounding him.

He pulled to free his ankle and found he couldn't reach the end of whatever bound him. He kicked harder, yet still was unable to free his leg. Realizing that a control cable could stretch longer than his remaining distance to travel, he gave up on extricating himself and kept swimming.

It was a mistake. The viscous stuff only thickened as he

proceeded. Soon it hit him that he was no longer floating in water but sinking in the goo. He felt the loop tighten around him and knew then he was in trouble.

He struck something hard and broad. Reaching out, he wiped at it with his palm and saw, in brief ribbons of clarity, the white fiberglass of the submarine's hull. He pressed farther on and came to a spot of transparency. Plexiglass. A window.

The diver recoiled. A wide-eyed, terror-stricken face was a mere foot away. A frantic smile creased its features, and a hand signaled to him.

He signaled back tentatively. Another flashlight beam crossed his mask, and he noted that at least one more of his companions had reached the site.

Suddenly a loud eruption sounded all around him. He reeled backward and waved his arms in an effort to right himself. Bright, heaving reflections engulfed and seemed to attack him, buffeting his body violently from side to side.

Then he raised his flashlight and realized the truth.

They were oxygen bubbles—pouring out from a breach somewhere in the shattered casing. In his many years of diving, he'd never seen anything this fierce and profuse underwater. Wherever this oxygen was coming from, he realized it was draining a large reservoir with astonishing speed.

He swam away but only succeeded in ramming into an out-thrust heap of deck planking. He felt a tug at his foot and remembered the cable remained looped around him. After kicking at it repeatedly, he finally shed the stubborn cord. The commotion opened up a larger viewing angle, and he saw, just ten feet to his right, the vessel's quarter-mast and mid-propeller.

The sight gave him an idea. Maybe, the diver reasoned, a strong enough tug could free the submarine from its smothering prison, thus causing it to surface.

So he grabbed the cable that only seconds earlier had bound his ankle, swam ahead, and looped it around the propeller's base, forming a rough knot.

He kept the cable loose in his fingers and backed away while pointing his light at the two divers now near him, motioning them over to assist him.

All three grasped portions of the cable and, paddling with all their strength, began to pull as hard as one can when underwater.

Something finally broke free, the force of which sent the lead diver flying back into the darkness. In the process, his flashlight tilted at his waist, showing him a pair of divers also tumbling into the void.

Then he saw it—the propeller. And behind it the submarine's shell, still attached.

Only, instead of the triumphant rising to the surface he had envisioned, he witnessed the sub sinking precipitously, along with an unbearable weight in its midsection. Vast convections raised by the plunging vessel cleared away the muck so that he saw clearly what lay beneath.

He felt buried under a wave of horror. He had done the unthinkable; he'd sent the submarine into even greater peril.

CRACK!

He screamed into his regulator.

Where the nearest surface of the sub had stretched only a moment before, now the upthrust edge of a maritime boulder cruelly protruded. Then from a shard of hard plastic, he noticed a trail of blood float away.

Next, a huge portion of the fuel slick drifted off, and he caught sight of the whole picture. One-third of the sub's shell had just been pulverized against the massive outcropping.

The lead diver shook his head, inwardly conceding defeat, declaring the rescue attempt a failure, and began kicking furiously for the surface, his companions close behind him.

RESCUED

26

THE SURFACE—BOARDING PIER

Jeff reeled in shock as he listened to the horrors now searing his radio speakers during the submarine's last roll. The screams and moans of people being torn apart, dying a horrible death, along with the wails of others, perhaps even more wretched, those who loved the dying and now were forced to witness their agony from close quarters, chilled him to the very center of his being.

What followed was a deafening metallic crunch, and what Jeff imagined as the awful meaning of the sound: his father's last seconds on earth.

He found himself shouting into his handset.

"Dad! Dad! Are you okay? O God . . . God, do something!"

He repeated the words over and over again for perhaps a full minute after the noises subsided.

Soon, the divers' heads broke the water's surface. The men yanked off their masks and began shouting at one another about some disaster in the rescue attempt. Jeff could hardly make out what they were talking about.

A minute later, an exaggerated rustling sound came through the speakers—that of the sub's handset being dragged along a hard surface. Jeff could hear all that had transpired from the switch of the sub's handset being stuck in the Talk position.

"Jeff . . ."

The voice was flat, weak, yet it was recognizable as his father's!

"Dad, it's me! I can't believe I can still hear you! What happened?"

"Jeff?"

"Dad! Can you hear me?"

"Jeff . . . I think I'm the only one alive."

Then, under a torrent of grief and regret, Jeff realized the sub's incoming radio channel had been destroyed. His father could no longer hear him.

Alan found it difficult to tell which felt more oppressive—the weight of Jenny's body, and many more behind hers against his back, or the despair and loneliness mercilessly crushing his spirit.

The loss of Jeff's voice pierced him to the core, and with it came the loss of all comfort and solace. If only he'd known the link would disappear so quickly, what would he have said? He desperately wanted another chance to talk to his son, to say something . . . before the end came.

He peered into the darkness of the crumpled sub, trying to ignore the low, almost inaudible moans of the dying. There was nothing he could do for them. Right now he could hardly calm himself or think straight.

The tiniest glimmer of color caught his eye, somewhere to his left. His lack of perspective made the sight disorienting, for he couldn't see enough of what was around him to even focus his gaze. Yet it was unmistakable. Something was glowing a faint red.

He reached out, fingers shaking, touching only air. But the color he sought lay farther ahead. He leaned forward. Still nothing. Seized by a desire to pursue the only sensory input left in his world, he risked falling over and leaned even more precariously.

Finally he touched something, an unexpected texture, like fabric. Someone's shirt, perhaps. Damp, but with what liquid, Alan did not want to guess.

So where was the light coming from? He brushed the cloth aside. There it was, closer now, small and round and red . . . but what was this light's purpose? He couldn't make out any print nearby but noticed a black coil that disappeared into a wall, and he remembered.

The radio. Of course.

His mind raced. Jeff's voice could no longer reach the P.A. speakers down here, somehow disrupted by the final roll. Yet for whatever reason the radio was functioning enough to leave this power light engaged.

What if . . . what if Jeff could hear him but not respond?

Could he bear to say what needed saying without being sure it was heard? The answer struck him with a resounding *yes*. Pouring his heart into a radio, despite a high likelihood of going unheard, was far better than the alternative of lying back and waiting for death to take him.

He pictured Jeff on the pier, hearing his father speak. He imagined the emotion Jeff would feel knowing his father had no idea whether his words were being heard, yet was willing to utter them anyway.

The image gave him an idea.

He seized the radio's handset. "Jeff, I don't know if you can hear me. I see the power light on in here, so I know there's a small chance. And a small chance is enough. Listen to me. In a few minutes, when I say the word, I want you to take the satellite phone and dial the church, then hold the phone up to the speaker. I need to talk with them. Okay? But before that, far more important, is that I talk with you."

Stop it! Jeff shouted inwardly to himself. *Stop the crying or you're gonna miss it! You're gonna miss his last words . . .*

But he couldn't stop. The sound of his father speaking again had thrown Jeff into an emotional state impossible to control. Since his father's first syllable through the speakers, he had dropped to his knees, his body heaving in gut-wrenching sobs.

"Jeff, you've given me so much happiness . . . I've never been more proud to be your dad. I love you, son . . ."

"Stop," Jeff said in a muffled whisper, leaning now with his face against the wheelhouse console in an effort to avoid the cameras. "Please, Dad, don't . . ."

"Do you remember boy-time, Jeff? How we used to get away, just you and me, like to the store, sometimes on a walk or bike ride, or just to play catch in the yard? 'Let's have boy-time,' you'd say with that six-year-old smile lighting up your face, the joy of leaving behind all the motherly attention for a little while, of being all boy. You'd grab my hand and look into my face with a grin that had no resentment in it, no defiance, no embarrassment. Just the pure joy of being with your dad. You'd take my hand, and it'd be up to me to let it go. Remember that, Jeff?"

"Yeah, Dad," said Jeff, wiping his eyes.

"It's been a long time since we had any boy-time, hasn't it, son? And it's all my fault. We stopped naming it years before it actually ended. But I killed it for good that night I left. And that's exactly what I did—I realized this at the time, yet it was so overpowering I couldn't admit it—but I left *you* when I left your mom, no matter how much I tried to deny it. I told you, and rationalized to myself, that we'd have even more quality time together, you and your brother and I, now that I was married in God's will, free from the oppression of the wrong marriage. But it never happened, did it? We never had boy-time again. Now I'd trade anything for another minute of it. I would, son."

Jeff straightened up in the wheelhouse, took a big breath. "We're having boy-time now, Dad," he whispered. "Best we ever had."

RESCUED

27

Denver—Summit Chapel

It was now afternoon, yet less than a handful of worshipers had even thought of leaving the sanctuary. If someone had walked in at that moment, unaware of the crisis at hand, the person would have likely considered it the most disheveled, disorganized excuse for a church service ever attempted. The usual arrangement of orderly aisles and rows of chairs was now in upheaval, with fifty or so groups of prone, distraught humanity huddled around the control booth, the epicenter. The great auditorium rang with a bizarre array of human sounds—of sobbing, wailing, praying, chanting, and the hoarse whispering of people for whom the trauma had become too overwhelming to endure.

CNN *Breaking News* still ran mutely up on their large screen, with its slowly reeling helicopter's perspective of the crystal blue Caribbean, the boarding pier, and now the divers who were dejectedly climbing from the water aboard the Kodiak boat.

The first sign of what was to come was a loud gasp from the control booth.

Then a voice through the sanctuary's speaker system.

"My beloved church . . ."

Thousands of faces snapped upward toward the screen at the sound of the voice hoarse with emotion but nonetheless recognizable.

". . . this is Alan. I'm speaking to you live, if you can hear me, from the interior of our submarine. As I'm sure you all know by now, we've suffered a terrible accident."

The sound provoked by Alan's words began as a communal gasp, then soon grew into a human shock wave that assaulted the sanctuary's ceiling. Just as quickly, everyone hushed so they might hear what their pastor had to say.

"Somehow radio contact was restored a few minutes ago, although a recent mishap took out any incoming signal. I don't know if you can hear me, or if even Jeff can hear me, but just in case, I've asked him to place his satellite phone next to the radio speaker. And I'm trusting God that you're hearing me, because even the chance that you're listening is making all the difference for me right now.

"First of all, I'm sure you have been praying with me for rescue. I don't know if anyone with me is alive. It's completely dark in here, and I have no way of helping or even comforting anyone. I know that Jenny is gone—" his voice broke—"along with Audrey and Hal Newman. I'm so sorry for any of their family and many friends who might be hearing this. Anyway, I have no real hope of being rescued at this point—at least by any human hand. So would you pray? I'm just going to sit here in silence and let you guys do the honors."

Larry Collins stepped up to the mike.

"Dear Lord, while our brother Alan, and perhaps others around him, still draw breath, we plead with You for a successful rescue." Larry paused a moment to control his emotions. "We need Alan, Lord. He is our spiritual shepherd, the earthly leader of this flock, and we need him. Please spare his life, and the lives of as many with him as possible. Send speedy help to his side, and sustain him in the meantime. We ask this in Jesus' name. Amen."

A long pause followed Larry's "Amen" as folks throughout the sanctuary continued to pray. Then . . .

"I'm back," said Alan weakly. "Thank you all for your prayers. Now, I'm wondering if you'd indulge me in one last message. Despite not knowing if you can hear me, this word is about what you do with your time, or to be more specific, your moments. Because the bottom line is how things come down to the moment. And since it appears I've reached my final moment on this earth, I want to spend it with you."

His words were accompanied by the sounds of louder weeping.

"You people are the best on this earth, and it's been my greatest privilege to be your pastor. I'll never forget how you've stood beside me. Most of all, that moment when I stepped before you to say I had found the damsel of my knight-errant's dream—Jenny, who lies here beside me as I speak. It seemed the most perilous and high-stakes mission of my life, to move beyond the mistakes of my past and embrace the future, the love that God had in store for me. And while I had already endured a lot by the time I stood before you with the difficult news, I considered your acceptance the biggest victory of them all. You stayed with me, literally and figuratively, while I explained to you the bitter journey I'd been on and the chance at wholeness that I had found and embraced. You came to our wedding, stood and prayed with us. You made that day a day of triumph, that moment a moment of victory, and I've never forgotten that.

"Right now you have the luxury of not facing your final moment. You all have more time than I do, though maybe not much more, only God knows. Yet however short the time is, you have the advantage—or maybe, depending, the *dis*advantage—of not knowing. And now I have a precious gift, this chance to order my dwindling moments in the manner I think best. Yet what a blessing it would've been to have known a day in advance. Even an hour. Well, you all have that. You have the time to consider that final moment. Because one thing's for sure.

When that moment comes, you'll never get another. And once it's gone, it's gone with a finality that will make your head spin if you've dared to think about it." His voice grew stronger.

"So what will your last moment be? Will it be spent cursing someone on a freeway somewhere? Or spent gritting your teeth, screaming at an emergency-room doctor? Or yelling at your spouse or your children? Will you be alone in a big house, paid for but empty of love? Will you be at work, trying to beat a deadline that will never come? Or will you have a final moment that your family and friends will feel inspired by, their faith affirmed?

"It's up to you, my friends. I choose *you* for my final moment. And I choose my boys. And my calling—to be your pastor. Each of these is worthy of occupying my final moment. I just plead with you to fill every blessed moment you're given with that same amount of awe and reverence. Will you?

"I know what kind of final moment I'll have, because I'm living it right now. I'll be with my brothers and sisters in Christ, grateful to share these precious seconds with them. I'll be anticipating my appointment with my Creator, to see Him face-to-face and ask Him the great questions of life, like why children are allowed to suffer and die. I'll spend it holding on to you like I'm doing right now. I'll spend it talking to my two boys.

"But yours? Yours is up to you. But let me say this, which I just now learned: Your final moment defines you. Please believe me. It's the culmination of your whole life, the final proof of whether you built your life on solid ground, or not. You choose. You choose . . ."

And then, faintly yet unmistakably, Alan Rockaway's voice began to falter, then fade in strength.

BARBADOS—BOARDING PIER

Jeff jumped to his feet, immediately recognizing what was starting to take place. He whirled around and impulsively struck the side of the wheelhouse in frustration.

"Son . . ." came a soft whisper through the speaker, confirming the worst. "Oh no. Oh, please . . ."

Then nothing.

RESCUED

28

Jeff realized that the worst moment of his life was now upon him. His father lay within yards of him, dying for lack of a few cubic feet of oxygen. Fresh air stretched for miles in the sky above them both, but not in any form Jeff could deliver to his father.

The bitterness and irony of his helpless state threatened to overwhelm him, including his ability to think rationally. He was pacing the deck, in a futile attempt to push back the building rage and grief assaulting his mind, when he saw the Barbados cutter pull alongside the divers' Kodiak boat.

"Come aboard! You cannot dive again," the voice roared through a bullhorn. "I repeat, come aboard! You just destroyed evidence of narcotics trafficking!"

Jeff shook his head, incredulous. Again, the captain's behavior didn't make any sense to him. Although the divers had failed, they seemed to be regrouping for a second attempt. But the Coast Guard officer, by ending their mission and pressing them to come aboard, had once more shown a blatant disregard for what lay below the waves.

Jeff suddenly stopped. For a full ten seconds he did not move a muscle.

He stared down, out over the water, his gaze drawn to the severed leg floating there. Yet what compelled him was not the limb but something else, something nearby. A pale, oblong shape floating several yards to its left seemed to beckon him, to embody a message that was desperately trying to break through his stalled mental faculties.

The scuba tank . . .

Jeff kicked off his shoes, rushed over to the wheelhouse. "I'm going in!" he shouted at the satellite phone that lay on the control console, the line still connected. "I've got a scuba tank and I'm gonna go for it—swim down there. I've got to *do something!*"

Within seconds Larry's voice was pleading to him through the phone.

"Please, Jeff, be careful! As much as we want an answer to our prayers, we don't want you to risk losing your own life in the process."

Jeff snatched up the phone. "I appreciate your concern for my safety, Larry. But I'm not gonna spend the rest of my life wondering what might have happened if I'd taken the chance and gone down there—done something while there was still time."

"Praying *is* something, Jeff," the minister insisted.

"Fine. Then pray. I'm sure I'll need all the prayers I can get. Talk to ya later."

Without another word or moment's hesitation, Jeff set down the phone, ran from the wheelhouse, and dove into the sea.

A rush of bracing cool water engulfed his whole body. He had always been a good swimmer, having taken all the requisite lessons as a boy. He even had five hours of scuba training, abandoned halfway into the course like so many other of his impulsive pursuits. After standing on the boarding pier for so long, going out of his mind just watching events unfold, it was exhilarating to get in the water, move his limbs, and take some action. Before he knew it, he was upon the tank.

He lunged forward and grabbed it and was horrified to discover the tank was still attached to the one-legged diver whose body lay just beneath the water's surface. Strangely, Jeff found that such a ghastly sight, which normally would have struck him as nauseating, now filled him with a renewed sense of determination.

Turning the body over, he pulled the mask from the swollen white face, then removed the regulator, buoyancy compensator, and tank, and then, while treading water, slipped on the gear as fast as he could. He wiped clean the regulator, then shoved it in his mouth and checked to make sure there was oxygen in the tank, flowing freely. It worked! Finally he took hold of the dead diver's foot and yanked off the one fin. Pulling it on his own foot, he turned and swam over to where the severed leg floated, then did the same with the second fin.

Yeah! He was ready.

His adrenaline surging, Jeff plunged into the water and started kicking with all his might. Behind him the brilliant, restless surface faded away as he paddled. Before him the deep blue reached out to challenge yet another diver.

He looked down to where the grim destination awaited him. His surface perspective had shown him only a vague darkening in the water somewhere far below, so what he saw took him completely by surprise. Just like the other divers, Jeff couldn't help but stop, stare at the wavy mass of sludge and wreckage, and peer desperately for a glimpse of the sub trapped within.

All he could make out were brief patches of the vessel, seen in a second's opening of the debris cloud. Jeff's will temporarily weakened as he confronted the vast, forbidding obstacle. Without even deciding to, he found himself praying.

I haven't talked to You much lately, God. But I need Your strength to carry through with this and save my dad. I can't do it by myself. Please, God, will You help me. . . ?

Not bothering to wait for any kind of confirmation, he forced his body into action, the fins propelling him downward while his arms and hands groped ahead into the dark amber mass of debris. He felt a length of pipe poke his leg, a protruding piece of fiberglass strike his side. He grimaced, leaned sideways, but kept kicking onward toward his goal.

The last five feet nearly defeated him, for the innermost layer of debris had coagulated into a thick mixture of engine oil and gasoline. His attempts at forcing himself through the viscous layer were unsuccessful. Still, he kept at it, hacking again and again.

On the fourth stroke he felt something break in his hand and drew it back, wincing in pain. A thin blood trail followed the motion's path, spiraling away. The sight enraged him. He turned and rammed his elbow through.

It worked—the mass bent and sagged open. Jeff rushed through and only a second later was peering through a window into darkness. The buoyancy compensator vest that held the tank had a small flashlight clipped to it. Jeff removed the light and shined a narrow beam into the sub's interior.

What he saw made him almost retch into his regulator.

The sub had become a death chamber, lined with the contorted torsos and vacant stares of the dead.

Quickly Jeff swam from window to window in hopes of identifying his father.

In the third window from starboard, he saw the face. His father was still holding the radio handset to his chest. His mouth hung open, and his eyes bore straight into Jeff's.

Jeff struck the side of the sub in frustration.

He was too late.

29

*R*EMAINING OXYGEN: *0 MIN. 0 SEC.*

In the midst of his anguish, forcing himself to think back over a mishmash of late-night survival documentaries and novels set in the wilderness, Jeff suddenly remembered something. *Asphyxiation can take a long time to run its course. If oxygen can be restored within ten minutes or so, sometimes a reversal can occur . . .*

He recalled the safety manual he had devoured topside. There was one page, one paragraph he'd forced a mental note about—*Emergency Oxygen.* He was sure he'd read the phrase. *Emergency oxygen and . . . a valve!* It all came rushing back. There was a valve, somewhere on the top of the sub, that released a substantial amount of emergency oxygen. He even remembered seeing a diagram of the valve, including the two words stenciled on the hull that marked the spot.

With the aid of the flashlight, he began sweeping his hands over the sub's shell in search of telltale signs. His fingers found a series of barely raised shapes. He swam closer for a better look.

Of course. Because the sub lay upside down, the oxygen valve was now buried beneath, against the ocean floor, and also several feet from his grasp.

The memory of his father's face propelled him downward without another thought. Fortunately, a seam running across the hull's width told him the exact location of its midpoint. He followed the seam down, still fighting his way through the floating wreckage, finally reaching a refuse-strewn bottom.

He began by moving aside all the junk piled up against the sub's upside-down roof. Once he'd cleared away most of the rubbish, the sand became his biggest problem. His frantic digging served mainly to stir up the sand into a thick cloud. But he told himself it was not necessary to see what he was doing; he was digging to get hold of a valve wheel, an object that would immediately tell him when he'd found it.

Realizing his spare minutes were about to run out, his anxiety level rocketed. He had to do this! He dug on, groping with his hands. He couldn't come this far and fail to uncover a simple valve . . .

There it was! At the very edge of his reach, with his hand extended as far as his shoulder would allow, he felt a metal curve consistent with a valve wheel. More like a badger now than a human being, he burrowed in deeper toward the shape with every ounce of energy left in him.

Though the sand was giving way for him to move closer, the remaining challenge was the valve's location at almost midway across the roof. This forced Jeff to lie on his back and shimmy far beneath the curving hull.

Any shifting now on the sub's part, and he would die instantly.

Jeff was now breathing heavily into his regulator, fighting not only extreme stress but sheer exhaustion.

Another minute of digging and crawling and finally he had a solid grip on the valve wheel. He started to pull. It wouldn't budge. Again he pulled, but still no progress. He kicked the fin off of the foot closest to the wheel and used his foot for greater leverage and strength, pushing against the wheel with everything he had. Still, it wouldn't move. The wheel felt as if its metal had been cast solid with its base, never intended to open.

Not knowing what else to do, Jeff kept at it, pulling and straining against the valve with both hands and a foot. He groaned into his regulator. He felt his biceps tremble, his hands begin to cramp.

All at once his furious tension gave out. He was through. The thing simply was not going to turn. He grudgingly relaxed his muscles and rolled away from the valve.

What now?

That face reappeared before his mind's eye, floating past horrifyingly close. His dad. The face of a thousand childhood memories, now a pale and sightless corpse, forever unable to communicate with him even the slightest word . . .

He had to try again. He had to find a way.

Maybe a different approach to the wheel?

Filled with dread, Jeff turned back, this time coming at it from another angle. He wedged himself in closer for a better grip, preparing himself physically and mentally. Then his muscles clenched into action as he put his entire body into one final attempt. *Please, God . . . help me!*

The wheel twisted free, so smoothly that at first his mind didn't register the victory. He thought he'd just lost his grip and slipped backward. But then he realized that the wheel was still firmly in his fists and his fists had *moved*.

Just as rapidly, an onslaught of gigantic air bubbles began to assault him. He released the wheel and nearly floated out from underneath the sub, swept away by the fury of the escaping gas. Even though it was frightening and sudden, Jeff celebrated. Like a solitary cheerleader, he pumped his arms and kicked, propelling himself higher in the water.

Okay, you can quit now, he thought as he watched the frenzied bubbles. Surely, after the initial blast, they would subside as the air filled the submarine back up to a normal level.

But they did not stop.

Jeff raised his arms helplessly, his elation now turning into confusion. Had the accident disabled the emergency oxygen valve? Had he succeeded in releasing it only to waste this precious air into the vast sea?

He paddled up to the nearest window.

A sigh of relief came over him. The window, which only minutes earlier had been clear, was now covered with condensation.

He knocked hard against the glass, just in case someone inside had recovered and was nearby. Nothing happened.

Then he sensed motion in his peripheral vision, over to his left. He swam closer to the spot and saw a hand wiping a different window clear! And then a face appeared.

His dad! Looking bleary-eyed and very pale, yet without a doubt it was him!

Jeff rushed to the window and stuck his face to the glass to show his father who he was—his son come to the rescue.

His dad nodded, gave Jeff a weak thumbs-up gesture, then his face retreated back into the sub. Jeff peered in, holding up his small flashlight to illuminate the interior.

Alan was crawling back among the mass of bodies. He crouched with agonizing slowness and then straightened back up with something black and shiny in his hand. His lips began to move as he raised his arm in a familiar gesture, and Jeff recognized what his father was up to.

He was holding the radio handset, still in contact with the congregation in Denver. Was he back to preaching again. . . ?

Immediately Jeff thought about the fleet of air bubbles that continued to spew upward from the valve. He might have released the emergency oxygen supply, but obviously there was a leak somewhere.

The air wouldn't last.

And Jeff would not, could not, let his father squander these precious minutes on some final address to the home crowd. After all, he told himself with a gathering certainty, there were more important moments to live for.

He peered back into the sub and shook his head emphatically. *No! No!* Seemingly oblivious, his father saw him but still went on speaking, smiling weakly now.

Jeff turned away and raised his head toward the surface, wishing he could rip the mask off, toss away the tank, and start screaming curses to the heavens. *How could this be happening?* he thought. After all of the day's cruel twists and turns, how could he win the victory only to have it snatched away again, and by his own father's insistence on picking up where he left off in some sermon!

The clock was ticking, the air running out, and his trapped and dying father didn't seem to care. And what, Jeff asked himself, nearly overwhelmed with exasperation, did the man consider so important to say anyway?

30

The CNN news feed, displayed on the sanctuary's large screen, had closely and relentlessly broadcast the six rescue divers' retreat, Jeff's impulsive dive, his gruesome appropriation of the dead man's diving gear, followed by his disappearance undersea.

But it was unable to show much of what happened after that—except for, just minutes later, a sudden explosion of bubbles to the surface. That event had prompted a flurry of speculation, all of it somber, from the panel of marine experts summoned by the network to provide play-by-play commentary of the catastrophe as it unfolded.

None of those watching was prepared for the voice that interrupted CNN and was broadcast once more across the auditorium.

"Church, here I am—again . . ."

The voice which filled their sanctuary was now a mixture of surprise, exasperation, and relief.

"I cannot believe I'm back here."

Alan Rockaway sounded drastically different from even the altered man they'd heard from just minutes before. His voice was shallow, weakened by half, seemingly exhaling final words. Yet, paradoxically, it was also driven by a sincerity and intensity no one had ever heard coming from the ever-casual, ever-hip Pastor Alan.

"Everyone," he breathed, "you really must pay attention, all right? I don't know how much time I have left, how much strength, or how much air . . . but I have to tell you what just happened to me. I still can't believe it. It's literally a matter of life or death. Actually, it's even more important than that. It's a matter of . . ."

He took a deep breath, and it seemed the entire congregation took it with him, wondering if he would speak again.

"Let me start this way. I died. I died and . . . well, let me start at the beginning."

A FEW EARTH-MINUTES EARLIER

An incredible silence.

A peace as deep as eternity swallows Alan Rockaway, accompanied by a stillness as sudden as being pulled underwater. Alan feels like his existence up to now has been one long jangling commotion just waiting to be turned off. He can almost hear its tinny echo waft away as though floating off on the softest of breezes.

He is in total darkness. He does not stop to analyze any of this; he does not need to. Its quality, in less time than the blink of an eye, has overcome his senses, simply morphed into his new reality.

After another brief moment, he realizes that this blackness, this emptiness, is far more than the absence of sound or light. It exudes a rich sensation like the softness of silk, the patina of gold. All is hushed. A great expectancy hangs suspended in the air. Something is imminent. Something inexplicable.

He feels a light pop, like the snapping of a flower stem.

He begins to float. Something is pulling him upward—through the submarine wall, the surrounding cloud of debris, then the water itself. Effortlessly he continues to rise, swiftly now above the coast and the green hills of western Barbados.

As a child, Alan dreamed of flying—of flapping his arms with utter conviction and seeing his determination rewarded by a feeling of lightness, of air gathering beneath him. The wonder of the front yard slowly falling away, a summer wind bearing him up and wetly kissing his cheeks, his brother and sister receding, pointing at him from below with jealous, excited cries. His chest swelling with the knowledge that, sure enough, it could be done. He always knew it somehow. You just have to flap your arms hard enough and never stop. Soon the horizon would appear, then the clouds, then the infinite expanse of the universe.

Since waking from such dreams, he has never shaken the quiet suspicion that on any given summer day, should the conviction well up within him and animate his limbs fiercely enough, he might wave his arms and see the reverie come to life.

This present floating is all he had ever dreamed, and more. He feels buoyant, an errant balloon tugged every which way by puffs of air. He glances down, and a bittersweet ache pierces him. This is his body, this his death. Yet the malaise lasts only an instant, as regret gives way to an odd feeling of detachment, an emotional counterpart to his leaving gravity behind.

So this is what it's like!

He becomes aware of music—multilayered strains of a sound not unlike that of violins playing. Then, floating atop the strings, disembodied choruses of female voices. Together they weave melodies out of minor chords so complex their notes seem immeasurable.

He gulps a startled breath, tries to contain his exhilaration. In the time this takes, he fails to register that he has already left the clouds behind. The Caribbean has receded to an arc of cobalt blue. To one side, Earth's curvature traces a graceful bend against the blackness of space, fringed by the turquoise veil of its atmosphere. High above, a blanket of light shimmers over the white of the North Pole. He cries out in astonishment and remembers. *Aurora borealis*. Northern lights.

He turns away and sees a spray of brilliant stars he has never seen before, so close it seems he could reach out and pluck them from space with his fingers. But for now, the intricate detail of Earth interests him more. He turns back to view the edges of the continents spread out beneath him. He sees the Atlantic, a violet jewel in a blaze of reflected sunlight. He shifts the other way and sees the opposite shore engulfed in shadow. Europe, he realizes, where it is night. There the lights of great cities peek through the darkness.

He wants to control his direction but realizes that he is awash in a grand adventure, and it will do with him as it pleases. He feels a presence and a fierce glow at his back.

He turns and stares straight into Splendor.

At first he thinks it the sun, for it is enormous and shining brightly, but then recognizes that this is no impersonal celestial body. Before him blazes a light so sublime and of such magnitude that to take it in fully would strike one blind forever. Then it occurs to him—he is not seeing with human eyes any longer. And the light's dimensions are only the beginning. This celestial bonfire seems to beckon him, to fill him with great anticipation, with a sense of beauty.

The light's warmth grows closer. He feels his inward being soften and blur into something like an embrace—a total surrender to the current flowing all about and within him. Had he been standing on Earth, he would believe himself in a windstorm, his hair and clothes rippling in a seaborne gale. Yet the force pulsating around him here and now seems composed of emotion somehow. Love pouring forth in an intensity that would have shattered his mind were he back in the world from which he has just ascended.

Exultant, he tells himself, "Alan, Alan, why did you fear death for so long?"

RESCUED

31

ETERNITY

With Earth and all its visual delights behind him now, Alan would give anything to enter the light that looms ahead, to lose himself inside its joyous glow. It seems made up of emotion and color and energy and life all at once. It is the most dynamic, thrilling thing he has ever seen.

But then he becomes aware of something else and is flooded with a sense of foreboding.

Something is wrong.

He notices the light is drifting farther away. It is hard to tell for certain, for it's so big that its proportions and distance from him cannot be determined with any accuracy. The feeling comes more from a sense of halted progress, a pause in an experience that up to now has unfolded inexorably and breathlessly before him.

Dread now engulfs him. Even if this drift were to signal his return, whole and healthy, back to his family and his comfortable life on Earth, such an outcome would strike him now as a disaster. For at this moment, Alan longs to join that great fire with a ferocity that surpasses anything he has ever felt.

Yet he feels himself falling away as vividly as he felt himself rise when this adventure first began, as vast currents of space rush past him in a solar wind strong enough to ripple his hair and clothes—except he does not have hair or clothes as he once knew them. Or, he realizes with an inner chill, any physical body at all. Nevertheless, he is most definitely falling. It becomes a breathtaking plunge, and he is buffeted now by a cold wind on his way downward. But there is no air here, he somehow knows. The feeling is more real and terrifying than if he were hurtling from an impossibly high cliff or suspension bridge.

Yes, he is falling—falling with no bottom in sight, without knowing whether a bottom even exists. Will he keep plummeting forever? Will he spend an eternity in free fall, a state that even the most unfortunate of earthlings experience for no more than a matter of seconds? The sensation is worse than falling with a known impact in sight. And all the more abrupt because, only a second ago, he was being pulled by an invisible force toward a warmth, a light of great beauty and joy, the fulfillment of his dreams.

The great light now blazes overhead, its glow hanging palpably above him. He has descended far from the course he was on earlier. Suddenly his head reels back as he hurtles through an oppressively dark hall of some kind, and he is overpowered by claustrophobic thoughts. After plunging seemingly forever, finally the blackness begins to appear less impenetrable. There is a faint brightening up ahead—or down below, he cannot tell, for he has lost all sense of direction while traveling through this void. What approaches seems not to be a lessening of darkness, or increasing intensity of light.

What approaches him is a . . . *presence.*

For an instant he welcomes the presence of another soul other than his own. The desolation of being alone in such a vast, alien universe has crushed his spirit even more cruelly than the sensation of falling or even the disappearance of the wondrous light.

The feeling of this presence begins to grow ominous. Where once he felt something pull him upward from the scene of his death, now he feels for the first time a distinct force pull him fiercely downward. A force comprised of thin, invisible fingers he can feel curling around his being, dragging him down into what no longer feels like a well, or mere vacuum, but the stifling interior of a panting, ravenous throat. The presence is foul in a way he cannot articulate in words: its vicinity makes his skin crawl and his mind recoil in combined revulsion and panic. He tries to scream, but his voice is drained of sound, his lungs swallowed up in dread.

Then what he has felt for so long abruptly stops. He has arrived somewhere, landed on something solid without even feeling the impact. The dizziness of the void gives way to specificity. He can distinguish up from down again, and that where his body ends, someplace else starts. Gradually what surrounds him begins to seep into his mind.

He feels the void in his chest now—like choking, though having nothing to do with the lungs. Something is missing, something vital. He cannot make his mind stop racing. Next he feels intense heat like that of a blast furnace. He wonders how his body is surviving the onslaught. He remembers then he has left his physical body behind. The body he inhabits now does not burn like human flesh and bone, which surely would have incinerated instantly.

He sees only blackness, and somehow it is not just the absence of light but something else. It is a maliciously willful blackness, like a being that assaults all his senses at once.

It comes to him that he can barely see. His eyes can make out shapes only, against a dim backdrop. He squints, tries to discern the landscape before him, obscured by swirling gray mist so thick and endless it seems ubiquitous. He looks up and notices there is no sun here, no place of concentrated brightness overhead, but only darkness stretching, bleakly, all the way to a faraway ring of barely discernable flickers. Fire. The fluctuations tell him the flames are the only source of light in this awful place.

Devoid of color, devoid of life. An eternity of black and gray. Somehow being in such a place fills him with unimaginable fear and alarm.

He looks down. The surface below him is composed of dark stone, scattered cinders, and piles of a powdery gray-brown dust. The mixture extends to a flat horizon, which he can glimpse through patches in the mist. A sharp smell hits him. The striking of a billion matches at once. *Sulfur.* The air, in addition to its heat, is damp and stuffy. A low, sweltering wind brings him another smell: the scent of decay, the odor of refuse and rot.

The same wind blows a sound to him that chills him to the core: a sighing moan of a single note and pitch, thick and echoed as though exhaled from the throats of millions of dying people. A groan conveying profound despair, loneliness, suffering. Sobs punctuate their lament, the dirge continuing without pause. The sound cuts through Alan like a knife.

He feels hopeless, desperate, and terrified. The feelings do not subside or even fluctuate but grow stronger and stronger.

Then, among the troubling shadows, he catches sight of a shoulder. A face, whose ghastliness rattles him, takes his breath away. His mind cannot process the sight approaching him, the horror of it. For the tatters of skin on this withered mask have no color, and this person, this being, is in fact transparent, its opaque flesh nothing more than a washed-out gray. Behind its head Alan can see a dimmer version of mist and stone. Jagged pools of black occupy the place of eyes, and a thin line droops from where a mouth would be. The face remains slack, empty of life. Its expression fills him with a crippling sense of despair.

Beneath this head sways a long, cadaverous body that lurches forward in slow, mechanical steps. Watching the creature shuffle near him, Alan feels smothered by misery and gloom. The being moves to within ten feet of him, yet its dead eyes take no note of Alan. They do not seem incapable of seeing him but simply indifferent to his presence. The being turns and walks just a few feet from where he stands, then veers to the left, then back to the right again. At first Alan thinks it is searching for something, but then he realizes it is aimlessly wandering this plain, its gaze fixed on the ground. It does not pause in its futile trudging. It seems to have no idea where to go, no plan of what to follow or look for.

Alan's eyes tell him something his conscious mind has been avoiding since arriving here. The plain is filled with these hideous beings. And as he realizes this, the sound of their moaning rises to an unearthly roar. He wishes he could shut out the noise but finds he has no defense against the thunderous lament.

Their transparency makes them hard to distinguish from the surrounding mist, yet as his vision adjusts, he now sees innumerable crowds of these figures wandering the cursed plain like a vast throng of cellophane mannequins. None speaks, none looks at the other. Each traces its own unceasing, meaningless path. And each issues from its drooping mouth an impossibly loud moan that blends as one, rises on the wind, and reeks of such pain and loneliness that Alan is compelled to join them.

He turns back to the first being, whose meandering has brought it nearby. Alan wants to flee, to put some distance between him and this monstrosity, yet he feels himself frozen in fear, unable to move. The smell of decay grows stronger with its approach. A step away from colliding with Alan, the thing finally raises its head and looks at him for a split second. In that brief moment Alan sees straight into eyes so dull and vacant that he feels stricken as by a hammer. The creature says nothing. Not a muscle on its blank face even twinges. It does not have to. Its expressionless gaze is message enough.

We are both condemned to this place, and there is nothing whatsoever we can do about it. Nothing. Ever.

Get used to it.

Alan returns the stare, and in that instant he feels himself become a little more like the creature he is repulsed by. Something tells him it has been here for a very, very long time.

So that's why he doesn't care. Soon I will be like him. I will linger here for ages. Years will pass beyond numbering, and still I will do nothing but walk aimlessly like him. And become an apparition, one so destitute of life and hope that nothing can stir me.

He experiences an almost physical sensation of vitality draining from him and realizes the meaning behind the choking he felt when first entering this place. It was not a lack of air, but of something even more essential. *Hope.* Life itself. Both have flushed from him in one thick flood, leaving behind despair of a potency he had never known possible.

Alan feels frantic, panicked as a lost child. He begins to moan. He wonders if he can bear these emotions another moment longer. But another moment comes, and with it the agony, unabated . . .

He rears back and shudders violently. Despair surges through him once again, floods every cell of his being.

He knows where he is.

But it can't be!

Oh my God . . .

Even the thinking of that name seems out of place here, alien and odd. Yet he thinks it anyway and is seized with a thousand questions, questions that poke at him, mock him.

Why am I here? Is this some kind of tour . . . on the way to heaven? To show me what so many poor souls must endure? To give me a taste of what the lost will suffer?

Maybe I'm here to find someone. Yes, to find a soul I love and tell them something . . . tell them how I feel and maybe give them one more chance to repent. It's assuming a lot, but then, I am a servant of God . . .

He turns back to face the plain and its ocean of wandering souls. It seems hopeless—the task of finding one person, one being in particular, especially if he doesn't even know who he is looking for. But maybe, Alan reasons, finding the one he was sent here to speak to will prove his ticket out of this vile place.

He attempts to walk back toward the plain when a fresh horror hits him. He cannot move like he once did on earth. He looks down at his legs and sees that he also inhabits a long, ungainly body without life and color, lurching awkwardly like those of the other living corpses. For a moment, overwhelmed by the shock, his brain refuses to accept this fact.

This is taking it a bit far, don't You think, Lord? he mutters to himself.

Doing his best, he tries to make his way toward the others, slowly and painfully, while staring at each one, hoping against hope to recognize someone, some thing, some trait . . .

But he cannot walk, cannot maintain his momentum. He stumbles forward and strikes another tall, unbearably ugly being. The impact is strangely muted and light, not unlike striking a placard on some city sidewalk. The being he bumps into curses at him and jerks backward but just as quickly turns away and wanders down another path. The loneliness of the response enwraps Alan like a shroud. He tries to right himself, but again he cannot seem to control his momentum. He sways backward, jostles against one, then two more. Low, growling curses roll out into the musty air.

"It's me!" he calls. "Alan Rockaway! Does anybody—do I know any . . ."

The futility of his shouting becomes as clear to him as the fading of his voice across the sulfuric expanse.

Realizing that, no matter what, he will just have to find this other soul. He starts off again. He attempts a swifter stride but falls again and strikes the hard soil.

This is not right! he tells himself. *And not at all what I expected. Whoever arranged this horrible excursion, can we please just end it? Can I get on to the good stuff now? The glory and splendor? Can I see God, and forget all about this place? That, or go ahead and meet whomever I'm supposed to meet, so we can move on?*

32

Alan turns and focuses on a ring of shapes approaching him from the plain. He wants to beg his sight to have mercy on him, to revise itself and blot out what now stands before him. His mind rebels, refusing to make sense of it. Alan sinks to his knees in a physical and spiritual heap. He no longer has the will to fight, no strength to keep asserting himself against the horror of what surrounds him. He wants to lie on the ashy ground and weep forever—just give in to the suffering and cease to exist.

What Alan sees are beings of an infinite variety—all of them foul, grotesque, demonic—that writhe perpetually and embody a perversion of the human or animal form. In fact, the sight of them seems less like a form than a contorted concentration of screaming horror, of evil itself.

They wave about with limbs of vastly unequal length and shape, displaying no symmetry or proportion whatsoever. The body of the nearest beast is covered with boils and scales, like a being that has been parboiled for millennia. Its jaw extends into space like the mutated maw of a barracuda, its eyes stretching over half its head, sunken in and ablaze with a lustful rage. While Alan watches, it leans down and with one arm snatches up one of the fire's victims, tosses the wretched being into space, and, extending a foot-long curved jaw, catches the victim mid-fall in its gullet.

Even from a distance, Alan can hear the damned one's screams as the monster gnaws on its wraithlike body. He has never heard such sounds as this. And he sees hundreds, perhaps thousands, of these beasts upon the Pit's edge and across the infernal plain behind him.

Backing away from the sight, almost of its own accord, Alan's soul cries out.

"I'm sorry!"

He has no idea where this compulsion to cry out to God has come from. If there is one thing he has learned here, it is that God is nowhere near this place, His Spirit nowhere to be found. Alan cannot conjure Him in his mind, cannot even imagine Him in the crudest of ways. And this unleashes a torrent of grief-ridden, anguished screaming to God, prompting Alan's soul, despite the apparent hopelessness, to continue calling to the void where God used to be.

"I AM SO SORRY!"

If this were earth, his voice would have carried the words across canyons and valleys, returning a woeful echo.

Feeling nothing, convinced that his cries have gone unheard, he takes another look around him at the infernal plain. The millions of gaunt creatures continue to mill around in their endless shuffle.

He fights the desire to gouge out his own eyes, yank out his hair, to tear the flesh from his limbs. He hates himself with a rage he cannot contain. Then he feels a presence approaching.

He feels it as the approach of a predator, rapacious, like a hot breath along the spine. The sensation washes over him in an instant, making Alan want to take off running forever. He turns. What he sees chills him more deeply than any of the horrors he has seen thus far. Carving a path through the crowd of transparent beings less than a hundred yards away is one of the revolting creatures, moving intently toward him. Through the mist Alan watches as a huge head lunges up and down in a relentless gait—a round, reptilian mass of horns and crusted skin with two leering eyes. It looks like something between a warthog and a decomposed corpse, its body hunched over with bony protrusions, its stomach bloated. Scaly arms wave greedily toward him, fingers forming the shape of flexing claws. An overpowering stench assaults him as the beast draws closer.

Its eyes contain a hunger in them, a desire to consume Alan's soul, and in the most loathsome of ways. He now realizes how newcomers to this place are drained of their last ounce of hope and individuality.

They become the playthings of demons.

The last shred of his will to survive seems to die, and although it may be useless to try to resist, instinctively he begins running . . .

Screaming, fighting to make his cursed body move, his washed-out legs churn as fast as they can, pale gray feet slipping in the cinder dust, he sees that up ahead a sheer face of dark stone beckons him. He veers for it, hoping it will provide some sort of refuge. Finally he reaches its wall and looks up. A rock tower rises and disappears in the mist. With one desperate leap he flings himself upon it, finding only glassy smoothness. His fingers slide slowly down its surface. He looks back.

His pursuer is only yards away, its twisted body rippling through the mist and the hordes of helpless ones trying to escape its path. As it approaches, the certainty of its impending feast turns to a broad leer across its monstrous head.

Horror grips Alan afresh. The fear paralyzes him, cements him in place to be served up to the beast bearing down on him. He is seconds away, he knows, from beginning to suffer torment that makes what he has seen thus far feel like a pinprick. His eyes refuse to do anything but stare at the abomination approaching. His thoughts grind to a halt. His knees begin to seek the ground.

In a flash of insight, he sees himself as the most pathetic of victims—one who embraces his fate, who not only refuses to fight but in resignation reaches out its arms to its tormentor.

But then an impulse to save himself suddenly shoots through him. Alan screams.

The creature halts in its tracks. It stands there for a moment, so close that Alan can smell the odor of flesh and rot steaming from its nostrils. He looks in its eyes, askew and bulbous, staring at him with hatred in them. He notes the mouth of the beast, pale lips stained with gore, constantly twisting and smacking in anticipation.

Something happens then that Alan did not see coming. He sees it begin with the demon's features contorting in a spasm of grotesqueness, which he slowly recognizes as terror. To his surprise, he watches as the beast quickly turns away to face something—something that should not be happening here, a tear in the fabric of the place—some sort of glowing light and alien wisp of hope that has punched through the putrid mist.

The demon leans its head back and howls. It throbs with rage and fright, and this fills Alan with nearly forgotten sensations he recognizes as relief, pleasure.

Without explanation the demon narrows its eyes, grimaces in disgust, then lopes away.

Alan finally sees what has driven off the beast. Another being is approaching, and Alan immediately brightens, for it is not an apparition. It is a alabaster-clad male figure about whom everything seems out of place. Its face bears an expression that, while somewhat grim, is neither hopeless nor inhuman.

The newcomer walks straight up to Alan and looks him strongly, sharply, in the eye.

"Alan. Please come with me."

33

The stranger turns without a word and starts walking briskly away from the ghastly crowd, apparently expecting Alan to follow. And follow he does, for he has no wish to spend another second in this place.

He follows the pale, billowing robed figure toward a hill that drops away from the plain, sloping down to the mouth of a long, gaping canyon whose bottom is lost in deep shadow. Just before the grade bends into a steeper angle, however, the stranger stops and allows Alan to catch up with him. He faces the chasm while holding his hand out toward Alan, who without hesitation steps beside him and grasps it.

"Are you with me?" the stranger says.

"Yes," answers Alan.

"Do what I do." He extends his foot far ahead of them and steps forward, Alan with him. Nothing happens. They do not sink or fall but merely find themselves walking again. Only, now they are making for a storm of flashing lights that rush up to surround them on every side and swirl like the center of a tornado. There is little sound, except for a mild breeze and the faintest crackling.

"Why did I have to go to that terrible place back there?" Alan asks the man.

"You were waiting," says the stranger.

Alan studies the man more closely. Granted, nothing since leaving his world has looked quite the same, yet this individual is unusually strange. The light seems different around him and sends forth a quality that is warm, even *loving*.

As he ponders this, Alan suddenly realizes he is walking more easily. He glances down at his legs and sees he inhabits a body again, one that resembles his old earthly one.

Furthermore, his guide's attire has now turned into a robe of white so pure and dazzling that he is difficult to look at.

"Who are you?" Alan asks.

"My name is not to be revealed in this setting," he says.

"You are an angel?"

He smiles. "I am honored to serve the Son who rules from the White Throne."

"Is that what I was waiting for? To go before the White Throne?"

His guide nods and stops walking.

Alan has never been much of a student of the Apocalypse, and so the mention of the White Throne provokes in him only a faint sense of uneasiness. Yet that sense soon strengthens exponentially.

All at once, the corridor of swirling lights vanishes and before him appears an entirely new landscape, one dominated by a giant doorway. Alan cranes his neck to take it all in, for he would guess it over four hundred feet high, carved whole from some kind of translucent jewel. The towering structure stands less than thirty yards ahead, on the other side of a bridge spanning another chasm.

The guide motions to Alan, indicating that he should enter first. Alan obeys and proceeds across the bridge. He glances over the span while crossing it and hears the rushing of water far below, past a bend in the stone.

The angel, standing on the other side now, calls out, "You are about to enter the Great Hall of the White Throne of Judgment, and shortly you will face your King. Though you've never met in person, the Son has seen you. He has beheld your heart and discerned your fruit. He knows your innermost desires, your motives, your thoughts and feelings, as well as all your works. Nothing has been hidden."

Eager to begin, Alan leans for the door, but his guide restrains him. The angel is not finished.

"You will approach when your name is called. At the gold rail you will kneel, where you will have a chance to address the Son of the Most High, the King of the Universe. That is, if you have the courage to speak, or if you are even able to speak. Your words to Him will not alter the judgment, however. Do you have any questions?"

"I don't . . . understand," Alan says, visibly shaken now. "You're saying this is it? This is to decide whether heaven or. . . ?"

"As it is written," the angel says. "This is the most decisive and solitary moment you will ever face. Did you not read in the eternal Scriptures where it speaks of the King's judgment seat: 'Knowing therefore the terror of the Lord, we persuade men'?"

Alan fights a sudden surge of panic. He feels weak, as though his knees might buckle at any moment.

The angel steps forward, lifts a gleaming latch, and pushes open the enormous door.

"May your name be found," he says.

"What?" Alan asks, aghast.

"The Book of Life," the angel says. "May your name be found there."

"Oh," Alan says, finally understanding. "In other words, *best wishes*. Well, I died while on a church trip. I'm a pastor, you know."

The angel does not respond but looks blankly down at the

ground as he steps inside. He seems to have heard that before.

Alan closes his eyes against the glare, yet moves forward following his guide inside. In a flash, he finds himself on his knees.

His world is unmade.

How can he find earthly words—originally created to describe human and earthly experiences—to describe the wonders of a different realm? The room before him is more vast, more grand, more beautiful, luminous, and ultimately more intimidating than any place his dreams could ever imagine.

And that says nothing about the incredible beings within it.

In the next second, Alan forgets everything that came before. If he were asked what earthly century he comes from, what nation he belongs to, he would have to stop and think hard for a very long time. For in three steps' time, it has all been dwarfed. In a moment, everything he ever considered "earth-shattering" shrinks to nothingness.

What he sees carries an invisible weight, and gravity, more crushing than anything else in the universe.

RESCUED

34

When Alan rises and begins inching his gaze toward the radiant One seated on the Throne, he is afraid he will cease to exist, that he will simply explode into millions of tiny particles. He fights to keep his fear under control as the self-recrimination floods his soul.

Without even looking at the Son straight on, he realizes again that, compared to the presence before him, everything he has ever considered important—and as a pastor, he has spent more time than most contemplating supposedly weighty matters—is the flimsiest of trivialities, the most laughable of follies.

To think he had worried over money, job performance, his children's grades, personal appearance, the tidiness of his house, the car he drove, the thickness of his waist or the darkness of his hair, the state of the world economy, and a thousand more . . .

. . . in a single glance toward the outer edges of the Throne, he realizes it all has been distraction, foolishness.

It is *this moment* he should have cared about, the thing that should have consumed his earthly life—his waking hours, his dreams, everything. It is this moment he should have prepared for, the reality of this encounter with . . .

He tries again to look upon his Maker, and once again he cowers before the intensity of His presence.

Alan is overwhelmed by the torrent of love that flows from the Throne and nearly threatens to drown those who enter the Hall. Or the paradoxical holy fear that instantly seizes the mind when approaching His presence. Or the light pouring out from His person, brighter than the white-hot core of the sun. Or the flashes of lightning that seem to burst forth all about him, with great rumbling peals of thunder.

Any one of these alone would undo a person back on earth. Yet it takes all of them and many more to evoke the indescribable awe that Alan feels as he steps deeper into the Great Hall of the White Throne.

Alan decides that the best way to preserve his sanity is to begin by concentrating on the Hall itself, as well as the lesser beings who inhabit it.

He looks up at the ceiling, which appears to be a thousand feet . . . no, five thousand feet high? He is not sure. He realizes then the earthly properties of light and shadow that usually help guess dimensions of things do not exist here. Light does not come from outside, through windows or from overhead light sources. It pours evenly from the Throne.

Instead, he tries guessing the dimensions by sizing up the figures at the room's opposite side, but still he can't. They are simply too far away.

He looks toward the wall closest him. It bears no flaw or texture to help him calculate its surface, its approximate size and material.

Finally he gives up trying to comprehend the Hall's structure or its grandeur and decides to continue moving farther in. He glances to his guide beside him and is surprised to see the angel grown both in stature and in brilliance, transforming into one of the angelic host who number in the thousands about the Hall.

Besides the angels, Alan spots an innumerable crowd of ordinary-looking human beings, whose downcast eyes and trembling bodies reveal their states of shock.

He nearly jumps when his sight is bombarded by images cascading rapid-fire through his mind's eye. They feature a dark-haired woman through various stages of her life-span, starting as a young girl and moving quickly through adulthood. All is revealed—from actions to words and thoughts, even motives. Alan frowns, for some of the images are embarrassing and offensive.

"What is happening?" he asks the angel.

"You are seeing her life. This is part of the Judgment. One's deeds are replayed for the King to judge."

"*All* of them?"

"That is correct, and everyone here witnesses them being replayed."

"But—"

Then a voice louder than thunder interrupted, saying, "Is Rosa's name found in the Lamb's Book of Life?"

"No, my Lord," replies another strong voice. "It is not."

"Rosa, you have refused My salvation. You are to be bound hand and foot, taken away, and cast into outer darkness where there will be weeping and gnashing of teeth."

Before the pronouncement of Judgment is complete, an odd and unsettling flash sweeps through the place. It is a flash not of light but of transition, a lightning-fast temporal shift. Alan sees something like the blinking of a great eye, like the dropping of a slide into an old-fashioned projector—one angled just a little askew from the slide preceding it, yet which orients itself again with but the slightest jostling.

"What was that?" Alan asks the angel.

"Time moving," the angel replies. "We are in the fullness of time and are moving about its corridors. It is the same thing the apostle John experienced when moving about different major events recorded in the book of Revelation. You are being shown things you might not have seen otherwise. This is not your

Judgment, but it is being shown to you nonetheless. Soon you will understand why. Prepare yourself."

"Hal Newman," comes the great voice once more. "Give an accounting of your stewardship."

"What?" Alan exclaims.

He looks down and notices, for the first time, the small figure of his old friend.

"Hal!" Alan cries.

Alan's guide says, "He cannot hear you."

"You'll be all right, my friend," Alan shouts anyway. "You're one of the most godly men in my church. If you aren't accepted, then my whole life's work has been for nothing!"

Another guide places a large hand on Hal's shoulder and begins to guide him down toward the front, his hold on the man a combination of insistence and tenderness. Despite his words of reassurance, Alan feels a wave of panic overtake him as he watches a dear, longtime friend enter such a frightening situation.

"I've served You, Lord," Hal says in a voice that echoes across the span. "My whole life has been about serving Your name. And serving Your people. It's been an honor, my Lord."

"Gabriel, is the name Hal Newman found in the Book of Life?"

Watching from farther back, Alan tells himself, *What a blessing this is to see someone with my church ministry, a real servant of God, to see him enter into his reward after a life of serv—*

"No . . ."

The word resounds like an earthquake.

". . . it is not, my Lord."

Shock like an electrical charge runs through Alan's body from head to foot.

Before him, Hal drops to his knees, not in prayer but in utter disbelief.

"Hal Newman, you are guilty of denying Me. You will be taken to the Lake of Fire, where you will spend eternity beyond

My presence, in the company of Satan and his demons and all those who have denied Me."

"But, Lord," Hal says, half shouting, half weeping, "*how* have I denied You? I accepted You as a boy and have been a Christian my whole life! I tithed faithfully and gave beyond that for all sorts of projects. Youth camp. Mission trips to Mexico and Haiti. Missionaries all over the world. I helped troubled kids. I sang in the choir. I was practically the only one supporting my church during its early years. How can this be? Why. . . ?"

His voice breaks.

"Did you not read in My Word where I warned of those who claim to know Me, yet deny Me by the way they live?"

"How has my life denied You, my Lord?"

Suddenly the onslaught of light and color throbs back to life in Alan's vision once more. Images begin flickering, rapidly yet vividly.

Hal's hand flies to his mouth in a gesture of dismay. Even from Alan's distant perch, he can see that these are deeds Hal was certain no one would ever see. As the chronology reaches his adult years, Hal covers his head with his arms and sinks to the floor.

The images cover many embarrassments, iniquities common among men. Sexual sins. The lusts of the eye. The debaucheries of youth.

But the ones that indict Hal the most arrive during the last twenty-five years of his life. By then, the images reveal the trappings of his success as a homebuilder and real estate developer. One in particular shows him standing before a young couple, who scrutinize Hal with anxious faces.

"*Look, trust me,*" Hal tells them. "*We tested the soil, so there's no need to worry. I've taken care of you. This is the best foundation known to man.*"

The next image is of the house's basement, strewn with boxes and toys that indicate the home has now been lived in. What stands out is the floor—a spider web of cracks and sloping surfaces.

A total loss.

Next, Hal is yelling at a construction worker. *"That's what fire departments are for! I don't care if the fireplace is undersized. This model is what I'm paying for, and it's what you'll install in these living rooms if you want the contract!"*

Next, Hal is talking to a man, with piles of lumber and trusses stacked high behind them. *"Look, I'm not gonna go broke just to satisfy some sissified bureaucrat who wants to make the world safe for humanity. This grade is fine. I don't care what the code says. Nobody will get hurt with this stuff. It's fine, and you're gonna sell it to me!"*

Next, Hal is talking over the shoulder of a man with a ponytail, who is sitting in front of a computer. *"No, it has to say 'Finest old-world craftsmanship.' That's what they like to hear. Think quality. The finest building materials known to man. Stuff like that."*

Then in an open field where Hal is looking at a large survey map draped over the hood of a pickup and yelling at another of his associates. *"Floodplain, my eye! Look at that soil. Hasn't been a flood here in thirty years, and there won't be after we build. Now, here's what you're gonna do. You know Marty, over at the planning commission. You take him this"*—Hal removes a thick, stuffed envelope from his pocket, hands it over—*"show up at his home, not his office, and go for a little walk around the block, slip this envelope in his hand. And make sure he knows this parcel doesn't need any geological surveys. Got it?"*

And on and on it went. The replay deteriorates into a sad litany of corruption, greed, slander—even while on Sundays Hal puts on his suit and displays the compassion and dedication to others for which the congregation of Summit Chapel respects him.

Finally, mercifully, it ends. Everyone around the room focuses back on the Throne.

"Hal, I would have gladly forgiven you of these deeds," the Master says. "I died for the chance to do just that. If you had come to Me with a broken and contrite heart, I would have joyfully erased these from all memory. For you see, these deeds are not your condemnation. You are condemned because I do not know you; therefore, your nature was not changed from a condemned state. And these deeds are merely evidence of that. Harold, you led two lives—one as a corrupt man of business, the other as a church person who basked in the praise and adulation of others. Neither involved knowing Me or walking in My ways. Unlike the worst of sinners who humbly repents upon his deathbed, you never truly invited Me into your heart and soul. You prayed a prayer decades ago, but it meant little, and this was evidenced in the course of your life. It was shallow and insincere and did not lead to your following Me in your daily life. Sadly, your prayers as an adult were also insincere, whether said privately or publicly, composed for eloquence and the impressing of those in your church."

"But everything I've done has been in Your name," Hal whimpered.

"Why do you call Me 'Lord, Lord,' and yet do not do what I tell you? At the Judgment many have told Me, 'Lord, we told others about You and used Your name to help them.' It saddens Me, but I must reply, 'You have never been mine. Go away, for your deeds are evil.' Therefore, bind him hand and foot, take him away, and cast him into outer darkness, where there will be weeping and gnashing of teeth. For many are called, but few are chosen."

Alan watches and feels his spirit drenched in holy terror, a fear made all the more chilling because of his recent journey. His friend is seized by a mighty angel and dragged screaming and cursing to the back of the Great Hall and out of sight.

If he still possessed the same heart as in his earthly body, Alan is sure it would have failed by now, stricken down by the crushing load and the chill pouring through him. He reaches out for support and feels his hand graze the angel's arm.

"I can't . . . I can't believe this," he pants. "This is worse than anything I ever imagined in my wildest nightmares. A man who spends his life in church, yet doesn't—"

"Did you see, Alan," interrupts the angel, "how he cursed

God, and even you, as he was led away?" The angel turns, stares straight ahead at the Throne. "That was your friend's true self coming out, his underlying nature."

"I suppose," Alan mumbles. Alan's shock only increases when the next name is announced, spoken from the Throne and echoing across the Hall.

"Carrie Knowles . . ."

RESCUED

35

DENVER—SUMMIT CHAPEL

The impact of Alan's story upon the worshipers in the sanctuary was like that of a bomb going off. Members cried out, recoiled, held each other tightly, while others appeared shell-shocked, standing to the side with blank expressions on their faces. One woman fell to the floor as if struck in the chest. Four more were thrown back in their chairs so strongly that one might have thought they'd been pushed. And weeping became the predominant sound throughout the auditorium.

Meanwhile, in the sound booth, a shouting match broke out between Larry Collins and one of the church technicians, Tom Scully. Tom was poised to cut the feed from Pastor Alan entirely, convinced he was delusional and saying things that would deeply wound the church, not to mention inflame grieving family members.

"This is no delusion!" Larry said through clenched teeth. His face grew red and splotchy, as it always did when he felt the need to defend a decision. "This is actually the most important message ever delivered at this church, and if you dare switch it off, as much as I'd hate to lose you right now, I will have you thrown out of the building."

"Fine," said Scully. "But you put it in writing that you gave me the order. I'm going to have it framed and carry it around with me for the years ahead when I'm accosted for having played that horrible, hurtful rant."

"My prediction? You'll have people coming up to you and cheering your courage."

"Why? For undermining every bit of teaching this church has ever stood for?"

"Exactly."

Larry turned on his heel and moved quickly away.

BARBADOS—BOARDING PIER

For Jeff Rockaway, his father's refusal to stop talking and preserve his remaining oxygen was like the bitter climax to the cruelest nightmare imaginable. For ten minutes now he had swum from window to window, banging on the glass and motioning wildly to his father to put down the handset and stop talking. He tried using the index finger in front of the lips, the hand cutting across the neck, a simple hand over the mouth, even mimicking the sight of air bubbles leaving the submarine. His father would occasionally make eye contact with him, take note of his gesturing, then smile, look away, and return to his monologue.

Jeff could not hear his father, but he could see that the man was weeping as he spoke, his face gleaming with tears, his eyes red and puffy. He could not tell whether this meant his dad was in the grip of perhaps a psychotic response to oxygen deprivation or truly conveying something of the utmost importance.

Finally, Jeff's once-unshakable determination to do something, so recently crowned with apparent success, began to lose strength inside him. Surely he had done his best. He had fought to restore oxygen to the sub, rousing his father from either death itself or at least its very threshold. Jeff consoled himself with the thought that what his father was doing, in his brain-addled stupor, to thwart that victory was now beyond his control.

Jeff glanced up at the surface, furious at the absence of more rescue divers. He could make out the shapes of news helicopters hovering just above the surface, looking like giant bugs through a kaleidoscope. But nothing military, nothing that looked remotely like a rescue operation. He held a fist up toward the surface. Had the authorities simply given up after their mishap?

If there was one tiny bit of good news Jeff could identify, it was that over time the brown mass choking the submarine wreck had finally begun to dissipate. There remained a substantial halo of debris, yet it no longer had the cohesion and the sheer mass it once possessed. In fact, Jeff told himself with a bitter shake of his head, if the divers had come now, they surely would have succeeded in their task.

To occupy his frantic mind, he resumed his mental playback of the safety manuals. He had found the emergency air, but was there something else? Somewhere, somehow, he had a lingering impression of another contingency, possibly something he had overheard the boarding pier operator say, just before the man leaped into the water and met his death.

What was it? Jeff shouted inwardly, racking his memory. *Please, God, cut us another break!*

Nothing came. Frustrated and angry, deciding he should check on his dad again, Jeff whirled around in the water.

Clang!

Something had come into contact with the hull when he'd turned, something behind him. He reached around to grasp whatever might be caught on his scuba equipment.

Sure enough, his hand caught on something—something flat, hard, and attached by a clip. He managed to get the clip open and finally grab the object.

It was one of those magnetic writing pads.

He stared at the thing for several seconds, then got an idea. He scribbled on the pad, quickly swam over to the window nearest his father, and held it up, pointing at the letters.

His father frowned, trying to focus, then leaned closer. It read, *New air is leaking out! Sit still, don't talk if you want to live!*

His father stood still for a moment, his eyes fixed on the message. Then Jeff saw tears well up in his eyes and begin to run down his cheeks.

Alan looked his son in the eyes and shook his head no.

Not knowing what else to do, Jeff nodded back. He could read his father's expression.

Alan understood he was using up his final minutes of oxygen, perhaps his last chance at life, but he wouldn't stop. Couldn't stop. He reached up and formed the *I love you* sign again for his son, then slowly reached back for the radio handset.

And continued on.

Alan had never pushed himself harder than he did now. Spurred on by the trauma and glory of what he had witnessed, he concentrated on articulating each word, fighting through weakness, grief, spotty vision, nausea, aching in his heart and lungs from lack of oxygen and a rising panic that he would not finish what needed to be said before his air ran out completely.

To make matters worse, with his son motioning to him through the window, he seriously began to doubt whether the radio link was still functioning. It seemed unlikely that his words were reaching anybody, let alone the members of a church in Denver three thousand miles away.

Even so, he told himself he had to keep trying. This was the only worthwhile manner in which to spend his last moments on earth. And so he spoke.

"I breathed a sigh of relief after Carrie's name was announced. After all, even though what happened with Hal was an incredible shock, here was a woman whose ticket to heaven was as good as punched. At that point I longed to hear a *yes* to that momentous question, to see someone being told 'Well done,' and ushered into heaven.

"I watched Carrie walk down to the front to account for her life, surrounded by angels on every side, hardly even visible against the brightness of the Throne. I thought of how many times I'd seen her walking the halls at church, holding a crying baby, or a frightened toddler by the hand, or a stack of Sunday school literature on her way to teach her class. And I saw that smile I'd seen her flash at me in passing maybe a thousand times over the years, a smile that was definitely wilted when she started the long walk that was ending just now. I wish she'd been able to save the full smile for God at that moment, because she so richly deserved the reward that awaited her.

"When Carrie and her angelic escort reached the Throne, no words were exchanged. Rather, the replay of her life's deeds immediately flooded my senses.

"I reeled under sensory overload, wondering how this was accomplished. For although it appeared to show every single moment of the person's life, it felt as if the entire presentation took only three or four prolonged minutes. Then I remembered the angel's explanation—that time is bent here, somehow, traveled through like some kind of ethereal hallway.

"Then I found myself caught up in the replay itself, and my expectations were ruthlessly shattered once again."

36

WHITE THRONE OF JUDGMENT

"Did you hear about Pastor Rockaway? He left his wife, took up with that trashy little worship singer . . ."

"I'm not here to gossip, but if you're thinking about making that woman head of preschool, there are some things you should know . . ."

"I'm just sharing this with you out of concern. After all, she is part of the church ministry, so she really needs our prayers . . ."

"Oh, I'm so sorry. I only mentioned it because I thought everybody knew . . ."

"Well, everybody knows they spent the night together in some love nest in Cairo . . ."

"You can't tell anyone. It could ruin a marriage . . ."

"Oh, thanks. I didn't mean it that way. But if they're choosing based on seniority, naturally I should . . ."

"Hey, somebody has to set the example . . ."

At last, Carrie Knowles's life-review ends, vanishing in a flash from Alan Rockaway's inner vision. He has learned more about the scandals of his own church, including rumors about himself in this rapid-fire replay of Carrie's gossiping career, than he learned in decades at the church helm.

He has also just learned the shocking truth about Carrie herself. He remembers that his first wife never really appreciated her. Terri had never said why; it just seemed her internal radar had received an odd return signal.

From his perspective, Carrie Knowles was the kind of woman pastors are always looking for—eager to volunteer, self-starting, willing to follow guidelines. Low maintenance . . .

"Carrie Knowles, give an accounting of your stewardship."

Carrie squares her shoulders and smiles nervously. "My Lord, please . . . those statements were taken out of context. They don't represent what I'm really about. I've been honored to invest my time in the service of the most vulnerable and overlooked of my church's members—the children. The children were my joy and my greatest concern. I gladly served them for twenty-one years of my life—"

"Carrie, did you not hear My Word when I said, 'Not all who sound religious are godly people'? They may refer to Me as 'Lord,' but still will not get to heaven. For they are unwilling to obey My Father."

"But I do, I have . . ."

"Your deeds reveal otherwise. My host, is the name Carrie Knowles found in the Book of Life?"

"No, Lord. It is not."

"What?" Suddenly Carrie's voice takes on the sound of an angry parrot. "But, Lord, I've been nothing but a servant since . . . well, for as long as I can remember."

"You already received your full reward for that service, Carrie."

"You mean that's it?" she shouted. "That's the thanks I get for all my years of wiping noses and changing diapers and helping others, all for Your sake?"

"Carrie, did you not read in My Word the seven things I hate? The seventh, which is an abomination, is sowing discord among brethren. And again I state in My Word that I cannot tolerate those who slander their neighbors."

Without raising her eyes to Him, Carrie snarls, "Didn't I pray? Didn't I ask forgiveness for my sins?"

"Yes, you did, but in an unspecified way, with a heart void of true repentance. And I know not to whom they were addressed, for My Spirit, My life, was not in you. Though you stated you knew Jesus Christ, you never came to Me with a humble and contrite heart for salvation. Therefore My life never was imparted to you. You trusted in your works as a substitute for a genuine relationship with Me, and I clearly recorded that by the works of the law no flesh will be justified. Had you sincerely given your life to Me, you would have had a changed nature, which would have produced works of righteousness. You then would have loved what I love and hated what I hate. That is the evidence of one who really knows Me and has My Spirit within them. I do not know you, Carrie, and therefore you must depart from Me and go to your eternal punishment, to the place prepared for those who reject Me. For many are called, but few are chosen."

She is dragged then, screaming and cursing, away from the holy place, her true nature also now revealed before the entire assembly.

Alan stands in absolute shock, shaking and speechless. Everything he always believed has just been turned on its head. He can hardly form a coherent thought. He doesn't know what to do, what is even possible to do at this point. His indecision is not allowed to fester long. Another one of the jolts in time and space startles him, and he finds himself in a moment that he can sense, for some reason, is highly charged.

"Alan Rockaway," the great voice echoes.

In the seconds that follow, Alan observes something surprising. Even though it is awesome and forbidding, the very sound of his name being called by that voice, by Him, also fills him with a warm thrill.

It is his Creator, calling to him.

Then it hits him . . .

This is it.

He looks straight ahead and allows himself to be led down, along the narrow path between crowds of angels. After what seems an eternal walk, he now reaches the golden rail.

Standing alone at this most momentous of spots, he feels he occupies the very center of—more than mere *universe*—the core of all that is. He feels infinitely large and impossibly small.

This truly is the loneliest moment a person could ever dream of, he tells himself. No one to consult with, no intermediary or counselor, no supportive parent to help cushion the trauma.

But despite this encounter's terrifying prospect, he reminds himself that he *is* a man of God. If his chosen career had held any real perks, surely the greatest should be the ability to approach the White Throne with a lack of trepidation, with confidence even.

He forces himself to look up and finds he is able, just barely, to glance ahead in the general vicinity of the Throne of Jesus Christ.

His peripheral vision reveals more than he can possibly absorb. Blasts of dazzling light, sun-like heat and roaring power combine with a paradoxical blend of piercing beauty and wisdom deeper than time, love sweeter than all the longing Alan has ever felt. Each of them no longer emotional abstractions, but somehow transformed into elemental forces as tangible as gravity itself.

And then the voice speaks to him.

"Alan, it is time for you to give an accounting of your stewardship."

The sound comes in waves and plunges Alan into a keen awareness of each divine attribute, and more: the vast, echoing timbre of that voice causes him to sense close-up the heart of his Creator.

He takes a deep breath and wills himself to speak.

"Thank You, my Lord. I . . . I don't suppose it accounts for much, but as You know I was a pastor for most my life, almost thirty years. I led many people into praying to accept You as their Savior—"

"Yes, but did *you*?"

"Did I what, Sir?"

"Accept Me as your Lord and Savior."

"Well, that goes without saying."

"No, Alan, it does not go without saying. How did you live your life?"

He starts to form an answer to this, but then his mind goes alarmingly blank. He finds he has nothing to say, so hangs his head in silence as a sense of impending doom rolls like thunder over him.

"Host," the great voice intones, "is Alan Rockaway prepared to enter My kingdom?"

Alan takes a deep breath. The seconds that follow seem to last an eternity.

"No, my Lord. He is not."

It takes his brain several echoes of the words to process them adequately.

The scene before him, extraordinary though it is, suddenly washes out white. Then gray. A whiny hum breathes to life somewhere at the back of his head. Everything begins to sway, turn slowly, as a filmy mask descends before it.

All thoughts shut off. All emotion locks down tight. Another voice inside him screams at his immobilized self like a drill sergeant. *Say something! Make your case!*

Finally his mouth moves, seemingly powered by someone or something beyond himself.

"But . . . Lord, I served You. I healed people in Your name. I baptized, I prayed, I taught Your Word. I devoted my life to Your cause . . ."

"Here are your deeds, Alan."

Alan turns away, wishing he could dig a hole, climb inside, and hide himself from this place. He closes his eyes, but the lights are dancing through his mind and he cannot escape them. What he sees embarrasses him deeply. Bright within him, magnified a thousand times or more in the vision of every occupant in the Hall, comes a series of clips that shows every shameful act he can remember, and many more he managed to forget. The very things he had done while quietly saying to himself, *Thank God nobody can see me doing this.*

Now he laments inwardly, *If only somebody had warned me.* But of course he knows that had anybody tried to explain to him the reality of this moment, he would have shrugged it off.

The replay continues.

Adolescence is a particular torture, with his getting caught up in all manner of licentious behavior, sexually explicit material, then exploring these urges further with girls in high school, taking advantage of them at parties, indulging himself in all that is lewd and indecent while hurting and deceiving others.

Mixed in with this are good things—Bible studies, youth camp bonfires, worship singing, church retreats—yet they are inevitably followed by more regressions. A trip home in the backseat of a friend's car, not sober enough to step from the door without falling to the ground. His breaking a young man's nose in a fistfight. His nearly killing himself and his girlfriend during a late-night drag race down a busy boulevard.

If Alan were not still reeling from the verdict just handed him, he would have been both fascinated by the retrospective look at his life and repulsed by what it reveals. But now the result is sheer agony.

He looks up again and views the heart of the matter.

He is explaining to one of the church elders why he left Terri. *"Look, like any other man, I have needs. And Jesus understands those needs. He's the One who created them . . ."*

He is preaching, only now his words are audible. *"Forget the angry, vengeful God of your childhood, of your negative formative experiences. I preach grace! Jesus Christ offers you grace today!"* He remembers delivering those words—how the rising of the sentences had proven hypnotic for him as well as his audience, and how their jumping to their feet had sent chills down his spine.

"Look out these windows on this fine spring day," he preaches

on another Sunday, *"and ask yourself whether the One who created the Rocky Mountains wants His highest, most beloved creation— you—living in a dark box of do's and don'ts!"*

Next, a private conversation with a fellow pastor. *"That church is so extreme, so completely under the law, it's not even funny. They have no clue of the full revelation of grace . . ."*

And then the *coup de grace.*

It is Jenny, walking down the center aisle of Summit Chapel in a dazzling white wedding dress, his beautiful bride. The church is half full, which is to be expected, although the stage is jam-packed with pastors and evangelists from across the country, come to lend their support and blessing.

"O Lord, we thank You for the sweet, slow journey You led these two souls on to find each other this day," prayed one of the pastors, this man from the Deep South. *"And for the even sweeter truth that You specialize in making lemonade out of our never-ending supply of lemons . . ."*

The images fade, and the focus returns to the Throne.

"You did all these things in My name, Alan, yet I knew you not. My life was not within you. You preached what would make you popular and successful. You tickled the ears of My people with empty words that let them think they were safe living their lives without knowing Me, without submitting their lives to My will, without allowing My presence to grow within them, without bearing fruit."

"No . . ." Alan cannot tell whether he voiced the word or is just inwardly recoiling at what he sees taking shape.

"Alan, without knowing it, you taught people how to keep their own walk with Me at arm's length, just like yours has been. You neglected to teach them what it means to truly follow Me, to love Me with all their heart, with all their soul, and with all their might, and to walk in My ways, abiding in Me, with My Word abiding in them. You even paraded your adultery and the destruction of your family before the church, justifying it in My name. This was an abomination."

The last word strikes Alan with an almost physical force.

"Had My life been within you, you would not have gone so boldly against My Word into adultery. For I clearly stated in Matthew's Gospel, 'Whoever divorces his wife except for sexual immorality, and marries another, commits adultery.' I also stated in My Word that the evidence of those who truly know Me is that they will keep My commandments. Those who really know Me, if they break My commands, will repent and confess their sins. Alan, you never confessed your willful rebellion of My commandment. Rather, you justified it, because you did not have My Spirit and Word in your heart. Paul clearly warned the church at Corinth, 'Do not be deceived. Neither fornicators, nor idolaters, nor adulterers, nor homosexuals, nor sodomites, nor thieves, nor covetous, nor drunkards, nor revilers, nor extortioners will inherit the kingdom of God.'"

"But, Lord, King David divorced, and You forgave him . . ."

"David sincerely repented," came the solemn reply. "And that is why he rests in his reward today. But you did not. You continued to twist My Word in your attempts to justify yourself. And worse yet, preached it to the sheep I had entrusted into your care. That is the difference."

"But I, too, was deceived," Alan pleads, as the sensation of ultimate condemnation begins to tighten around him like a noose. "I was led astray. I preached what I knew! I taught what I had been taught!"

As in response, another image bursts to life above them. *Terri.*

At this moment, in this place, the sight of her causes him overwhelming distress. He knows, before the words even leave her mouth, just what she is about to say.

They are in the kitchen of their old house, the small parsonage they occupied until money and success had brought them to the mini-mansion of their breakup. Terri is in rare form.

"Alan, I've listened to your sermons for years now, and I'd like to know—have you uttered the word 'sin' once in the last decade? Or how about the word 'righteousness'? Or 'justice'? Tell me this: How does someone receive Jesus Christ at Summit Chapel? You

keep talking about how Summit Chapel is a safe place to check out the faith, to 'kick the tires,' as it were, but how do these poor seekers ever find anything? There are no calls to repentance or explanations of how to find and follow Christ."

"Terri, I'm not going to debate this with you," Alan hears himself answer. *"Because no matter what point you may have, the bottom line is, you just don't get it. You are in such complete bondage to outdated, legalistic dogma, you don't get what my ministry is about, and you don't care to find out."*

"Oh really, Alan? Is that why I'm sitting here asking you, and you're the one refusing to answer? Who's the one who doesn't care?"

Alan doesn't have to look to see what comes next, because he remembers. He turns away from her. Anyway, she was right—he didn't care to educate her in his vision, to win her over. She was his wife, after all, and it should not have been necessary.

"Alan, you knew," the Lord continues as the image fades away. "You were told, and warned. Did you not read in My Word how those who are teachers in the church will be judged by God with greater strictness?"

"Yes, Lord, I did. But I believed I had been called to this work."

"You were called to it, but it would have turned out much differently if you had only surrendered your life and ministry to Me. But now you must depart from Me, for My presence is not within you, and your name is not found in the Book. Host, bind him hand and foot and cast him into the deepest darkness."

"Why the *deepest*, my Lord?" he pleads, the futility of his question ringing hollow in his ears.

"When I was on earth, I said that whoever causes one of these little ones who believe in Me to stumble, it would be better for him if a millstone were hung around his neck, and he were thrown into the sea. For such persons, I said that I would reserve a place of greatest torment, in a place of deepest darkness. Host, take him away."

The words are tinged with unbearable sadness.

A resignation and sense of doom falls upon him as an angelic hand on his arm begins pulling him, and he hears himself screaming.

The next few moments are a blur. He feels the presence of God recede quickly away and suddenly realizes he's feeling it for the last time in all eternity. The rising absence of Him feels familiar. And it should, for it is the same stifling hopelessness he felt earlier, on the plains of Hell. It is the bleakest and most terrifying sensation in the universe . . .

And it will be his lot forever and forever.

It is all so monumentally horrific that Alan blacks out.

When he awakens, he is someplace new. Someplace where the horror is fresh, and raw, and even stronger than the former place of suffering.

He looks about him, but it is useless. He is in a place of darkness so oppressive that if it was not broken by a single, central light source, it would be impossible to see anything at all.

He turns toward the one light source and begins to wonder if sightlessness would not be a comfort. Moving closer, he looks down and shuts his eyes against a blaze of reds and oranges moving like tongues around a core of pale white . . .

Fire.

What seems like several hundred yards away, Alan sees an edge, an ending to the plain—and beyond it, a crater aflame. Smoke rises in vast clouds, lit by the dancing tongues of fire. The edge grows nearer, the fierce light stronger. Its low roar now drowns out the moans. The heat has reached the level he would have once associated with a pottery kiln, or worse, the surface of the sun. It is unbearable, and yet suffering seems oddly normal here. The burning of his skin could surely be no worse than what he is hearing, or seeing, or feeling. He reaches the edge and looks over to the sight of a pit as wide around as any basin he has ever seen—miles across, with no apparent bottom. It is a sea of fire.

His eyes focus, and what he sees causes the blood in his veins to curdle, his soul to rip itself open and melt into a horrified gape.

Like pale stumps bobbing across the surface of a flesh-strewn bayou, a swarm of hands and arms claw upward through layers of smoke. And down there amidst an endless sea of fire, he makes out the writhing figures of bodies too numerous to count, dancing the macabre jig of the enflamed. Momentarily suspended, he watches. His horror is now complete. Crackling reaches his ears, and shrieks of terror. The bodies continue to burn, their mouths to scream, their limbs to jerk horribly of their own accord, yet their flesh is not consumed. It is an endless torment. Staring into this holocaust, he rears back and shudders violently.

A hand nudges him forward, and at last the Lake's gravity exerts its hold. He feels himself falling, falling, a hot wind intensifying around him, enveloping him, taking him down, down into the blast furnace, ever deeper, with a rumbling horror bellowing up to greet him, raw fear manifesting itself by screaming like he's never heard, and a feeling of hopelessness that cannot be conveyed in words, yet which catches him with his mouth flying open as he joins the damned in a long, loud, piercing cry . . .

Striking bottom, he abandons himself to despair and dread. But even the surrender offers him no solace whatsoever.

He knows—this is his fate, for all eternity.

New Jerusalem—former Church for All Nations, years later

"I'm sure this description of what Alan experiences sounds familiar to each of you," Storyteller said in a somber tone to those gathered around him.

Every face was locked on him in a blank stare, each one alone in his or her personal horror. And each face nodded, to no one in particular.

Yes. I know that scene well. I saw it . . .

Lydia had a look of seriousness about her countenance, deeply absorbed in her thoughts.

"Therefore, that which you beheld, the Pit of Gehenna, is a

window—straight into the very Pit that Alan looked and entered into himself. The demons there are every bit as repulsive as what you saw, except now they are tormented along with those who did not follow the Lamb of God. The suffering is probably even more horrendous than what you witnessed, simply because of it being prolonged. For those who are there, there is no turning away. No end to it all, ever."

He took a deep breath and managed a weak smile.

"My only hope is that, by the time we are done, you will understand fully why it was necessary for you to see this horror in the first place."

RESCUED

37

Writhing in the Lake of Fire, it is impossible to describe how thoroughly Alan hates himself.

Is there anything more pathetic, he rages to himself, *or more wretched than someone who not only spent his life in church but preached the Gospel for a living, and yet failed to make its truth a part of his own life?*

And now there is nothing he can do about it.

The horror of it returns full force, and with it, regret. And panic. And despair. He screams out, *Why?*

Why did I wait?

Why did I keep God at arm's length?

Why did I mix my pride with my theology?

Why did I swallow a cheap, shallow teaching that told only half the story?

Why did I rebuff my Father's wish that I share my life and my innermost self with Him?

Why did I fail to embrace the simple truth of what following Him is all about?

He turns away. He cannot bear it anymore. Yet there is no respite, no mercy. He looks around him and sees others—other people—and then, to his further revulsion, the demons, who themselves are being consumed.

Because time in the Lake of Fire has a way of stretching itself beyond simple reckoning, he has no idea how long he has been here. He tries again to will himself into oblivion, to commit some sort of spiritual suicide that will erase him from this place, from all existence. But it is no use—there is no relieving himself from the constant torment.

And then he feels something. Something different, far above him. A brightening . . .

He looks up and cries out in wonder.

His angelic guide is back! The luminous face lowers itself toward Alan, seeming to repel not only the blackness but the despair and suffering from every side.

The angel extends a hand, which Alan eagerly reaches for. The two come together, clasping hands, and Alan is pulled up to the Lake's edge where he first observed his fate.

"Come with me, Alan," the voice says, audible somehow over the storm of fire.

"Wha . . . How?" Alan stutters.

"You have indeed left your body, Alan. You have seen the Judgment and been in the deepest region of the Lake of Fire. The Father has allowed you to see and experience these things for yourself and many others. What you have been through is real, and if you truly lost your earthly life at this moment, all this would have been your eternal destiny."

"Then what *did* happen?" Alan asks, trembling.

"The Father allowed you to see what would have happened if your son was not, this very moment, rescuing you from death. But because of your son's persistence and obedience to the urging of the Spirit, you are about to be spared. You see, the Father is going to allow you, Alan, to deliver a message to the world. He is granting you a second chance, a reprieve in which to restore truth to the unbalanced teaching you and your fellow colleagues have been feeding God's people."

Alan begins to reel, for even as the words reach his mind, he feels the terrible heat and the mental torture of the place pull away like a sticky, unbearable coating.

"And just at that moment," Alan said into the radio handset, "just after it had sunk in that I would spend eternity in the worst torment, I felt life, faint and distant, flowing into me."

Taking a precarious breath, he continued.

"It was the oxygen Jeff had just flooded into the submarine. And because of what my courageous boy just did by the will of God the Father, I've come back into this body with the taste and the crush of that despair still thick upon my mind and my spirit."

Alan turned toward the submarine window and waved at his son. Jeff smiled back, yet also used the opportunity to make one more *shush* gesture.

"Jeff is warning me that I'm using up maybe the last of my air as I speak these words. But what I have to tell you is more important than that. I must tell you this awful thing, my dear church, and I have to ask for your forgiveness. I've preached a false gospel to you, one that resembles key parts of the truth but ignores the most crucial aspects. One that focused almost exclusively on grace—only not the real thing but a cheap, easy kind of grace that glosses over whether we are truly walking with God. One that ignores the fear of God, His righteousness and justice, the evidence of our changed lives, with good works as proof of His new life inside us. More than anything, it ignores the reality of eternity—of heaven and hell and the Judgment. For the Judgment is real. I know that now."

There was a pause, which seemed like the end. But then Alan took a deep, shaky breath, and went on.

"I must repent of one last thing. My divorce and remarriage. It is clear to me now that I destroyed my marriage in an act of rebellion and adultery. And worse yet, I justified my adultery by distorting God's Word to avoid accountability for my sin. This was an abomination in the face of God, and I repent before all of you, and beg your forgiveness. Please, God. Please, church. Forgive me. And redeem my death by making sure you don't suffer the fate I did. Don't let the counterfeit grace that has inundated our Western church and shortsighted words keep you from a real walk with Christ. Will you pray with me. . . ?"

DENVER—SUMMIT CHAPEL SANCTUARY

Completely overwhelmed, the remaining members inside the sanctuary fell upon their faces in unison, arms splayed out toward the large cross suspended above the heart of the church. It was a spontaneous reaction to an unforeseen arrival, accompanied by a solemnity and sense of awe that swept through the place like a windstorm.

Larry Collins was among those who experienced this divine power and force—the presence of the Holy Ghost. But he also experienced something else, something he dimly remembered from his childhood spent in the Pentecostal churches of the Pacific Northwest, something he never thought would descend upon the hip, contemporary folks at Summit Chapel.

Like an electrical circuit instantly snapped off, Larry's will was disconnected from his knees, his waist, and his arms. His body was not his own, seized as it was by a sudden fever. Even as he felt his limbs flop down onto the floor, Larry saw the same thing happen to every single person around him. He smiled, tears of joy flowing from his eyes.

He knew it. He just knew it.

Their sanctuary had just been visited by the Holy fear of God.

None of those on their faces could have guessed how long they remained there. A silence and stillness held sway over them, making time feel as if suspended.

Larry, kneeling at the front, glanced behind him and took in the beautiful sight, the reverence that shone throughout the sanctuary. Lately, Larry had come to despair that a genuine moving of the Spirit would ever sweep over the congregation he helped lead. He had resigned himself to the occasional insight arising from individual sermons or specific speakers. And none of these anointed preachers, in Larry's mind, was named Alan Rockaway.

The fact that Alan—whom Larry was on the verge of giving up on as a source of substantive Scriptural teaching—would be the one to lead the congregation in calling down the fear of God struck him as the ultimate irony. Up to now, Alan had been the kind of energetic, polished, consumer-oriented pastor to talk only about the grace of God, the laughter and joy of God. Over and over again, Sunday after Sunday. But never *Holy Fear*. And nothing as intense as this!

Standing in the midst of this human tide, Larry laughed out loud. *No predicting what God can do when He decides to shake things up . . .*

Then the atmosphere changed as their pastor's voice returned in the sound system, growing weaker with every word he spoke.

"I started out this cruise," Alan continued, "flippantly talking about it being something like a baptism. Please, let those words become more than just a casual remark. Let them be truth. Let's open our hearts and make this a new beginning for all of us— individually, as a church, as a people."

His voice grew breathy and shallow.

"Pray with me . . . Dear God, I beg Your forgiveness for my sin, my rebellion, my pride. Please redeem these last few moments my dear son Jeff has given us and, Lord Jesus, enter our hearts through Your Spirit, dwell in us, and make us Your own. *Your will be done.* Take us, Lord . . ."

Now his voice faded to a whisper.

"Forgive us" were Alan Rockaway's last, barely audible words.

Seconds later, Summit Chapel's members were calling out to God in an odd diversity of voices and styles of praying . . .

. . . begging for His mercy.

38

BARBADOS—UNDERWATER, OUTSIDE THE SUBMARINE

Through the window opposite Jeff, the bubbles started to thin as the oxygen began running out.

"No! No!" he screamed into his regulator while pounding a fist against the sub's window.

He refused to believe what was taking place. After all the miraculous events of the day, he could not accept that it would all end with his father's death. Desperation had blossomed into an unquenchable hope and ripened into an indestructible thirst for victory. Giving up was simply not an option! ·

God, he prayed, *You've really stood beside me today. Thank You. But I've still gotta have Your help. I still have a dad who needs saving. And I know You're in the salvation business. So how about it? Please give me a miracle, an idea, something, anything. . . !*

Growing more and more frantic, Jeff started looking around—at the sub, the floating debris, thinking again about what he saw in the boarding pier operator's safety manuals—

then took off swimming, tearing away at any obstacle shoved up against the sub's hull.

On the other side of the sub now, to his left he caught a glimpse of something a few yards away, some words painted on the hull. He quickly paddled over and wiped away the kelp stuck to the words so he could make out what it said.

It read, EMERGENCY OXYGEN BALLAST VENT.

Again he thought back to the manuals. *Emergency blow*, his memory prompted. *A means of surfacing the submarine rapidly in an emergency* . . . Release the valve and several tons of air would force out the water ballast and jerk the craft up to the surface!

He could hardly believe it. Once more, his desperate prayer had been answered.

He reached for the valve and, straining as hard as he could, tried to turn it. The thing wouldn't budge. Not again! Shaking his head, he ignored its stubbornness and gave it another try, groaning into his regulator. *I will not quit!* he reminded himself. *This valve was made to turn, and I'm gonna make it do its job!*

Finally the stubborn metal cranked nearly a quarter turn.

There was a roar as the huge hull tore itself loose from its shroud of wreckage and launched upward, into the shimmering golden disc of the sun's reflection.

Jeff hung on by a single hand, his mask and regulator ripped free by the force of the water rushing past him, gripping the valve handle for dear life as the sub hurtled up toward the glow overhead.

An awful jolt buffeted his body. The sub's momentum pulled mercilessly on his arm, yet Jeff couldn't help but smile the whole way up.

"Thanks, God!" he shouted as he broke the surface like a dolphin, gulping mouthfuls of fresh sea air.

The sub's nose shattered the surface with a roar of lofted spray, then crested and seemed to hang briefly above the sea, finally coming down with a deafening splash that created a pair of great bow waves.

Amidst it all, Jeff felt himself reborn. Somehow he felt he'd become a man in those last agonizing moments, in the rock-solid conviction that he would not release his hold upon that valve wheel *no matter what*, even if his lungs burst within him, even if the chaos around him ripped the arm from his shoulder. In the teeth-gritting certainty that he and God would ride this adventure to its very end.

Jeff could hear muffled shouts and cheers from those in the news helicopters directly overhead. He waved and shouted back a cheer of his own, then sprang into action. Although his arm ached from being yanked in the ascent, he ignored the pain and pulled himself up like a rock climber, scaling the still-draining sub toward its top.

As if out of nowhere, the cutter *Triumphant* came in hard beside him and abruptly reversed its engines to halt its advance, sending an enormous wave into the sub's flanks. Jeff gripped the hull for dear life, nearly thrown off by the wave's force.

"Disembark the vessel!" yelled someone on the loudspeaker from the cutter's deck. "Disembark the vessel at once!"

Jeff clambered to the top of the sub and stood just as the final warning was shouted to him. He turned to the glowering officer, waved defiantly, and, emboldened by the cheers from overhead, climbed into the conning tower. He flipped open the main hatch and leaped in.

What greeted him was the most sickening of sights. The sub was truly a death chamber, crammed with jumbled bodies, familiar faces smeared with blood, eyes still open in terror and agony, limbs branched out at grotesquely skewed angles. He saw Hal Newman and Jenny, both of whom were obviously gone. He started forward, being careful not to step on anyone's arm or leg.

He heard whimpering near where Jenny lay. He tenderly pulled her back. There was his dad, who looked up at him, grimacing. Thankfully Alan appeared to be breathing the fresh air, although barely.

Jeff bent down and cradled his father in his arms.

"Dad. It's me, Jeff. We're on the surface now. We have to get you to a doctor . . ."

Eyes closed, Alan smiled at the sound of his son's voice and reached up shakily to hold him about the neck.

"You did me proud today, son," he whispered.

"So did you, Dad. But please, please hang on, okay?"

"Jeff, promise me you won't ignore what I told them today. Promise?"

"I promise," said Jeff, crying now, gently parting stray hairs from his father's face.

"I can see them, son."

"No, don't go!" Jeff pleaded.

"I can see them coming for me . . ."

Alan turned his face toward his son, and his smile grew broad.

Then he went limp.

39

NEW JERUSALEM—FORMER CHURCH FOR ALL NATIONS

The listeners had grown restless, with many raising their arms again. Storyteller could see that his tale had taken long enough without a resolution, and they simply did not have the patience to wait any longer.

"So what finally happened?" Lydia asked Storyteller. It was her first question since joining the group.

"Well, all the people on that submarine lost their earthly lives that day. For some, it was truly a tragedy. Hal Newman entered eternity and continues to suffer torment beyond imagining."

"What about the others?" said a young man.

"Carrie Knowles went to the same place," Storyteller replied, "and remains there today."

"I don't understand," asked another. "How could these people spend so long so close to the Gospel and yet not know Him?"

"That's a good question," Storyteller said. "First, remember that in those days, God was not actually visible on the earth, only to the impressions of our spirits and through other revelations such as His Word and creation. Human life in those times was like a mist. Some of you lived in that time, although its memory no doubt has since faded. People spent their days groping and clawing for traces of God through a fog of unbelief mingled with faith. They staggered through ups and downs of doubt and endless physical distractions. Remember, too, that their whole world was shot through with evil, not to mention the bombardments of the Enemy. Their very bodies were riddled with illness and approaching death, their minds with the trash of a cluttered culture, their souls with the temptations of a fallen nature. It was easy to miss the truth if you weren't honestly seeking."

"Yes, but still," insisted another, "how could they spend so long in a house of God and yet miss the mark completely?"

"It is amazing, I know. The greatest of heartbreaks occurred time and time again in front of the White Throne of Judgment. There, soul after soul that had called itself 'Christian' turned out to be Christian in name only. In the turmoil of living in the midst of earthly life, millions upon millions found it too easy to put off having an authentic walk with God."

"Was that a hard thing to do? A walk with God?"

"No, not at all, and that is the saddest part. It begins with true brokenness before God—a deep sorrow for living separately from Him and breaking His laws—followed by a sincere request to submit to the lordship of Jesus Christ, a total surrender of the life and will to His Spirit, humbly asking that He enter the heart, and then most would have avoided that fate and enjoyed eternity with Him, and with us. Instead, they chose to enjoy only the surface attractions of what they called 'church,' by which they meant the company of nice, like-minded people, the uplift they received from inspirational teaching, the good music, and the many, many activities.

"But let me stress to you the real happy ending here. You see, for several of the people on that submarine, the ending of their earthly lives was the greatest victory imaginable, for their old lives were but shadows, caught up in the mist and fog, of no comparison to the beauty they possess now. Audrey Newman, despite her sin of tolerating and covering up her brother-in-law's evil, did in fact follow Jesus Christ. Her name was written in the Lamb's Book. Jenny Rockaway, despite her sin of having helped convince a man to leave his family, repented during her final moments on the submarine, at the same time Alan was making his confession. Her name was found, and she was taken up to be with the Lord. Even Kathy, the wayward young woman, was found and taken forward into the light of His presence, where she was not only forgiven by Yahweh but, earlier, by the boy whose life she had taken through her addiction. He stood waiting for her on the shore of heaven with open arms and a smile on his face."

"What about the lady whose name Pastor Alan could never remember?"

Storyteller smiled and nodded in appreciation. "I am so glad you remembered her, dear one. Her name was Velma Epperson. She had been a member of the church for thirty-two years, a volunteer nursery worker for nearly that whole time. She had a peculiar knack for blending in and not calling attention to herself. She showed up, did her work, and went back to her home. But when she entered the Great Hall of the White Throne, suddenly everything changed. The Hall broke into cheering and applause. Velma was so unaccustomed to receiving any kind of praise that she started to clap and cheer, too, thinking it was for someone else, then turned around to see who was being celebrated. That set off a great, warm laughter that continued for quite some time. Even Christ Himself laughed at that one, which you know if you're anywhere nearby when He laughs out loud, is a most delightful experience.

"Finally He asked her, 'Velma, give an accounting of your stewardship.'

"'Well, it's not much, Lord,' she said in a soft voice. 'I tried to fill my time with service, and You should know, dear Jesus, with my talking to You all the time. You're awfully good company, You know . . ."

"The laughter erupted again.

"'So are you, my daughter. I delight in your company.'

"'And I delight in Yours, my Lord.'

"And then He called out to her, 'Velma, come and possess the kingdom, which has been prepared for you ever since the creation of the world. I was hungry and you fed Me, thirsty and you gave Me a drink; I was a stranger and you received Me in your home, naked and you clothed Me; I was sick and you took care of Me, in prison and you visited Me.'

"Velma cocked her head with a questioning look and replied, 'When, Lord, did *I* ever see You hungry and feed You, or thirsty and give You a drink? When did I ever see You a stranger and welcome You in my home, or naked and clothe You? When did I ever see You sick or in prison, and visit You?'

"Jesus replied, 'I tell you, whenever you did this for one of the least important of these brothers of mine, indeed, for the babies in their beds, you did it for Me! You are a trustworthy servant. You have been faithful with the little I entrusted to you. That is why I am appointing you governor of ten cities as your reward!'

"And so this very day," Storyteller said, "Velma Epperson is in the Throne Room of the Father, occupying a throne of authority. Velma is now the governor of the Javan Quadrant."

"You mean, Governor Jidia?" Rhonda asked. "I can't believe that's her—she's so strong and beautiful!"

"That's because being around Christ makes you that way. She has become a radiant and beautiful lady since coming here. Just like all of us were cleansed and made whole again when we first arrived. And by the way, you'll never believe what happened to Terri Rockaway."

"She married again?"

"She did, yes, though many years later. But what I was referring to is that Terri found a wonderful calling in the months following these events. As the story of that day grew in its influence, she found herself being asked to share her testimony in person, all over the world. As time went on, she emerged as a leading voice for what was taking place, as a person of credibility and respect, the one who had stood her ground and planted the seed for what Alan would learn at a terrible price. In an even greater blessing to herself, she was able to minister alongside her son, and the two of them shared many of their days serving the Lord together.

"When she arrived to heaven and approached the Throne of Judgment, Christ Himself came down to welcome her. As her reward, He appointed her an under ruler to the Quandrant of Lermain."

"You mean, Lady Gabrielle?"

"That is her new name, yes."

"What happened to the corrupt company, and the man on the Coast Guard ship?"

Storyteller laughed. "Indeed, your curiosity knows no bounds. All right, I will tell you. After leaving the surfaced sub, Jeff wasted no time in sharing his footage with the world. And one of the points he most emphasized was that the sinking of the *Aqua Libre* had been completely unnecessary. Eventually a probe was launched, and Lieutenant Soares's ties to the boat-builders were uncovered, as sins always are. The corporate officers and the lieutenant were all eventually arrested and sentenced to hefty jail terms."

"What about the people back at the church? What happened to them?"

"Ah," he said with a big smile, "that is the best part of the story."

40

NEW JERUSALEM—FORMER CHURCH FOR ALL NATIONS

"Indeed," Storyteller said, "for all those who happened to attend the nine-thirty service at Summit Chapel that Sunday morning, what took place sparked something that spread through the church community like wildfire. Soon the number of worshipers doubled to 3,143 when the eleven A.M. crowd joined them midway through. And for all those who lay prone in the sanctuary while their pastor's desperate confession had blazed over them and seared their spirits, they would leave the sanctuary that day with a whole new understanding of grace and what it meant to have their lives renewed and transformed by the true indwelling of the living God.

"Many others stayed put in the sanctuary for several days more, so moved were they by what they had heard and experienced. They refused to budge until they had thoroughly processed with their brothers and sisters the transforming nature of this new picture of God. Because at first they could not even visualize how to act now—how to respond, how to live—and so remained there at church until the image resolved itself and gained for them some degree of clarity. Other members brought food; a small buffet table was set up at the back of the auditorium, although many fasted. And cots and blankets were discreetly installed along the far aisles.

"But once they did *get the picture*, these renewed believers had no idea how powerful and compelling their story would be to the rest of the world.

"The first evidence of this lay just outside their doors, within five steps of leaving the church lobby. Because their personal experience had been so engrossing, the worshipers had forgotten that the whole world was watching the unfolding tale of Alan, his son, and their church back home. As it turned out, a slow news cycle would conspire to keep their story at the top of the global media for several days afterward. So the network news trucks and anchorpeople were still there, poised for interviews, days later when the most reluctant church members finally left for home.

"The journalists, and the world they covered, could not understand why a man would sacrifice his last breaths of air to convey a spiritual message to people who could not help him. Because they did not know or understand the Gospel, Alan's distinction between justice and grace proved far too difficult for them to reduce to simple sound bites, so it became necessary to release the recordings of Alan's final words to the world, which in turn were replayed on the planet's talk-show circuit.

"Alan's words—not only their meaning but the tangible pain and suffering exuded with his speaking them—communicated far more powerfully than anyone had anticipated. It was not only Christians caught in shallow theology who responded, but also atheistic non-believers, as well, drawn, ironically, by the grace and love emblazoned in Alan's sacrifice. The majority of the world, however, disregarded Alan's words, viewing his experience as nothing more than a man hallucinating due to the shock of the accident.

"Nevertheless, because of the lives changed, because of its power and profound truth, the story of Alan Rockaway and his son Jeff—who would later enter seminary and one day pastor his father's church in a triumphant new direction—crisscrossed the planet over and over again as the story continued to grow. Untold thousands of Christians, a whole generation, listened to Alan's tortured last words and turned from ear-soothing, unbalanced doctrine to a true walk with God, to a rightful understanding of the balance between God's justice and righteousness and the need to fear Him on one hand, and His love, grace, and forgiveness on the other. And a great number were spared the horror of hearing 'Depart' as they stood before Jesus Christ at the White Throne.

"They would come to call this the 'Great Return,' for it was seen as a returning to a true and balanced view of God and experience of Him. As a result, many came to know the Heavenly Father—infinitely loving and gracious, but also the holy and righteous Judge who will render to every man according to his deeds."

"Tell us more about Jeff—how did his life turn out?"

Storyteller smiled. "It turned out wonderfully. As I said, after attending seminary, he became pastor of Summit Chapel. He married a beautiful girl, Sharon, and later became a father to three children. He dedicated his life not only to serving the members of Summit Chapel, but the nations as one of the leading lights in the Great Return. He wrote a book about his story, which was read by millions whose lives were changed as a result.

"The only wrinkle for Jeff was the inevitable aftermath of his role in the story's events. Until the day he died, Jeff would be tortured by thoughts of whether he could have done something more to save the doomed church members, perhaps by obeying God's urgings earlier, perhaps by showing more faith in what his father was trying to communicate.

"You see, the great question in Jeff's mind, which lingered for years afterward, was whether his father had actually voiced his own prayer for salvation during those final seconds or merely led the others in repentance. Had he actually neglected his own soul in those frenzied moments, his own sacrifice would have been even more enormous, because it would have meant setting aside an eternity of bliss in order to atone for misleading his church. To make matters worse, Alan's near-death testimony had already established that someone could lead many others to Christ without his own name appearing in the Lamb's Book of Life. So it remained at least possible that when he led his congregation in the prayer of repentance, and publicly repented of his greatest sin, he had run out of time to make his own peace with God. It wasn't a likely scenario, yet it somehow blossomed into a minor controversy, persistent and pernicious enough to afflict Jeff terribly as time went on. So much of that day remained unsettled and untidy. Ultimately, Jeff found the final scene after opening that submarine door, along with the last words of his father, impossible to interpret with any certainty. He would rarely voice his anguish on the subject, but as the years passed, the question dug a deeper and deeper hole in his heart.

"Where is he now?" asked a young man from the back row.

"Well, one day many years later, Jeff found himself quite an old man indeed. Remember that in those days, even those who walked with God were subject to emotional pains like loneliness and longing. His father had died many decades earlier, as well as his beloved mother twenty years hence. His wife, Sharon, was in a nursing home, her mental faculties fading. Even one of his own daughters, Lenora, had passed on as an adult, less than five years before, from a lingering illness.

"Don't misunderstand, for Jeff was generally a contented man. He had invested his earthly days exceedingly well, in walking with Christ and serving Him to great impact all over the world. He was a man beloved and respected by many. Still, like many people of advanced age, he fought against an encroaching melancholy. He could sense eternity approaching. What they called the 'afterlife' hung on his every word, his memories, and his prayers. He longed to see his Heavenly Father in person. And his earthly father, too. Yes, Jeff was ready.

"And on that one morning, an unusually warm spring day, Jeff rose from his porch chair overlooking the Brazos River that bordered his Texas home. No one else was with him to establish where he was headed, or what had prompted his walking forward. Perhaps he heard someone call his name. Or maybe he had been seized by a mysterious curiosity about something beyond the edges of his front yard. In any event, Jeff suddenly fell over on the stone path that wound through his flower garden.

"Then, grimacing in pain from his fall, he rose to one knee and glanced over at the cottonwood trees that marked the path leading to the Brazos River, or *los Brazos de Dios*, which in the Spanish language means 'The Arms of God.'

"It was an unconscious solace for him, to search out his beloved river. As he aged, the river for Jeff had come to occupy an increasingly recurrent place in his thoughts and dreams. He liked to blame its persistence on those pivotal minutes spent in the waters of the Caribbean so very long before.

"On this particular day, Jeff looked back around him, sure that he had merely tripped and stumbled on a pesky rock, when he was taken aback to find the figure of a strange visitor. Someone, he saw, as his eyes moved up the body from toes to crown, who looked out of place somehow. The stranger was clad in a robe of a color he could not readily name, whose face seemed lit from another source, from somewhere else.

"Someone Jeff's father would have recognized in an instant.

"'Good morning,' Jeff said to the visitor.

"'It certainly is,' the stranger replied, shaking Jeff's offered hand. 'It is a very fine morning, in fact.'

"Then the stranger pointed at the ground. Jeff's eyes followed the finger down to where it was pointing, and his whole body jolted in surprise.

"There lay an old man, motionless in the dirt. An old man whom Jeff promptly recognized. Or at least an old body that had finally relinquished its hold on his own spirit.

"The stranger, or angel, as Jeff now clearly knew, extended

an arm away from the sight and announced, 'The time has come, Jeffrey. I have been sent to be your personal escort. Let us go from here . . .'

"As they turned to leave, Jeff realized they had already risen quite high in the air, far above his home. He looked down on his house, his town, his continent, and although he felt a twinge of nostalgia for the place he had always known, he knew he had lived a long and rich life. He was ready, even anxious, for what awaited him. He so longed to meet his Lord in person!

"Then he became aware that his body had been transformed and his old world was behind him forever. A light appeared across the horizon, instantly growing larger and brighter, more intense and vivid and wondrous than anything he'd ever imagined. He was overwhelmed with indescribable joy and a sense of well-being, with exhilaration and pure energy, infinitely stronger than what he'd enjoyed as a young man.

"Above all, there was the warm feeling of his coming home, of returning to a place where he *belonged*, of being embraced by God Himself, the One who had created him. It was the culmination of all the premonitions and strange longings for heaven Jeff had harbored all those later years.

"Another of the wonders was sound, or music. But it was music of a sort he had never heard. He would have hardly known whether it was vocal or instrumental in nature. He could not convey any notion of what, or who, had blessed his ears at that moment. All he knew was that the sound seized him with something similar to—although magnified a thousand times— the old shivers he once felt cascade down his spine at the opening notes of some favorite song. In fact, it hardly seemed like something apart from him but rather a force that resonated through every cell of his new body.

"He wasn't just in the middle of a song—he *was* song.

"And all of these sensations were merely background, or backdrop, to the sights now streaming all about him.

"Jeff had now entered the light. Far ahead stood a crowd of waiting people, and even though he could not see their faces, which were silhouetted against the light, he somehow knew they were people he dearly loved.

"A single form stepped out and began to approach even faster than the others. Striding along the center of this great fiery sun, it was the silhouette of a man walking, then running toward him. A man in the prime of his life with thick, light brown hair, and features that instantly resonated in Jeff's memory."

"His father!" exclaimed a man sitting next to Lydia, tears streaming down his face.

Storyteller smiled.

"Yes, that's right. *My* father."

41

New Jerusalem—former Church for All Nations

There was a pause while Storyteller smiled knowingly at his listeners, giving them a minute to absorb his last sentence and its implications.

"Yes, I am Jeff," he said, "although the King of Kings has given me a new name, Storyteller, and a new mission."

"I knew it," said a woman from the back.

"I'm sure many of you had guessed it already, and I hope it did not spoil the story for you."

"But it's not finished, is it?" Lydia asked. "The story?"

He glanced at her and chuckled. "Of course it isn't."

"So tell us about being reunited with your father!"

His smile grew even wider as he stared up at the building's ornate ceiling as if to refocus his thoughts. "It's hard for me to describe how I felt when he reached me and we threw our arms around each other. I felt foolish over the doubts I'd had about his eternal destiny. Still, I have to admit that gratitude and relief washed over me in great waves of joy and delight.

"'My son,' I remember him saying, 'if you only knew how much I've longed to see you, to tell you how proud I am of you.'

"He finally pulled back to look me in the eyes, and I marveled at his appearance. Although it was obvious he was every inch my beloved father, his whole countenance and being had changed, literally beamed with a new light, a glow of contentment. His eyes sparkled like the sun glinting off a shining sea beneath a cloudless sky. His smile, his skin, his hair—all of him shone forth with an impossible health and vitality.

"'Dad, you have no idea how much I agonized over you,' I managed to say. 'I worried and worried . . .'

"'I know you did,' he said, 'and I would have done anything to set you at peace. Tell me, did our Lord send my old friend Demeter to escort you here?'

"'You mean the angel?'

"'Yes, the same friend who led me to the first Judgment. He came for me the second time, as well, pulling me away from your arms, back in that submarine. I wanted to console you, to reassure you and tell you that I'd repented, too, that I was made confident of where I was going. Isn't it amazing—the journey here?'

"'It all seems too much to take in,' I said.

"'And you haven't even entered the gates yet! And the Believer's Judgment! When you're His, when your name is in the Book, it is such an amazing encounter. I'll never forget the sheer joy and delight that swept over me, and the entire Hall, for that matter. You'll find out soon enough for yourself. The laughing and praising. Jesus is so overjoyed at receiving us home. You have so much to look forward to! And to see heaven itself, and then the New Creation . . .'

"I'll stop there," Storyteller said, "because, of course, the New Creation is something you all know too well. It's your daily life. When you contrast it to the Former Times, it's almost too much to imagine. In fact, for many of those who were condemned, it was *exactly* too much to imagine, for they refused to think of it, to even consider it. They never realized that their loss was so much more than imaginary.

"But I'm so happy to tell you that, even though God's grace did not come as cheaply or as easily as my father once portrayed it, it is still powerful beyond all description. My proof is that he, despite having the experience of standing before the White Throne and been told to 'Depart,' was given back his earthly life and those additional minutes in which to do the right thing. Occasionally such a thing would happen, thanks to the triumph of medicine or resuscitation. God gave my father a second chance through helping me find the submarine's emergency oxygen so I could bring him back, at least for a little while.

"And as you heard, my father did not miss his final chance.

"Because of that, we were able to be reunited at the heavenly gates. I can't tell you how blessed that moment was.

"Soon afterward I felt a tug at my arm and turned into the arms of another beaming soul whom I recognized in an instant as my mother. I don't remember there being many words said, mostly just hugging as we basked in each other's presence. And if there was any passing of my former life before my eyes during this whole time, it happened then. I returned to my earliest days of my childhood years, feeling my mother's love seep back into me like water into parched soil.

"Then my father approached and reached out his arms, and the three of us held each other as we had not done since I was a boy. All had been forgiven, of course, for as you know grudges do not exist here. The three of us talked and laughed together for the longest time, all in the warmth and healing light of our Heavenly Father."

"Is your father a governor, too?" one of the listeners asked.

"No, my father is not an influential man in the New Earth. He does not occupy one of the thrones or rule over provinces and principalities. His earthly life was too misspent for that. He is one whom God's Word describes as having been saved 'as though through fire,' which means he came to Christ only moments before death—and *that* is true grace. But he is overjoyed to be here, in the splendor and joy of God's presence, rather than the place he was headed. And so am I."

He crossed his arms and assumed a thoughtful, introspective expression for a moment.

"I suppose this concludes my story."

"But wait!" cried one young woman two seats over from Lydia. "You told us your story would have something to do with the Pit, that it would help us understand the horrible things we saw there."

Nodding, Storyteller replied, "You're right, Natalie. We talked earlier about what kind of story this was, remember?"

"Would it be considered a cautionary tale?" Lydia offered.

"Yes, but I would put it differently. It is a rescue story, or more precisely, a story of *being* rescued. And that is derived from far more than simply my attempts to save my father's life. Or even what my father did with his last moments on earth to try to rescue his church from his own bad teaching. No, the ultimate rescue was carried out by God Himself. You see, that Pit that horrified each of you does not exist by accident. God has allowed it to remain there, on the outskirts of His most blessed city, for a very specific purpose. Even back in the Days of the Mist, He inspired His prophet Isaiah to write about the coming of all mankind to offer praises. This passage spoke of people like you coming out from the Holy City and looking upon the bodies of those being consumed in eternal flames."

"But why?" came a question from the second row.

"If you remember, the original rebellion against Him, which set off the War in the Heavens, was given birth without provocation—there was no tempter. Lucifer's pride and betrayal grew from nothing. It had no antecedent, no prior existence. Therefore, it could conceivably happen again. And so our Lord allows this window, even here, to remind us what happens to those who turn against Him. None of us should ever forget."

The listeners remained silent for a long moment as they absorbed this.

"I don't understand why I didn't notice the Pit until today," said a man at the center of the crowd. "I've been coming here and offering praises since arriving, yet never realized it was there until now."

"Today was your appointed time," he answered. "There is a different reason for each of you. God established that this be your time for your own personal encounters with this reality."

"But . . ." Lydia began, "somehow it doesn't all connect. Why us? That still doesn't make this story relevant to us."

He smiled again, deeply, as though expecting, or even hoping, for someone to raise the question.

"You're absolutely right, Lydia! There's one final, important reason why this story matters, why it fits in. You see, every one of you sitting here is a spiritual descendant of the Great Return. You were led to your salvation by someone who came to Christ as a result of the revival that followed my father's story. So in many ways this story is yours, too. I am not a stranger to you. One reason why I know your names is that I am your spiritual ancestor. For some of you, I am a grandfather in the Lord, for others a great-grandfather. But no matter our relation, one fact remains. If it wasn't for what happened, each of you would quite likely be down at the bottom of what Gehenna reveals. You would be in the Lake of Fire, forever, and suffering a torment so terrible that we otherwise do not speak of it here in New Jerusalem."

With that, Storyteller raised a hand in farewell.

"I love each of you deeply," he said. "Thank you for your patience, for your listening. Please place the horrors you saw in Gehenna in the right frame of mind, as our loving Father's protective warning. And let us enjoy the wonders of the New Creation and the wonderful tasks God has bestowed on us. We are all family now, and I look forward to more fellowship with each and every one of you."

As Storyteller turned to leave, three arms went up with more questions.

It was always that way, he had found. Telling his story had a way of provoking a flood of pent-up curiosity. But for now he had nothing more to say.

He smiled as he walked toward the door, his right hand lifted high in goodwill. It sometimes struck him as altogether sad that he so rarely was able to speak of the thousands upon thousands of years of earth's rich, if tragic, history, and the memory of so many countless souls who once lived, perished, and were consigned to such agony. Ignoring it was like they had never been born. He had lost so many friends to the Falling Away—good, well-meaning friends who even now were being tormented . . .

No, he thought as he opened the door to step out into the brilliant light of New Jerusalem. He turned back, then reminded himself it was better not to think of it. The joy of this new life deserved to be sheltered from such bitter ponderings. Outcomes over which he had no influence whatsoever. ·

He walked down the golden steps leading away from the building. A reflection of lesser light—here it was not called shadow, for shadow required darkness—stretched out behind him, its source the intense glow of the very presence of God Himself, less than a mile away across the expanse of the blessed city.

Halfway down the stairs, Storyteller, the former Jeff Rockaway, stopped and turned to face a man who was crouched over a bed of the city's famous roses. The man's robe and his countenance revealed to the listeners—who had poured out of the building's sanctuary and stood gazing down after their Storyteller—that the man was one of heaven's gardeners. A man of modest yet worthwhile service in the Holy City.

Storyteller bent down and placed a hand on the man's shoulder. The man stood, laughed warmly, and embraced Storyteller in a hug.

The two men walked away, arms draped across each other, as more hearty laughter drifted up to the listeners.

"Boy-time?" the gardener said, his voice echoing up the steps. "Yes, a little boy-time sounds like heaven right about now."

A Note from John Bevere

Dear Reader,

When I first began thinking and praying about the possibility of writing a novel, I knew I would need help since I had not written one before. But along with that, I also knew I had a very clear vision of how the story could and should impact its readers. With my collaborator, Mark, I can tell you we spent hundreds of hours in prayer, in plotting the story and developing the characters. Then countless further hours involved line-by-line editorial review in light of the Scriptures concerning the consequences of sin, the power of redemption, and the certainties of the afterlife—for Christians and for unbelievers.

Since the first release of *Rescued* in the Fall of 2006, I have been blessed and blown away by the realization that thousands of readers have responded to the novel in exactly the ways I had envisioned. This phenomenon is probably captured best by a Georgia pastor, who told us he was dramatically touched after reading the novel and felt every person in his congregation should have the book. He purchased over 4,000 copies, and these are being used as teaching materials in the congregation. Additionally, he has bought 1,000 CDs of the *Rescued* Audio Theatre, a dramatized version of the story, to expand its reach and effectiveness. He is encouraging everyone who has been blessed by the novel to pass it along to people they know who are far too casual and unaware about what happens after a person passes on.

The themes of life, death, and the Hereafter woven into this story are gleaned from my nonfiction work *Driven by Eternity* (FaithWords Publisher), and in it you will find further expansion of the two certainties I keep ever before me: what I do at the cross of Jesus Christ determines where I will spend eternity, and the way I live as a believer determines how I will spend it.

You may have friends and loved ones whose spiritual condition causes you concern and for whom you have been praying. It may be that *Rescued* will provide an opening into their lives for the Holy Spirit to speak, to convict, to woo to the foot of the Cross.

I would love to hear your own story related to *Rescued* and its ministry in your life and others. Please contact me by mail or through our Web site: *www.messengerintl.org*.

In the service of our Lord,
John P. Bevere Jr.

Responses to *Rescued* from Readers

My husband passed away on May 10 from a heart attack in the middle of the night. . . . The last four months of his life God rescued him . . . it started with reading the *Driven by Eternity* book, then a couple weeks before he died, he read the book *Rescued* in one sitting. I had these two books beside him in the casket because these books were instrumental in him being saved.

" "

It is 2:45 a.m. and I just finished *Rescued*. It is incredible and amazing. I sense the presence of God and feel very sobered and deeply impassioned. . . . I am overwhelmed.

" "

The edge-of-your-seat suspense captivated me! I laughed, cried and was afraid throughout the novel but experienced love in its truest form.

" "

As I read *Rescued*, I was completely pulled into the story! Never before have I had such a vivid picture painted of how I need to live my life now to prepare for eternity. Tears streamed down my face as I finished the story and realized that what I do every single day matters. I will never live life the same!

" "

I could not make myself put *Rescued* down. It was so well done I could do nothing but keep going. The message reached me on many levels.

" "

I started reading *Rescued* around 11 p.m., and before I knew it, it was 5:43 a.m. and I had finished the entire book! From the very first paragraph I was enthralled with the story.

Not only was *Rescued* a marvelous read, it was also a convincing book of compassion and mercy.

" "

I literally feel as if I have been snatched from the fire.

" "

I have been in a constant state of prayer and repentance since I finished the book *Rescued*.

" "

Your description of the White Throne Judgment had me in tears. All I could do was bury my face and cry, asking God to have mercy on me.

" "

Thank you so much for shaking me to the core of my spiritual being.

" "

I started reading *Rescued* yesterday afternoon and I could not put it down. It is very sobering and anointed.

" "

When I got to those chapters where the "Christians" are told to depart, I could actually feel their disbelief and shock. As I was reading those chapters, I couldn't stop repenting and asking the Lord to reveal any wicked thing in me.

" "

This book has changed me and how I view my salvation!

This book brought me back to my salvation, my first Love for God.

"   "

This book may be the most powerful vehicle that I have ever seen to reach those who are not saved and those who are far away from their first love.

"   "

Until I heard your message and read this book, I did not understand what God's heart was for the church.

"   "

As I read your book, I truly felt the holy fear of God and came to a place of deeper understanding of His Sovereignty.

JOHN BEVERE, who has a doctorate in ministry, is passionate about seeing individuals deepen their intimacy with God and capture an eternal perspective. An international bestselling author, his award-winning books and teaching materials are available at the conferences and churches where he speaks around the world. John co-hosts "The Messenger" TV program airing in 216 nations. He and his wife, Lisa, also a bestselling author, founded Messenger International in 1990, currently with offices in the United States, Australia, and the United Kingdom. They live in Colorado Springs with their four sons, and they all enjoy sports, whether scuba diving or skiing, wherever their travels take them!

More information can be found on their Web site:
www.messengerintl.org

MARK ANDREW OLSEN, whose novel *The Assignment* was a Christy Award finalist, also collaborated with Tommy Tenney on bestsellers *Hadassah* and *The Hadassah Covenant*. The son of missionaries to France, Mark is a graduate of Baylor University. He and his wife, Connie, live in Colorado Springs with their three children.

ALSO BY JOHN BEVERE

NONFICTION
Victory in the Wilderness
Voice of One Crying
The Bait of Satan
Breaking Intimidation
Enemy Access Denied
The Fear of the Lord
Thus Saith the Lord?
A Heart Ablaze
Under Cover
Drawing Near
How to Respond When You Feel Mistreated
Driven by Eternity

ALSO BY MARK ANDREW OLSEN

FICTION
The Assignment
*Hadassah: One Night With the King**
*The Hadassah Covenant: A Queen's Legacy**
The Watchers
*The Road Home**

Rescued also available in Spanish

*with Tommy Tenney

Looking for More Good Books to Read?

You can find out what is new and exciting with previews, descriptions, and reviews by signing up for Bethany House newsletters at

www.bethanynewsletters.com

We will send you updates for as many authors or categories as you desire so you get only the information you really want.

Sign up today!